EUROPE 1942

IRELAND

ENGLAND

· London

Southampton

White Cliffs of Dover

THE ENGLISH CHANNEL

Dunkirk

Ostend

· Brussels

Lille

BELGIUM

Germany

· Paris

OCCUPIED FRANCE

VICHY FRANCE

Bilbao ·

Pyrenees Mountains

PORTUGAL

SPAIN

Rock of Gibraltar

Foxford Press, Asheville, NC

First American Edition, June 2018

ISBN-13: 978-1948907002

Library of Congress Control Number: 2018947185

Printed in the United States of America

TELEGRAM FOR MRS. MOONEY

ALSO BY CATE M. RUANE:

Message For Hitler

COMING SOON:

Letter Via Paris

TELEGRAM FOR MRS. MOONEY

Cate M. Ruane

Foxford Press

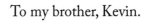
To my brother, Kevin.

PROLOGUE

Somewhere in Belgium

WHEN THE CALL COMES to Gestapo headquarters, Otto Ulbricht sits at a roll-top desk eating a lunch of cold chicken with a side of over cooked red-cabbage slaw.

On the first ring, he's thinking about his wife back in Dresden—the meals she makes: pork chops braised with brown sugar, dumplings as light as clouds. He sighs. The phone rings again as he wipes grease from his hands. On the third ring he lifts the receiver, while he throws the remains of his lunch into a trashcan.

"*Ja*," he says, nodding his head as he folds back a pad of paper, ready to take notes. "*Das Flugzeug Spit-feuer.*" The airplane is a Spitfire. He continues to make notations. The repeat of "*Ja*," and the forceful pressure of his mechanical pencil, punctuate each period mark. He says in German, "I understand—yes—somewhere north of the tracks."

Returning the receiver to its cradle, he looks at the clock that hangs above a portrait of the Führer. It will be at least an hour before the others return—longer if the beer is good. If the Royal Air Force pilot survived the crash, an hour will give him a good start at an escape. *"Verdammt,"* he says, cursing under his breath.

It's like a race: the Belgian Resistance will try to get to the crash site first. He looks again at the clock and then lowers his eyes, looking into those of Adolf Hitler. Rising from his seat, he approaches the portrait, which always gives him strength.

He scribbles a note and leaves it on his officer's desk.

Walking to a coat rack, he grabs a long black leather trench coat, even though it's a sweltering day. He'll be on a motorcycle; and, besides, when approaching an enemy officer it's always best to be properly attired. Before buttoning the coat he pats the Luger that fits into a leather harness strapped to his torso. He takes a fedora from the shelf above the rack, pushing it snugly onto his head.

Before he turns the ignition key on his BMW motorcycle, he scans the road that leads to the timber and lath city center—the opposite direction of the crash site. For a moment he hesitates, thinking he should pull one of the others away from his lunch. They might be in any number of cafés or pubs...there's the problem. A waste of time.

Then he thinks about the glory that will be all his. When finding the RAF pilot, he puts the Luger to his head and pulls the trigger. He's never gotten a shot at a British officer—only at a few Jews, and Belgians who won't get in line.

He kick starts the motorcycle. It backfires as he pulls the bike onto the road—tar sticky in the merciless sun.

I will bring honor to the Fatherland.

Thinking this, he gives the bike full throttle, feeling the power of the engine pulsating between his legs.

CHAPTER ONE

Long Island, New York

WHEN THE BOY ROLLED UP TO OUR GATE, I was up in the O'Leary's oak tree, playing hooky and hiding out from my ma. I seen him lean the bike against our picket fence, reach into his saddlebag, and open the gate latch—which always gives trouble. Next, he swooped up the brick path to our front stoop and knocked three times. I seen it all from above, like a bird sees it, or like an airplane.

The boy called out, "Telegram!" My ma called back that she was coming.

From my brother Jack, I figured.

He's famous—bold letters in *The New York Times*: same exact paper President Roosevelt, a New Yorker too, gets delivered to the White House every morning. The president is proud of my brother, I bettya. Edward R. Murrow interviewed Jack on the radio. His voice came through the air and hit the antenna on our roof. Everybody on the block heard it. He was in a movie with Jimmy Cagney, *Captains of the Clouds*. On top of all that:

he shaked hands with the King of England.

His letters came all the way across the Atlantic Ocean—in the belly of ocean liners—the stamps engraved with a portrait of the king, which my ma let me keep if I was careful steaming them off the envelopes. He sent us a black and white of the house he was living in—a hoity-toity place near the sea, once an earl's.

I'd get the news from Jack at 4 o'clock, when everybody expected me home from school. I was supposed to be in sixth grade grammar class reading *Fun With John and Jean*, the Catholic school version of *Dick and Jane*— like the original wasn't mind-numbing enough. Sister Bridget at Saint Brendan's I'd handle with an absentee note typed up on my sister's Underwood, Da's signature traced using his fountain pen. That wouldn't work with Ma and I needed to stay out of her path, and how.

Hanging from a branch was my lunch pail—baloney and liverwurst sandwich, an apple, and a nickel for milk. I wouldn't go hungry and could wait it out. The nickel was better spent on an ice-cold bottle of soda anyways.

"Jack's faster than a speeding bullet," I said out loud. Opening my arms wide I became an airplane, buzzing low over the house and the corn fields beyond—flying over to Manhattan, circling the Empire State Building and the Statue of Liberty, then buzzing Ellis Island before cruising all the way to Southend-on-Sea, England, and Jack. Then I put my head back in my book: *Treasure Island*.

By the time I climbed out of the tree, hours later, my

head was filled with pirates and treasure and I'd plum forgot about the telegram.

When I entered the house, the first thing I noticed was that the radio was turned off, and the place was as quiet as a church on Monday. A yellow jacket buzzed against a screen window in the parlor. My ma wasn't in the kitchen, where she should've been fixing my after school snack and winding up to quiz me about the day's learning. And another thing was that somebody left the icebox door open and water was spilt all over the linoleum floor.

I called out for my ma but got no answer. Then I seen that her bedroom door was shut closed, which was just plain abnormal. Wondering if my ma was down with something, I tapped.

"Ma? Are you in there?" I asked in a whisper, so as not to wake her if she was taking a lay down, which she hardly ever did in broad daylight.

Had to put my ear flat to the door to catch her words: "Not now Tommy," she said, fast and sharp.

Sitting on the parlor sofa, I tried to think what could be the matter. I didn't make the connection to the telegram, not even then.

I looked around the bare room for a clue. We didn't have fancy things, because my da was laid-off and we was stone-broke. That's when I seen the telegram put next to the photograph of Jack in his Royal Air Force pilot's uniform. It took a brave man to fly a Spitfire. The Nazis were always chasing after Jack and trying to shoot him down.

I'd read it in the paper. My brother chased a Messerschmitt AG and got within 10 yards of it before letting loose his guns. He looked the Luftwaffe pilot in the eyes right before the German plane went into a tailspin and then hit the ground in a blaze of fire. He had another German plane on his tail—a Focke-Wulf 190. Jack did an aerial flip, coming up behind it. Two kills in less than five minutes.

The memory gived me a jolt. I stepped to the side table where the telegram was. Very slowly, like it was a booby trap. I read it over a few times before my heart started beating regular again.

Turned out my brother was missing, was all. It didn't make sense to me that somebody went to all this trouble to tell us. I went missing all the time—like today, missing from Saint Brendan's. One time I went missing for two days to practice survival skills for a Boy Scout badge. Nobody sent a telegram.

Only once or twice do I remember getting lost for real. There was the day I got a new Schwinn Camelback and was testing it out on long distances. One wrong turn and I ended up in Oyster Bay at Sagamore Hill—that place of President Teddy Roosevelt's where he kept that taxidermy collection. All I done was ask one of those gardeners to help me make a phone call to my ma. In no time Jack came in his pick-up. While I waited, I examined a few moose heads. The bear and tiger rugs was terrifying to step on. I didn't get in trouble with Ma, because it was an honest mistake.

My brother was always the one to find me—when I was lost by accident, or hiding out on purpose. He knew all the hiding places, because he'd used them before me. When I was holed up with a good book in the hayloft and late for dinner, Jack came to get me.

Once I got lost in the woods. In the middle of escaping wild Indians, I ducked behind an oak tree. Changing parts, I became an Apache scout and climbed up a dogwood. Somewheres in the switch, I lost north. Starving to death, now just a plain ol' Irish-American, I was miles from home near a muddy creek when Jack found me. It was astonishing how he'd drive up alongside me in that old Ford pick-up of his whenever I got more than ten blocks from home. The reason I was able to play hooky now, was because my brother was off fighting Hitler.

Every once in a while, Jack showed me a new place to hide. There was an abandoned house he took me to—a creepy place where an old widow once lived. Her husband was killed by a Confederate cannonball in the Battle of Gettysburg, which made it so the house was never painted again. The front porch was rotten and fallen in and there was snake nests up around the dowel trim. We entered through a back window and found ourselves in what used to be the kitchen pantry. Cans of food from before the Great War were still stacked on them shelves. Jack said you could get botulism if you ate from them. Once a bunch of folks died eating olives out of old rusty cans. I didn't like olives myself but got the point and didn't touch them cans except to check and see if there was money socked in one of them.

People don't trust banks anymore. That's good news for people like Jack and me who like to hunt for treasure. The obvious hiding place is a cookie-jar or under a mattress. Problem is, thieves know this, so people have to be cleverer these days. Cans and jars left on shelves and in iceboxes are good options. And cornflake boxes.

Some fools will ruin a perfectly good book by cutting a hole out of the center of the pages. They'll find a thick one, like the "S" volume of an encyclopedia. They put treasures inside—small things like diamonds, rare coins, and postage stamps. Or Babe Ruth baseball cards which will be going up in value now he's retired. Then they put the book back on the bookshelf, thinking no one will notice. It's one of the first places any halfway decent thief or treasure hunter will look. And what happens later when that same fool needs to learn about the Spanish Inquisition?

One good hiding place is inside of walls. A person good at carpentry can make a hole, put treasures inside where the insulation goes and then patch it up with plaster. People forget to attach a treasure map to their Last Will and Testament, and in that case, it's fair game. Jack and me tapped around the walls in that abandoned house listening for a change in tone. A couple times we used Da's hammer to bust a hole.

In this way we stumbled on hidden newspapers dating from March 15, 1889. We looked them over cover-to-cover, hoping for clues to a real treasure but never could find nothing. The funny thing was that on that day in '89, the German Navy tried to take over an island called Samoa. That was the first time I learned that we Americans owned an island in the Pacific Ocean. Most people didn't find out until last year when the Japanese tried to steal Oahu, Hawaii. Back in 1889, it took three American warships to scare the Germans off. Made you wonder—all these years later and my brother fighting the Germans off again.

People are always asking me how it is my brother became a fighter pilot. Well, he learned to fly while working for the A&P. He started out with the supermarket chain when he was not much older than me—mopping floors at night when the store was closed. We live around the corner from Mitchell Field and he worked his way up to a position as a driver—ferrying goods from the airfield to a warehouse.

Jack got in tight with the pilots who worked for the A&P. Before long, he'd learned how to fly and was hired on as a pilot. You could say Jack was a self-made man.

His job was to bring fresh fish to markets around Long Island—fish stinking to high heaven if delivered in the back of a truck. Once he came home with fish-eggs, which he said rich people called *caviar* and ate on crackers. I left some of them eggs on my sister Mary's pillow that night. Another time he bringed home a live lobster, which he flew with all the way from Maine. My ma refused to let it in the house. She said she'd be satisfied with a fresh flounder on Fridays.

At the cinema one Saturday night, Jack seen a newsreel featuring the First American Eagle Squadron—a squadron of American pilots flying for Great Britain. The squadron was sort of like the famous Lafayette Escadrilles of the Great War. The Eagles were American pilots who enlisted in The Royal Canadian Air Force and later joined forces with The Royal Air Force—The RAF. Already they'd seen action against the Germans and were heroes in the Battle of Britain. All Jack planned on that night was seeing a good Western but he left a changed man. For my brother Jack, being a fighter pilot was just the sort of life he wanted.

In the summer of 1940, he hitched up to Montreal. America wasn't in the war yet. Funny thing is, he'd enlisted the same day France fell to the Jerries. At the time I don't think my brother had anything against the Germans. Jack had a kind word for everybody, even for my sister Mary, the thorn in my side. He wanted to dogfight and who could blame him?

My ma wasn't happy about him joining the RAF and fighting on the side of Britain. She and my da were born and raised in Ireland—before independence, when the Irish sent all the good potatoes to England and were left with the crummy ones. My da, in his heart, wanted Jack fighting against the British and not for them. Not for the Nazis, mind you, but for the Irish Republican Army. Problem was, the IRA didn't have Spitfires.

Then Pearl Harbor was attacked, America jumped into the war, and my ma was looking forward to Jack's transfer to the U.S. Army Air Force. He'd fight for America—that was the main thing. Ma was hoping he'd be sent somewhere like Texas to train new pilots. Jack mentioned that as one possibility. I knew better. My brother would volunteer to go to the Pacific and fight against Japan. That was more his style.

Ma still hadn't come out of her room. I was back sitting on the parlor sofa, with the telegram in my hand still baffled why we got it. Jack was a grown-up and was allowed to go missing if he wanted. So why'd somebody rat on him to Ma? He was old enough to drive a car, a motorcycle, and an airplane even. Ma teared her hair out when he joined up with England but there was nothing she could do to stop him. He was getting married in two weeks, for Pete's sake, even though my ma wanted him to marry a girl from the old country, not an English girl. It didn't make sense, none of it. If Jack was lost for real, the RAF needed to go find him, was all. Maybe they was too busy fighting off the Nazis and couldn't spare anybody for search and rescue. Maybe they'd telegrammed us hoping my ma and da would find him, so he'd keep fighting.

That's when an idea began formulating in my mind. I was the best qualified to find Jack, what with all my treasure hunting experience. If he was hiding out from the Gestapo, I'd know the sort of hideouts he'd pick.

Jack was always the one to find me. It seemed only right I should help him out when he was in a tough spot. Besides, my da needed to find a job and be the breadwinner. That left me the only man in the family to take on the responsibility of finding Jack. I wasn't even able to find ten-cent lawn mowing jobs. What with the depression and all, people was either mowing their own grass or just letting it grow tall. And I was afraid of dogs, so being a paperboy was out of the question. I was no use to the family staying here in East Hempstead.

I put the telegram back on the side-table and went to find myself a snack. Maybe I'd go out to the abandoned house, come to think of it. It was a good place to begin planning my trip to Europe. My sister Mary would get home from school at any minute and she'd start pestering me. I needed somewheres quiet to let the wheels in my head spin smooth. An abandoned attic was the perfect place to do it.

CHAPTER TWO

TREASURE HUNTERS GOT TO have a knack for observation—20/20 vision and big ears. King Tutankhamen's tomb was discovered by Howard Carter's trusted Arabian worker, who spotted a small step covered in sand—a step that for years other archeologists strolled over on the way back and forth to their tents. Down that staircase was the Egyptian Fort Knox.

By applying powers of observation, I avoid ever coming face-to-face with my sister Mary. All five senses can be used, even though two will do the trick.

Smell: She uses Ivory soap, which she thinks will clear up her pimples, and setting lotion to tame her frizz. Smoky house and you know she's in the kitchen cooking.

Hearing: She wears a charm bracelet. The Washington Memorial clinks against Sacagawea, the Indian lady who helped the Lewis and Clark Expedition. If that fails, I listen for the Chrysler Building clanging against a heart locket—who gave her a heart locket is anyone's guess.

One night a month or more after the telegram arrived, I sat at the dinner table eating mashed potatoes with ketchup—a combination my ma said was a sin. She believed the only proper way to eat mashed potatoes, or baked potatoes for that matter, was with a dab of butter and a sprinkle of salt. Tonight I observed she wasn't eating much at all and skipped the butter all together. The spuds sat in a big lump on Ma's plate, and she picked at them with the prongs of her fork. She got skinny this last month—I'd say from size 16 to 12. This normally would have her boasting as she put darts in the waistbands of her skirts. Now she let the clothes hang baggy on her. Her wedding ring was loose, too. While she was washing up one night, it slipped down the drain. Da had to take apart all the plumbing to retrieve it and meanwhile flooded the whole kitchen.

On top of that, she wasn't applying Woolworth's "Lustre-Cream" to her hair and she'd stopped plucking the white ones out. She stopped putting on the cameo brooch Da got her when they was courting. These were all bad signs. But the worst thing was she stopped baking cakes. I wanted more than the world to make her happy again—happy like before the telegram arrived.

My da sat quiet at the head of the table eating his fair share of boiled cabbage, shame-faced because he'd drunk our meat money down at the Cold Stream Pub and there was no ham to go with it. He was drinking more than usual since Jack went missing. Da kept to himself, but we knew he was worried about Jack by the way he stared at the ketchup bottle. My da was what you'd call the silent type, so I wasn't too troubled. My ma, on the other hand, had what the Irish call the gift of gab. She enjoyed telling us stories about the old country. Now all the stories had dried up in her worry.

As far as I could tell, nothing was being done about finding my brother—nothing but a whole lot of worrying, and my ma lighting a candle every day at Saint Brendan's Church. What was needed here was action.

All we knew was his plane was shot down in German-occupied Belgium. The closest I'd come to that place was the Belgian Pavillion at the 1939 New York World's Fair, which happened on Long Island. It seemed obvious someone had to go over to the real place, find Jack, and bring him home. Seeing my ma like this, day after day, fortified me in my plans to be the one to do it.

On the best hand, the Belgian Resistance was hiding Jack from the Nazis. On the worse hand, he was somewheres deep inside Germany, a prisoner of war, and he'd need my help to escape. Never once did I entertain the notion that Jack was dead. Every adventure story I ever read ended happy, like in *Treasure Island*. If Jim Hawkins, just a boy like me, escaped fearsome pirates and got home to his mother, it stood to reason that so could Jack. Escape the Nazis, that is.

"Tommy, help your sister clear up," said my ma, folding her napkin into a perfect triangle and sliding back her chair. There was very crucial tasks to accomplish before bedtime, but I didn't want to upset her, so I said, "Yes, Ma," in my most obedient voice. I was rewarded with a shrug.

Only one of my two sisters was home that night.

My older sister Anne (who we called Nancy for a reason I never got) was working nights as a waitress at a Greek diner out on Hempstead Turnpike. Each time I visited her there, she snuck me a big piece of Boston cream pie, and I loved her for it. She was a knockout—a female version of Jack, who could be in the pictures if he wanted. My friends were all carrying a torch for Nancy and always nagging me for information about her. They wanted Nancy's measurements, offering me a year's worth of Cracker Jack prizes for the three numbers. I found their obsession revolting. Still—it made me proud to be blood related.

Mary was the third child in the family, after Jack and Nancy. She was 14 and the thorn in my side, as I might've already said. When my ma was out of the room she bossed over me in a way made me wish aliens'd snatch her up and take her to Pluto.

"Be careful to let the water get hot before you wash the dishes, Tommy," she said, as she sat on her duff examining her fingernails. Them nails were sharper than a samurai sword. Plus, she was taller than any boy in her class and had five inches on me. So I went to the kitchen sink.

One day, when I shot up tall as Jack, the tables would turn on Mary. For the time being I had to get my revenge on the sly. My da's straight edge razor blades and erasers were my weapons of choice. The last ten pages went missing from a romance novel took her three months to get to the end of. The night before she handed it in to the teacher, several sums were changed on her arithmetic homework. Best of all, on her final paper for history class, I replaced the word Henry—as in King Henry VIII—for Harry.

Now she was getting back at me by throwing dishes in the sink without wiping the food scraps first. "Oops," she said, as the leftover mashed potatoes from my ma's meal floated to the top of the soapy sink water, splashing onto the plates I'd just placed on the drying rack. I loathed her with the same intensity that people hated the Lindbergh baby kidnappers.

"Looks like you'll have to start all over," she said with that smirk she perfected by watching Betty Davis films.

"I'll finish up without your help, thank you," is how I solved the problem, just as she'd hoped. She went sauntering out of the kitchen, leaving me in peace to finish with the washing up, alone in my thoughts.

While drying the dishes and stacking them in the cupboard, I mentally went down the list of supplies I still needed to gather before leaving East Hempstead for Nazi-occupied Europe. A duffel bag hidden under my bed already contained a spare pair of blue jeans, a flannel jacket, and a baseball cap. Knowing I'd have to go undercover, I removed the Brooklyn Dodger insignia from the cap—a crying shame. In the likelihood I'd need a disguise, I packed the tie and dress jacket I was forced to wear to Mass on Sunday. For the same reason, I added to the bundle a pair of aviator sunglasses. Jack gave them to me before leaving for Canada. The sunglasses were one of my prized possessions because Jack wore them during flight training. They made me look as dashing as Robert Taylor, the movie star. It was Nancy who made this observation and so it was a fact.

But I still had to find a compass and a map of Europe. The map I'd cut from a Rand McNally World Atlas at the public library, using the same razor blade I applied to Mary's novel. By then the blade was dull, useless as a weapon. Jack left his boxing gloves with me, but I'd need more than my two fists to duke it out with a real Nazi. There was Jack's bow and arrow set—the one he used for shooting possums that came at night and ate our chickens. I was sharping my skills by aiming at a target drawn on the barn wall. The bulls-eye was the nose of Adolf Hitler. If I missed a little, at least got his moustache.

I'd also bring along a pocketknife, a slingshot, seven darts, a boomerang, and a few boxes of firecrackers and matchsticks. Mary's nail file would go to Belgium too. If the SS had Jack locked up in chains, it would come in handy. The added bonus was knowing Mary's nails was getting ragged. Then there was the real four-leaf clover, glued onto a card, that my grandma in the old country sent me. That was coming along for luck.

When my da lost his job, I lost my allowance. There was only one place to get the dough needed for a journey to Europe, because banks had armed guards. I planned on confessing at a church somewhere far from Saint Brendan's—somewheres like Brussels for example. Three Masses on Sunday worked out to three collection plates coming my way. Normally I was moaning and groaning all the way to Mass, and so people began to notice.

My sister Nancy said, "Tommy, you'll become a saint if you keep this up."

"He's a good lad," said my ma, who was thinking I'd become a churchgoer so's to pray for my brother Jack. She'd attended Mass every morning since Jack went missing. She patted me on the head.

"Patron Saint of Brats and other Wayward Youths," said Mary in her nastiest voice. I flicked my rosary beads at her knee. "See what I mean!" she yelled out. But I'd managed the attack so nimbly, no one knew what she was going on about. I leaned back into the car seat and put on my cherub face. I felt for the wad of dollar bills I'd stuffed in my back pocket and said a Hail Mary just in case.

My departure was scheduled for September 2, 1942, the day that the school term began. All summer I trained, not only with target practice but also by running laps around the block, doing 100 push-ups every morning, and by climbing trees more than usual.

Mr. Fisch, our neighbor who lived in the green Tudor at the end of the street, was teaching me German. His lawn was filled with miniature dwarf statues standing under a man-made waterfall that flowed into a six-foot long river with a wooden bridge across. Mrs. Fisch said it reminded her of Germany. For more than a month I learned the lingo. Mr. Fisch emigrated from Berlin before the Great War and didn't like Adolf Hitler no more than me. I clued him into my reasons for needing to know German and he swore to keep my plans a secret. But I suspected he didn't take me seriously, even after I asked him to teach me to say in German, "Have you seen a downed Spitfire around here?"

Four years of Latin class, and compared to that, German was a snap. I already knew how to say airplane three different ways: *das Flugzeug, die Maschine* or *der Flieger.* I could introduce myself in German and ask for directions. I knew how to count to 100 and how to buy a train ticket. I knew how to ask if the Gestapo was anywhere abouts—important to know, because they were the dreaded Nazi secret police: G-men with a capitol G. I made sure I learned how to say all of my favorite foods—like ketchup and marshmallow, which lucky for me turned out to be *ketchup* and *marschmallow*. Whenever I came for a lesson, Mrs. Fisch offered me macaroons from a tin she hid behind the bread box—it helped me keep up the stamina needed for my training.

Mr. Fisch is the one first told me that the Nazis had it out for Jewish people, which included him and Mrs. Fisch. On one of my visits he handed me a book he said I'd better read, in the English edition because my German "*vus* leaving room for improvement." First thing I asked is if the book had pirates.

"*Nein,*" he said, in a hushed voice, "But *vay* many monsters." Then he warned me not to pass it on to bullies. That got my attention big time, so I dived into that book.

Turned out it was written by Adolf Hitler himself. Not since Professor Moriarty was there a villain like him. On the first page he's talking about gobbling up

Austria, now a done deal. Take this: "The plow will become the sword, and the wheat will be watered by the tears of war." Meaning my ma's tears, the stinker. Next he's describing himself as a boy: "I had somehow become a little ringleader among my group."

Well, no kidding!

I got to page two of *Mein Kampf* and gave up, but reckoned I'd better bring it along to Europe, being that Mr. Fisch claimed it was "Important reading if you *vunts* to comprehend the despicable Nazi agenda."

I needed somewheres to stay once I got to Europe. The only people I knew over there was in the old country. Irish people like to have big broods. I had grandparents in Ireland, plus hundreds of aunts and uncles. If I went anywhere near them, they'd give me up to the authorities—meaning my ma and da. I'd steer clear of Ireland.

Then it came to me—there was always Daphne, the 18-year-old English girl Jack was engaged to marry. I didn't know much about Daphne, only what I'd learned from a newspaper article, which mentioned a letter she'd written to Ma. She said, and I quote, "I've put away the trousseau for a while but I'll be taking everything out again soon as I know he'll be back." I had no idea what a trousseau was, but she had to be keen on Jack or why marry him? I'd have to find the letter Daphne wrote to my ma. It was the only way to get her address in London without raising suspicions. For all I knew Ma burnt the letter. She went ape when Jack sent word that he was marrying an English girl. My ma wore black for a week.

Still—it was worth looking for the letter. And come to think of it, this Daphne girl might even want to help me find Jack, as it might be between that and her becoming an old maid.

Ma kept all of Jack's letters tied up with a ribbon in her top dresser drawer. I figured that's where I'd also find Daphne's letter, if it still existed. This drawer was forbidden territory, because Ma said it held her private things. I happened to know she kept a stash of chocolate mints in there. Once when I peeked into the keyhole, I watched her sneaking one out. I'd a dickens of a time keeping myself out of that drawer once I knew what was in there.

Unless there was hitch-ups, everything was on schedule for my departure in early September. We heard on the radio that the American B-17 Flying Fortresses were now bombing Europe. This was good news to most Americans but worrying for us. Now my brother Jack was in peril. The clock was ticking and there was no more time to waste.

CHAPTER THREE

ON THE MORNING OF SEPTEMBER 2TH, 1942, hours before breakfast, I rolled out of our driveway headed west. The wheels was spinning so fast, my sneakers had trouble gripping the pedals. Any second thoughts, I ordered to get behind number one.

My plan was to go non-stop, but somewheres around New Hyde Park I had to untangle a shoelace that come loose and got jammed in the sprocket. Then, near the boarder of Queens County, the chain began slipping off. I stopped at an Esso gas station and the service boy helped me fix it free of charge. Wiping the motor oil from his hands he said, "Fill'er up, bub?" and we both had a good laugh. I gulped down a bottle of soda and was off again.

It took twenty minutes to pass alongside a cemetery. There was a million tombstones and still not enough space for all the people who had immigrated to the city. What with all the Irish who'd come after the famine, they was now stacking whole families one on top of the other like bricks. That's one of the main reasons my parents moved out to the sticks. Out on Long Island a person planted himself in his backyard if he wanted.

When I got bored, I entertained myself by imagining the scene back home:

"Mary Rose Mooney!" my ma yells at 6:30 AM. "Wake your brother!"

"Yes—hiss—Mother—hiss—dear," my sister says, while she removes a pin from a pincushion. Her hair is in curlers and her mind is bent on torture.

Entering my room, the first thing Mary notices is that the bed is made and I ain't in it. She knows I never make the bed except when I'm bullied: the first clue. She guesses I'm playing some sort of trick, and her back goes up as she braces for a surprise attack, but none will come—that's the sad part. She examines the bedcover and the way all the corners are tucked under. It's Ma's work—once a professional maid. It means one thing: I didn't sleep in my bed.

Mary runs straight for Ma, hiding the pin behind her back. I almost hear Ma saying, "What are you saying, girl?" Ma puts down the sandwich she's lovingly fixing for my lunch and begins making her way to my bedroom. All the way she's calling out for me: "Darling boy! Sweetheart! Apple of my eye!"

I've been known to sleep in all kinds of places—sometimes in the attic, once in the crawl space under the stairs, and lots of times in the barn—so she isn't panicking yet, just a little annoyed. This is the first day of the new school year and she wants me there on time.

Nancy, who worked the late shift at the diner, is woke up by Ma's voice and steps out of her room, wrapping herself in a satin robe. "I'm trying to sleep, Ma," she says, before joining in the search, which soon enough will prove to be a waste of time.

"Where ever could he be?" Ma says to my sisters and to Da. By now he's wide-awake and not too happy about it. He'd have a hangover from staying too late at the pub.

"He's run-off to avoid school," Mary says. "I'll be sure to let Sister Bridget know."

"You'll do nothing of the kind." I picture my ma saying this as she slaps Mary's backside with a rolling pin. "This is none of your business you good for nothing snitch. And now get off for school yourself. And try doing better than Ds this term."

"I'm trying to be helpful," Mary says. "Harrumph!"

Once Mary leaves the kitchen my ma says, "I hate to say it but the girl might be right. What else is the explanation? He's normally such a grand child. Maybe we should have switched him to the public school like he wanted. Tommy has a strong aversion to nuns."

They get it, only too late.

"Well, I'm going back to bed," Nancy says, because she likes to sleep in. "There's nothing to be done now. He'll show up this afternoon, once school is out, with a perfectly logical explanation."

But I wasn't returning home. Because later on that day, I was still making my way by bicycle to the Brooklyn Harbor to hop a ship headed across the Atlantic Ocean.

Coasting down a highway, being blasted by the

wind made by passing trucks, I stayed as close to the edge of the graveled road as possible, what with all the broken glass along the way.

One puncture and my mission was over.

A passenger in a Chevy tossed a chewed up piece of bubblegum at my head. Drivers laid on their horns as they swerved around me.

As I neared the city, I stopped to scout out a 1920's model Studebaker that was abandoned on the side of the highway. Sad to say, everything was already stripped, leaving nothing except a worthless, rusty skeleton. Standing on the roof, I was able to get a view of the city, which is always a thrill for anybody who's lived their whole life stuck out in the boonies. A Coast Guard seaplane trailed a plume of white smoke above the Empire State Building—on watch for German warships.

No thoughts of nuns right then, only nagging regrets that I hadn't kissed my ma good-bye. I'd left a note in her top-drawer though, in place of the letter from Daphne I took with me. All would become clear the moment Ma went for a chocolate mint. Besides, if I turned back now there'd be trouble, and if I kept with my plan there'd be...

What?

Forcing the answers from my mind, I kept on pedaling down Schermerhorn Street headed toward the East River—weaving between Checker cabs stuck in traffic, and sticking my tongue out whenever the cabbies honked their horns.

CHAPTER FOUR

About the same time the recess bell rang at Saint Brendan's Catholic School I made it to the Brooklyn Harbor. Sitting on a stack of newspapers, I checked my feet for blisters. Like I feared, bubbles rose off the surface of my heels and off the sides of my toes. Using the sharp point of my sister's nail file, I popped the blisters, squeezing out blood and water until my feet looked good as new. I shoved them back into the sneakers, thinking I'd earned a rest. I'd picked a good place for it, too, with a view of the East River and downtown Manhattan. The sun was full force on the skyline, rays of light shooting off skyscrapers and off the pure gold roof of the Metropolitan Life Insurance Building. Lady Liberty waved at me and I blew her a kiss. Already there was a fresh wave of huddled masses pouring into New York 'cause of Hitler.

Across the water was where bankers like J.P. Morgan racked in gazillions of dollars. To my right stood the Brooklyn Bridge and I was glad I didn't have to pedal over it. My calves burnt and my thighs felt like toasted marshmallows. I'd never cycled so far in my life.

For a fleeting half-hour I worried that I'd made a mistake. Something felt wrong but I wasn't sure what. Then I knew: I was troubled by being in New York City alone, a scary place with all sorts of lunatics running loose. The sooner I got out of there the better.

My Schwinn Camelback bicycle had to be abandoned, but it couldn't be helped. I loved that bike—its chrome hubcaps and cherry red paint, and the way the spokes buzzed at high speeds. Even though it was a long shot, I left a note in the basket with my address in East Hempstead. Underneath that I put REWARD in big capital letters, without getting into details. My ma would offer a dime to the good citizen who returned it, but by then it would be too late.

My plan was to find a boat leaving for England. I wanted to sail straight for Belgium but that wouldn't be possible. America was at war with Germany and the enemy now occupied France and Belgium. Rotterdam was out too. Most captains didn't want to risk being torpedoed by a U-Boat.

Once in England, I'd figure out a way over the English Channel. Why, the distance across was no farther than what I'd just bicycled. In 1926 a mother swum across the Channel—it was that easy. The only weakness with the plan: I was a cruddy swimmer. Once I came close to drowning in a rip tide and Jack had to bring me back to life with mouth-to-mouth resuscitation. Hopefully the English Channel wasn't turbulent like the Atlantic Ocean. An ocean undertow can suck you down to where the octopuses live. Better to stick to the low end of a swimming pool, I say.

I pushed thoughts of swimming out of my head. What I needed was an ocean-worthy ship, headed in the right direction. The harbor was a hubbub of men working to move freight on and off boats. One ship was bigger than Saint Brendan's Church. Easy to hide out on a jumbo ship, I figured. Beginning my observations, I ducked behind a wood crate that must've contained a bread truck. Two men stood nearby taking a cigarette break. They looked like bodybuilders, with tattoos covering their arms. I got close enough to make out a Hawaiian hula dancer on the buffer man's arm. His friend was wearing a red bandana around his neck. My ears picked up bits of their conversation.

"I'd prefer the navy myself," said Hawaii.

"Na," said Bandana, "I wanna see some action, not be stuck out on a ship for months at a time twiddling my thumbs while California gets invaded."

"Aircraft carrier. That's the life for me, nothing boring about that—fighter planes landing left and right and my job to make sure they don't crash into each other."

"Nevah thought a that." Bandana was beginning to second-guess himself. "But heck—I'm kinda sick of ships after this gig." He shifted his attention back to the crates in front of them. "Let's get these boxes loaded and be off to a cold one. I'll have enough fightin' to do with the missus when I get home afterwards."

Inching around the crate to get a better look at the big ship, I observed something a bit worrying. The crate was stenciled with black writing. Whether it was Chinese or Japanese I wouldn't know. But one thing I did know: what with war raging in the Pacific, I had to be careful not to board a ship headed for Tokyo. Then and there, I eighty-sixed all the cargo ships. And also any boat that looked too small or rickety.

Then my ears rang with the sound of a whistle blowing: a ship getting ready to launch. I followed my ears and ended up looking up at a boat berthed a few docks down. What a beaut: a sailing yacht with polished brass fittings. The wheel was made of wood oiled to a shine. And it was painted my favorite color: blue. My calculations put it at over 100 feet, big enough to cross an ocean. Something this fancy had to belong to J.P. himself or one of his millionaire cronies. Rockefeller probably used it to cruise himself to Florida. This was the sort of ship suited me fine. For one thing, the food would be something. And as a stowaway, I'd get the leftovers. My mouth salivated as my mind pictured a sirloin steak and cheese fondue, with chocolate pudding and marshmallow topping for dessert. The smell of imaginary cheeseburgers hit my nostrils. I almost passed out with joy, or maybe because I'd skipped breakfast and lunch. *No potatoes on a vessel like this,* I thought.

"Bingo," I said, noticing the British flag waving from on top of the masthead. "Welcome aboard Tommy!"

But there'd be no welcome aboard for me, not unless I looked like somebody who went golfing and ate caviar on crackers and lobsters that came all the way from Maine by private airplane. I knew the look, too, seeing that I'd once tried out for a job as caddie at the Piping Rock Golf Club. It was my job to retrieve golf balls from a fishpond, but I used my time to closely observe the rich folks, in the hope that their money would rub off on me.

Hurrying back to the Chinese crate, I ducked out of sight and took the Sunday-best-jacket and tie from my duffel bag. A white handkerchief got placed in the breast pocket with exactly the perfect fold. The aviator glasses came next, perched on the tip of my nose, playboy style. My baseball cap topped off the disguise. The sneakers were the only give away.

I removed a box of firecrackers from my duffel bag, planning to create a small diversion. But the matches were nowhere to be found. The whistle blew again, this time a long hoot followed by two short toots. My hands were shaking, knowing that all my plans were crumbling like oatmeal cookies. And all for the lack of a match. That's when I heard Hawaii's voice, like a foghorn to a lost sailor. I ran over and begged for a book of matches.

"Ain't you a bit young to smoke," he said.

"Ah, let 'im have 'em," said Bandana. I wanted to hug him.

I bolted for the yacht and thanked myself for forgetting to pack dress shoes, because without them sneakers on I'd'a never made it back to the yacht in time. As it was, the blisters slowed me down enough so that I arrived to find dockworkers loosening the ropes that attached the yacht to the pilings. Lighting a whole pack of firecrackers, I threw it up on the deck of the yacht, in front of the helm. This did the trick and had the whole crew running to the explosion with buckets of water.

I spotted a long rope and attached this to my boomerang, throwing it to the top rail with one elegant toss. My tree climbing practice came to good use, as I shimmied up the rope and leaped onto the deck. I did this so fluidly, no one noticed my presence when I slipped below deck and through the first door I found.

The room was used for storage. There were pillars of steamer trunks all embossed with little V's and L's. Some were locked but I found one that wasn't. It stood on end, and when I opened it, out spilled silky dresses of the sort that made my sister Mary drool. I pushed my way into the trunk and managed to close it behind me.

The early start that day, and all that cycling from East Hempstead to Brooklyn, had wore me out. I held my hand over my mouth as I yawned, making sure that no noise escaped. It was stuffy inside a trunk with all them evening gowns but otherwise comfortable. Suffocation might prove a problem and I was glad that once my eyes adjusted, I saw light seeping through a crack where the trunk closed, a good indication of airflow. That's when it came to me: I'd left the door open. Out I went, fast as an alley cat, and shut the door. Darkness filled the room and I felt my way back to the trunk. Before long, I was dozing off.

I woke and, by the feel of my bladder, knew I'd been napping for some while. I listened but heard nothing outside of the trunk. The boat was rocking and I guessed we were underway. I had to pee badly and didn't want to spoil the fancy dresses. Besides, my legs was cramping up.

Once out of the trunk, I seen there was nothing to fear. The only stowaway in the storeroom was me. I felt around for my flashlight and had a look around for a place to relieve myself. A bucket stood in the corner and worked better than plumbing. My mind turned to my parched throat and I went hunting for something to drink. I found crates marked gin and vermouth but I wasn't fool enough to start in with that stuff. I needed to find something less potent, and that's when I heard the soft jiggling of glass bottles which—*jackpot*—led me to a case of soda. Things were looking up. I'd packed a jar of peanut butter, another of grape jelly, and a loaf of Wonder Bread. With a couple Cokes and a Milky Way bar, I soon was settled down to a good supper. I knew it was smart to remain in the storeroom until morning. By then we'd be too far out to sea to turn back and I would be on my way to England.

All of a sudden it dawned on me that just because the ship was British, didn't mean we was headed to England. Maybe the owners wanted to escape the war by bolting for Miami or the Caribbean. I might be stuck on a beach for the duration.

There was only one way to know for sure, and so I took out my pocket compass. I'd used some of the money from the collection plates to buy a professional level one—the kind used by lion hunters on African safaris or mountaineers climbing the Matterhorn. The salesgirl at Woolworths said it was the best money could buy.

I opened the case, unlocked the needle, and watched as it jiggled into action. Facing the direction we seemed to be sailing into, I saw the red needle jolt left and hover over the letter "N." My eyes moved around the rim of the compass, toward the path we was headed—toward the letter "E."

"E" for East! "E" for England!

I was glad, because I hadn't packed my swimming trunks and was in no way willing to wait out the war in Bermuda. I had a brother to rescue.

CHAPTER FIVE

I HAD *THE ADVENTURES OF HUCKLEBERRY FINN*, which I'd checked out of the Hempstead library before blowing town. The book was banned from Saint Brendan's. Mother Superior says that Huck's grammar is an anathema, whatever that is. It's not all spit-polished like John and Jean's, that's one thing. At Saint Brendan's, Huck's kind a grammar gets you 40 lashes. Or worse: crucified.

I was reading with the help of my flashlight. As it turned out, Huck and me had a lot in common. His guardians, the Widow Douglas and her nasty sister, were the Protestant version of Sister Bridget and her sidekick, Sister Michael Ursula. I was rooting for Huck to make his break.

It must've gotten late and past my usual bedtime, because mid-way through the third chapter I was having trouble keeping my eyes opened—even though I was dying to know what come next. No way I was getting back into the trunk for the night, but I had to take cover until morning. I struck on the idea of constructing a fort using some of the steamer trunks, suitcases, and crates. With plenty of experience making forts, within no time I was holed up in my new hideout. I turned off my flashlight, made a pillow out of my dress jacket, and conked out.

Sometime later on I was jolted awake. We had sailed into troubled waters. I told myself a boat this size should have no trouble making an Atlantic crossing. Our biggest threat wasn't waves—it was German U-Boats. Still, I confess for a minute or two, as I was tossed against a case of booze, I lost my nerve. I'm not what you'd call a religious man, but I got to my knees, folded my hands, and prayed to Jesus *plus* St. Christopher—the patron saint of travelers. The storm only got worse. Obviously, I needed the name of the patron saint of sailors, since there was sure to be one. No matter—somebody up there finally passed a message to the right department. The ship righted herself and we avoided drowning.

It's time to survey the vessel, I thought, hoping to find the crew and passengers asleep in their berths. I would avoid the top deck, where somebody might be manning the helm even at this late hour. Opening the storeroom door a crack, I took a peek down the narrow hallway. I'd make myself invisible by removing my sneakers, which had an annoying way of squeaking on wood floors. Once before, while leaving the house on a clandestine mission, my sneakers gave me away. So in my bare feet, I creeped down the hallway toward the forward end of the boat. The bow, it's called. All the cabin doors were shut closed and no one was about.

From one of the cabins came a thunder of snoring. *Experienced sailors,* I figured, because they'd slept through the storm. Two snorers were synced to each other. When one took in air, the other let it out. It made me miss my brother Jack, who bunked with me up until the time he left for Canada. It seemed safe to open the cabin door and have a gander inside.

There was nothing to worry about, because the sailors kept sleeping as I entered a cramped space not much bigger than my ma's kitchen pantry. One sailor was a giant—taller than seven feet and crammed into his berth like a Catholic at Easter Mass. His knees were bent and he'd have a crick in his neck when he woke up. The man on the upper berth was pint-sized—shorter than me. This one was sprawled out, snoring away with a huge grin on his face.

While checking out the room, I spotted a wristwatch in the giant's cubbyhole. Unlike a sailor's cabin, my storeroom was portholeless, making it impossible to tell night from day. A safer bet was a pocket watch clipped to a chain hanging from Peewee's belt. As I slipped the watch into my back pocket, I made a promise to return it before the voyage ended. There'd be enough shucking and jiving to do next time I got into a confessional booth.

I returned to the passageway in search of the galley and a midnight snack, because both hands on my new watch pointed to twelve. The kitchen was easy enough to locate, it being the only room with a window facing into the passageway. Upon entering, I found myself face-to-face with a chocolate layer cake, left right there on the counter. It dawned on me that that cake might fall to the floor during another bout of stormy weather and be ruined. So I took the whole thing back to the safety of the storeroom. That was enough exploring for one night—no need to take no unnecessary chances. And besides, I now had the problem of the cake to attend to.

I woke the next day with a slight stomachache, meaning I'd've missed school even if I hadn't left home. And what a thing it was, to be left unmolested by my sister Mary, who I pictured sitting in Algebra class under the eagle eye of Sister Michael Ursula. I checked the pocket watch. It was already 11:20 in the morning, and the first time I'd skipped two days of school without having to fake a sore throat. That was the problem with having an iron constitution. Every other kid in the school came down with the chickenpox, but not me. Worms, no. Lice, no.

But to keep myself fighting fit, I took time for calisthenics. The exercises had to be done while standing in place—there was room for nothing else. After 100 jumping jacks, I followed with 100 knee squats, repeating the drill until sweat poured from my armpits. I rewarded myself with the remainder of the chocolate layer cake. To my way of thinking, the perfect breakfast. I settled back with *Huckleberry Finn* and the afternoon passed in a flash.

Fortunately, I was in my fortress when I heard the doorknob turn and two people enter the storeroom. I held my breath by shutting my mouth and pinching my nose. A lady's voice said, "O'Reilly, I know I left New York with the pearls. I'm quite certain I'd put them in my Louis Vuitton jewel case."

Jewels, I thought to myself. This was getting more like Treasure Island every minute! There might be some good pirating to do before we reached England. I listened close:

"I can't have lost them, O'Reilly. The pearls are a family heirloom. Part of a set passed down from my grandmother—believed to have once belonged to Catherine the Great. Of Russia. Pooh! We simply must find them."

"My lady," said the man called O'Reilly, who by his accent I knew was an Irishman. "Forgive me for saying so, but may I remind you that you frequently misplace things." He suggested she visualize herself removing the pearls. The trick had always worked for me.

"Jolly good idea," she said, talking like the Queen of England. She started in on a blow-by-blow of her last night at port. First there was dinner with Eleanor Roosevelt, the president's wife with the fat ankles. They ate at a place called the Russian Tea Room, where the First Lady tried to order chipped beef on toast but had to settle for *Boeuf À La Stroganoff.* This was followed by a "leisurely" stroll back to the Waldorf-Astoria, where the English lady: first, admires a bouquet of flowers sitting on her dressing table; second, notices that the roses matched her complexion; and third, admires the beadwork on her Schiaparelli jacket.

"The pearls, my lady. Get to the pearls," said O'Reilly, and I couldn't blame him.

"I'm getting there, O'Reilly, one can't rush these

things. Hum… In the mirror before me, I can see Lord Sopwith's reflection as he approaches from behind, whilst removing his bow tie. Oh, wait a minute… I've got it! It was my husband who last took the pearls from my neck!"

The Irishman was "bold to suggest" they look in Sir Thomas's kit bag for them pearls. (I figured out that Sir Tom was the husband.) O'Reilly said it would save them the headache of rummaging through trunks. I hoped with all my might the lady would go for his plan. If they found me, I might never see Jack again.

"Excellent idea," she said, and they left the store-room. I gulped for air and felt dizzy. Then I found my notebook and added deep breathing exercises to my training regime.

CHAPTER SIX

I WAS KEEPING TRACK OF THE DAYS by carving marks into one of the wood crates, the one labeled vermouth. A boat like this might take a week to cross the ocean, two weeks tops. Without food, I'd starve before landfall. Not the kind of starving you do before supper, but the kind the Irish did during the Great Famine. Killed half the country. So, using my fine-tuned hearing—developed over years ducking my sister—I hunted for food. One night there was a close call when a sailor who, diverting from his regular schedule, took a break from the helm while I was foraging in the galley. Luckily for me, he was whistling "I've Got A Girl In Kalamazoo," by Glenn Miller.

Peeking into the hallway, I realized it was Peewee. His back faced me as he leaped the stairs leading up to the deck. Sometimes my ma said, "Tommy, isn't this weighing on your conscience?" but I never got her drift. Maybe it was missing her, because now them words came back to me full force. For the first time, I felt a nagging feeling I suspected was this conscience thing she was always going on about. I fingered the pocket watch. It was engraved on the back: *Till death do us part, Martha.* Exiting the kitchen galley, I creeped to the door leading into Peewee's bunkroom. Once the door was cracked opened, I threw the watch at his bed using a junk-pitch, the slowest of all, so the watch wouldn't break. I must say—the second that watch rolled off my fingers my conscience all but disappeared.

I'd never be fool enough to take an entire chocolate cake again. If they noticed things missing, the game might be up. I managed to fill my stomach by sneaking slivers of goodies, which the naked eye would never see missing. In this way, I squirreled away cheese of the likes of which I never known existed. One kind had holes in it, like a mouse beat me to it. The package said it came from Switzerland. One nighttime raid on the galley pulled in a huge slab of steak, which was mind-bogglingly thrown in the trash. My ma would make a potpie with it or add it to a beef stew. The supply of soda pop was getting low though. I'd have to start rationing.

After a fourth day at sea, I bunkered down for the night. Everything in me wanted to keep reading *Huckleberry Finn*, but it was important that I bone up on the Nazi agenda, so I picked up *Mein Kampf*, spit on the cover, and started reading. Two lines in, and I began to get a creepy feeling, like Hitler was there in the storeroom with me, hiding in one of the trunks. I shoved the book into the bottom of my duffel and picked up *Huckleberry Finn*. By then I was drowsy, the words blurring on the pages. I was deep under when the sound of people entering the storeroom jolted me awake.

This time it wasn't the Irish servant and his absent-minded boss lady. It was none other than Hitler's dastardly henchman, Heinrich Himmler, and with him, a troop of SS officers. They began searching the room and I trembled behind a stack of steamer trunks. Then Eva Braun, Hitler's girlfriend—dressed in lederhosen—yelled, "Who is responsible for this?"

Spooky, I thought, *she sounds like my sister Mary.*

Eva Braun was pointing to her silk gowns strewn on the storeroom floor. She screeched, "Find the culprit!" One of the nastiest Nazis, a real bruiser named Wolfgang, made his way to my hiding place. He held a leash attached to a gigantic German Shepherd. The hound had teeth the size of a killer whale. I wasn't afraid of Himmler or the SS; I'd make fast work of them using my darts. But the second that dog's fangs came near my leg, I wet my pants that's how scared I was. And screamed at the top of my lungs, "Ma! Ma! Save me, Ma!" Then someone grabbed my collar and started shaking me hard. I opened my eyes and seen it was broad-daylight.

"Got ya!" he said, with a brogue just like Ma's.

I tried to think how an Irishman came to be a Nazi, but it didn't make no sense. Then he pinched my arm and that woke me but good. It was the servant O'Reilly talking. He said, "Jesus, Mary and Joseph, who in God's name are you?" My voice was wobbly, still shook-up by the nightmare. I was in a bad predicament. But at least my leg wasn't mauled, Eva Braun was gone, and my trousers were bone dry.

"Speak up boy," said O'Reilly, spitting out the words. He was wearing the uniform of a bellhop, the kind with two rows of buttons down the front. His white-gloved hands gripped my shirt collar. There was no getting away. So I told him I was on my way to Europe in search of my brother, missing in action. But he didn't look at all simpatico and told me to come along without making trouble. I had no choice but to do what he said. He pushed me down the narrow hallway leading to a door I'd never been brave enough to enter. My biggest worry was that he'd turn the boat around, making me go home, and I let him know it. He boxed my ear and said, "If I know Sir Thomas Sopwith, he'll want to let you off right here. Mid-Atlantic." Then he told me to wait outside and slipped through the door.

Once the door shut, I put my ear to the keyhole, but all I caught was the voice of a lady laughing her head off. O'Reilly opened the door again and motioned with his index finger for me to enter. That's when I got my first look at the main stateroom. It was paneled floor to ceiling in dark oak. Shelves lined the walls, filled with leather bound books. The room was cloudy with the smoke of expensive cigars that came all the way from Havana. A schmaltzy record was playing on a portable Victrola, skipping whenever the boat rocked. On a long sofa, sat a lady dressed in nothing but a thigh-length terrycloth robe, flung open to reveal a bathing suit. My ma would call it indecent, even though I'd seen worse at Jones Beach. The lady was tanned to a crisp, with sunglasses pushed up on her head to hold back her unpinned hair. Her feet were slipped into white tennis sneakers with the heels squashed down. She looked classy in her swimsuit—maybe because she was twirling a long string of pearls.

"Come here," she said, pointing to the floor in front of her.

"Look sharp, young man," said O'Reilly.

I did as the lady asked and stepped to the spot.

Seated near the lady was a man dressed in a yachting getup that put my own to shame. I'd seen a fella like this in a movie called *The Lady Eve*. Barbara Stanwyck played a gold-digger who takes a cruise hoping to swindle a millionaire. She goes after a sucker played by Henry Fonda, dressed just like the man in front of me. I figured this had to be Sir Thomas Sopwith in the flesh. His pants were made of crisp white linen and his jacket of fine navy blue worsted wool. The genuine brass buttons on his jacket gleamed in the light coming from a crystal wall sconce, nailed to the paneling behind him. The crest on his jacket pocket looked like it was made with one hundred percent pure gold thread. A yellow ascot made of silk was wrapped around his neck. His feet were clad in white leather oxfords, polished so they looked like glass. He didn't find a getup like that in the Sears, Roebuck & Company catalog.

"What do we have here?" he said.

"Obviously he's a stowaway," said the lady. "Whatever shall we do with him?"

"Put him to work on the press gang would be one option," said Lord Sopwith.

"There *is* the gang-plank, sir," said O'Reilly. "He'd make excellent shark food."

I looked Lord Sopwith up and down, trying to get his measure. He wasn't a pirate—that much, I was sure of—but he *was* the captain. The faster we made friends, the longer my life expectancy. I asked if he'd ever heard of *Treasure Island*, hoping to gain his sympathy. Maybe he'd think I knew the whereabouts of a treasure and spare my life. Lord Sopwith drew on his cigar, and let smoke escape from the side of his mouth. All the time he looked straight at me, like we was having a staring contest. I made sure not to blink. Finally he said, "A classic," and threw his index finger in the direction of the bookshelves, claiming to have a first edition. His first question told me he knew the story:

"Whom would you be, Jim Hawkins?"

I gave him my name, laying on the Thomas part. But since I didn't have a rank or serial number, I thrown in my address and phone number instead.

"Hempstead," said the lady, speaking to Lord Sopwith, "Don't we take the Hempstead Turnpike out to the Hamptons?"

"Yes, Phyllis, I believe that's right," he said.

"We have a son named Tommy, in fact." She dabbed her eye with a hankie. I wondered if the boy died in the war.

Turning to me, Lord Sopwith asked "what in confounded" I was doing aboard *Endeavour*. O'Reilly said, "Besides pilfering," and wagged a glove at me. When I explained about my brother and gave the details of my mission, Lord Sopwith clapped his hands and said, "Fantastic! Very brave, what?"

"Why, isn't the boy simply adorable?" said Lady Sopwith.

O'Reilly moaned. But you could see Lady Sopwith considered me the perfect boy. That is—until I opened my mouth again.

"My darling child," she said, "Please remove the chewing gum. It is rude to speak to your elders whilst blowing bubbles."

Lord Sopwith pondered his thoughts. Then, I'll be darned, he told me he'd designed one of the airplanes flown by my brother's squadron: the Hawker Hurricane.

I told him straight away that Jack was flying a Hurricane when he shot down his first Messerschmitt, describing the dogfight exactly how it read in the newspaper, but adding a few touches of my own. Lord Sopwith was riveted to his seat. "Capital!" he said. "And you say your brother was shot down over Belgium and is missing? I dare say, very distressing."

"This dreadful war," said Lady Sopwith. "When will the bloodshed stop?"

No one had an answer. Not even me.

Lord Sopwith promised to discuss my mission later but changed the subject, wanting to know if my parents were "apprised of the fact" that I was onboard *Endeavour*, headed for Weymouth, England. I hemmed and hawed a little, before saying that my da was too busy drinking whiskey at the Cold Stream Pub to care much about anything; that sometimes he'd forget my name, even though it was same as his; that he wouldn't notice I was missing until somebody sent a telegram saying as much. Lady Sopwith looked horrified. Lord Sopwith tapped the tip of his cigar in an ashtray, but his face gave nothing away. O'Reilly said, "The drink," and left it at that. Then I mentioned the letter left hidden in my ma's secret dresser drawer, next to the box of Whitman's chocolate mints. My letter explained everything, I said.

"Very clever, Tommy," said Lady Sopwith. "No doubt she's discovered the truth by now." She asked O'Reilly when luncheon would be served.

"At your pleasure, my lady," said O'Reilly, as he snapped to attention.

"Then inform the cook that we shall be having a guest join us," said Lord Sopwith. Then speaking to me, "That is, unless you have another engagement, Tommy."

O'Reilly shot me the evil eye as he left the stateroom. I suspect he was an Irish patriot who didn't like one of his own hobnobbing it with the enemy.

CHAPTER SEVEN

LORD SOPWITH WENT TO A SIDEBOARD and opened the cabinet. There inside—low and behold—was a mini pub. "Martini, Phyl?" he said, pouring liquid into a silver cup. He attached a lid and shook it violently. "Fabulous," said his wife, who turned to me and offered a Roy Rogers. "Fabulous," I said and licked my lips. I had a passion for ginger ale and sugar syrup with maraschino cherries. They served the concoction on the pizzeria side of the Cold Stream Pub, where kids was permitted. Lady Sopwith ate an olive straight out of the jar and I warned her about botulism.

A steward—much younger than O'Reilly—finished laying the banquette table that took up most of the far side of the stateroom, with more silverware than I'd ever seen in my life, and all of it for just the three of us. Lady Sopwith instructed me to bring my drink over and take a seat. Lord Sopwith sat at one end of the table, his wife at the other, me in between.

"Usually, I dress for luncheon," she said by way of an apology. "But when we are at sail, we tend to be rather casual. I plan to go straight back to sun bathing and miss pudding. Trying to get all the color I can. England is so dreary, and I so hate that ghostly look popular in the 20s. I'm hoping for a tan that will last at least a few weeks." She looked me over. "You are looking a tad ghostly yourself, young man." I explained that I was hiding out in the storeroom these last few days and only coming out at night. "You are positively like a mouse," she said. "And I assume you've been with us since New York?"

"Yes, ma'am, that's right," I said. "I hope you don't mind too much—my sneaking aboard without permission. I don't have the bucks for a boat passage and it's very important I get to Europe toot sweet."

"We quite understand," she said. "And to tell you the truth, I'm thrilled you've joined us for the return passage. You see—we just left our little boy in America. We couldn't have our only child killed in a bombing, consequently he's been evacuated." She looked like she might cry. "So many children perished in the Blitz. God only knows what it must be like on the Continent. I shudder to think." She looked at me and forced a smile, changing direction the way grown-ups always do, wanting to keep things from kids because they think it might give us nightmares. So now she had a smile on her face but still with the sad eyes: "I was dreading our Tommy's absence, and then, like a prayer—here you are to take his place!" She cleared her throat to get her husband's attention. "Isn't this a pleasant surprise, dear?"

Lord Sopwith had a pen out and was doodling on the tablecloth. I leaned over and seen that he was working on a design for an airplane propeller.

"Dear, how many times must I ask you not to draw

51

on the good linen? Pooh!" said Lady Sopwith. She made O'Reilly go and fetch a piece of paper. Turning back to her husband, she said, "For heaven's sake, this is family linen, Tom. An heirloom. Really, how maddening."

"I'm sorry, Phyl," said Lord Sopwith, capping his pen and putting it into an inside satin jacket pocket. "Had a sudden flash of inspiration. Couldn't be helped, what? You know how I must get these thoughts down right away or they fly from my head."

I laughed at that. Propeller. Fly. That was good.

"But on Victorian linen? And look at the lovely lace-work—hand work, no doubt, by Belgian Benedictine nuns." She turned to me shaking her head in a way that wanted a collaborator but I wasn't biting. Better not to take her side. I'd worked hard to gain the captain's sympathy and wasn't about to lose it. Just a few minutes ago I was about to be thrown overboard. Now I was being waited on.

Lord Sopwith wanted to know when my brother joined the Royal Air Force. When I answered, he said, "A long run really," pulling on his chin. "Dangerous business. You know, I'm a pilot myself." He went on to tell me that he was the 31st British pilot to get a license and one of the first to fly over the English Channel. "Now *that* was an adventure—"

Lady Sopwith cleared her throat and said, "I'm headed back up to the deck for some more of those lovely rays." She rose from the table, leaving Lord Sopwith and me alone in the stateroom.

"My first crossing was back in 1910, before the

Great War," he said. "I'd bought my plane from Howard Wright—no, not one of your Wright Brothers. A biplane, with—in theory—enough horsepower to lift to 2000 feet. Half-way over the Channel I lost altitude. For a moment there, I questioned the wisdom of ever having started on the trip. By George, seagulls were higher than I was—I had droppings on my clothing to prove it!" He flicked dandruff off his shoulder. "I was bundled up better than Ernest Shackleton on his ill-fated Antarctica expedition. There's a photograph." He pointed to the wall and I rushed over to take a look. Sure enough, he looked like a polar bear in that getup.

"Go on, sir. Give me the rest of the story," I said.

"So I crossed over the Channel finally. I was almost certain I had the French coast in view. Visibility was less than ideal, mind you. The sun was setting. And to top it off, I had a faulty compass."

"I've got a first-rate compass," I said, taking it from my pocket to show Lord Sopwith. "You're welcomed to borrow it anytime you want. It's how I made sure we was heading for England."

He took a close look at my compass and handed it back. "Well, I wish I'd had that compass with me that night. At one point, I nearly collided with a church steeple; but I managed to give it more throttle and get over the belfry without so much as a scrape. Then I hit an air bump and was nearly tossed out of the airplane. I was perched on the leading edge, you understand, with no seatbelt to hold me in. After that I decided it was best to land. Had I waited any longer, I'd have had trouble telling a field from a village. There was a quarter tank of petrol left, and I might have made it further if not for the lack of visibility, what?"

"You landed okay, sir?"

"Bumpy, what with having to land on a freshly plowed field. But otherwise, I'd say it was a pitch perfect landing." He pointed into the distance, narrowing his eyes as if he was viewing the long-past scene. He said, "Then, what would you know? In the twilight I saw a man who had his back to me. Seemed he was hoeing potatoes. I shouted out a greeting—in French, naturally. He slowly stood up, shrugged a shoulder, and went back to hoeing his bloody potatoes!'"

Was the farmer Irish?" I asked. "They love their potatoes."

"No, no," he said grinning. "Turns out I was in Belgium. Took me three hours and forty minutes to get there."

Belgium was exactly where my brother's plane was strafing a German supply train when he was shot down. I said I was worried about Jack.

"Well, Tommy," said Lord Sopwith, "I've done quite a lot of crashing in my day and walked away every time."

I thought for a beat and then said, "It's not a coincidence I ended up on your boat. It's what you call *fate*." I looked him in the eye. "Maybe we use that plane of yours to cross the Channel into Belgium and find my brother."

Lord Sopwith laughed at that one. "Tommy, that plane is long gone, and besides, one can't simply glide over to Belgium these days." He exhaled all his helium and now he looked like a deflated balloon. "The situation has become quite serious in Belgium from what we're hearing—eyewitness accounts of Nazi devilry from refugees pouring into England. Terrible inhumanities. Unspeakable acts of cruelty."

"The plow will become the sword, and the wheat will be watered by the tears of war." I said, surprised I'd remembered the quote. "Adolf Hitler wrote that in *Mein Kampf.* Them exact words."

"Good God!" said Lord Sopwith, shutting his eyes tight and shaking his head. "The brute."

When he seen how glum I looked, he slapped me on the back and said, "Cheer up. We pilots are made of resilient stuff. Your brother will turn up." I tried to cheer up but was having a hard time of it. That is, until O'Reilly returned to the stateroom holding a serving dish and announced that pudding was being served. Turns out it was coconut cream pie and not pudding, which was fine by me.

Things went a little downhill after that first lunch with the Sopwiths. O'Reilly nosed in and insisted I earn my keep mopping the decks and helping the cook with the washing up. O'Reilly, it turned out, had some of the same character traits as my sister Mary. But between work details, Lord Sopwith was willing to teach me navigation. It was a skill he said I had an aptitude for. I managed, single-handedly, to steer the boat all the way between N 61° 12' 4.1518 and N 60° 30' 59.0057, which is a big deal for a 12-year-old. That's like the distance between Manhattan and Cleveland, Ohio.

We was in a convoy, sailing in a pack with other boats—some of them navy vessels, one a fleet carrier. This was to avoid getting sunk by a German torpedo and ending up 2000 fathoms down. We sailed the long way to England, passing by Iceland. We might avoid a torpedo and get sunk by an iceberg instead. Lady Sopwith's tan started fading.

Since she had time on her hands, now with no sunbathing to be done, Lady Sopwith started giving me English lessons. "We do know how to speak English in England," she said. "Not like you unfortunate colonials. We shall have an hour lesson, every day until we make landfall." Turning to Lord Sopwith, she said, "How many more days, dear, until home and hearth?"

"Fourteen, fifteen days, tops," he said.

"—Now, that's a fortnight, Tommy."

"Forts?"

She explained that a fortnight is equal to two weeks. Said that by then she'd have me speaking like an Eton boy, with no trace of my dreadful Long Island nasal accent. I had to ask what being Eton meant. And, gee, was my accent really all that bad? They shook their heads yes, and from there on it was back to school. But unlike the nuns, Lady Sopwith knew how to teach a fella so it didn't hurt. Maybe it had to do with the tennis getup she wore while—I mean *whilst*—teaching me grammar.

Mostly we practiced what you call "irregular verbs." These are action words like run, jump, fly, fight, or explode. But somebody messed up the past tenses, making it near impossible for a kid to get it right. It was a wicked nun, I'm sure. She did it so's she could whack a boy every time he said *bringed* instead of *brought*, or *seened* instead of *saw*. It wasn't my fault I spoke like the son of straight-off-the-boat Irish immigrants, and I told Lady Sopwith as much:

"Them nuns at Saint Brendan are the culprits. They teached me wrong."

Lady Sopwith wrinkled her lips up so they looked like prunes someone had smeared lipstick on. Then she let out a little sigh. "Tommy, darling. Let's reconstruct your sentence, shall we?"

Now I had to rack my brain to remember what I'd said. "*Those* nuns at Saint Brendan?" I stared her in the eye.

"*The* nuns will do."

"The nuns at Saint Brendan are the culprits," I said, "They taught me wrong."

"Incorrectly—they taught you incorrectly."

"Glad you agree," I said.

The Sopwith's idea of entertainment was to sit around after supper acting out a Shakespeare play. I would've rather listened to *Captain Midnight* on the radio, but we couldn't get a signal out in the middle of the ocean. Shakespeare was a playwright like Gilbert and Sullivan of *Pirates of Penzance* fame but without the catchy tunes. Will had English down to a science, or so claimed Lord Sopwith. That's why it was important for me to read the words out loud and have the Sopwiths correct my accent. They had the man's *Complete Works* published by Methuen in the last century. The books were leather-bound with gold trimmed pages. If I rubbed hard enough, I got gold dust on my fingers.

We had just finished off *Richard III*—a rip-roaring story but one you needed an Oxford dictionary to understand. I made it clear to the Sopwiths that I would put up with Shakespeare as long as they didn't make me read *Romeo and Juliet* or his sappy sonnets. So we ~~was~~ were starting in on *Hamlet*, the Prince of Denmark, who spoke the King's English for some reason no one could explain to me.

After supper, on the eighth night at sea, Lord and Lady invited me into the stateroom. They were dressed to the nines, or tens more like it. Lady Sopwith was wearing a dress that made her look exactly like Glinda the Good Witch of the South. She had everything but the magic wand and the giant bubble that *The Wizard of Oz* witch travels in. She let me know straight off that dress was custom made by a fella named Norman Hartnell.

"I was Norm's first patron, and now he has a Royal Warrant as dressmaker to the queen. Of course, her majesty hasn't the right figure to carry off his designs." I caught Lady Sopwith taking a peak at herself in a mirror that swung from a hook, trying to angle so she could get a good look at her narrow hips. Every Catholic knows that vanity is one of the seven deadly sins. being a Protestant, Lady Sopwith was oblivious to the danger.

Whenever the boat rocked on a wave the dress sparkled and so did the tiara that sat perched in a beehive hairdo. I counted at least 130 diamonds—couldn't take my eyes off them—I mean *those*—rocks, trying to figure out how to chip one off without her noticing. Lord Sopwith was wearing a dark red velvet smoking jacket, tied around the waist with a satin rope—the kind of rope they hang murderous noblemen from in England. "It's a privilege of the aristocracy," he explained.

We passed *Hamlet* around, taking turns with the parts. Lord Sopwith started us off by playing the part of Bernardo. "Who's there?" he said, in a voice like a tuba. It's the first line of the play, and if you want my opinion, not a very clever one. *Treasure Island* starts off with the words "Old Sea-dog," which sucks you right in. The "Who's there?" line reminded me of one of them "Knock, knock, who's there?" jokes that were now so popular with grade school boys.

"Landon!" I shouted, and Lord and Lady took their noses out of the play and looked at me.

Then Lady Sopwith began laughing like a hyena. "Landon who?" she yelped, clapping her emerald, ruby, and diamond studded hands.

"Landon Bridge is fallen down!" I said. Lady Sopwith let out a hoot, but his lordship slammed *Hamlet* shut and went to fix himself a rum and soda.

While mixing his drink with a glass swizzle stick, Lord Sopwith was deep in thought. I figured he didn't get the joke. Then he said, "*Macbeth*, scene III." He pulled the *Macbeth* volume from the shelf, opened to the right page, and handed me the book. Sure enough, there it was:

Knock, knock, knock:
Who's there? i' the name of Belzebub.

"Etymologically speaking," said Lord Sopwith, "that would be the origin of your 'Knock, knock' jokes—Shakespeare." After proving his point, Lord Sopwith explained to me that *Hamlet* was not to be made fun of under any circumstances, because it was Shakespeare's magnum opus. I didn't even have to ask him to translate.

"Masterpiece," I said.

"You do know your Latin. One good thing to come of religious education, I dare say, is an appreciation for the classical languages." Why he thought I appreciated Latin was anyone's guess. But I let him roll with it. "You've read Cicero, no doubt?"

"I've read Saint Augustine of Hippo's *De doctrina Christiana*, sir. It was plain torture."

"Not quite *Treasure Island*, what?"

On the twelfth night at sea—surprise, surprise—we began Shakespeare's *Twelfth Night*. By then I was saying thou, thee, and thine instead of you, me, and mine. Thee had to do it. It was either that or get thrown overboard and end up like Jonah the Prophet. No kidding, we were spotting Orcinus orcas close to the convoy—killer whales.

Lady Sopwith was especially "keen" to improve my tenses, which she said were "dreadfully tangled." I was never to use the word *was* when *were* was what was needed.

"Surely, you must see," she said, "that improper speech is very *off-pudding*."

"Off-pudding?" I said, figuring this was a threat. Didn't matter if half the people in the five boroughs messed up irregular verbs. If I wanted pudding, I had to speak like a baronet.

"Not off-pudding," said Lord Sopwith, cracking a smile. "Off-puttttting."

The only thing keeped me from going nuts was time spent swabbing the decks with the crew, talking like a sailor, and learning words that would have my ma after my tongue with a Brillo Pad. It was dirty this and dirty that. Ol' Joe knew every swear word there ever was, and how to combine them for maximum impact. He even knew some in the Cantonese and Mandarin tongue, because he'd once sailed from England to China and back. With opium in the hold. They had stories to tell—some that put hair on my chest. (Especially the ones they told when the Sopwiths were out of earshot.) If I was to try and write out one of their sentences it would go something like this: %$@&*! @& * %$#@^%! *&.

On the afternoon of the fifteenth day we were up at the helm when I scanned the horizon with a Swiss-made spyglass. "Land ahoy!" I shouted.

"Ireland," said Lord Sopwith, and I begun to get jittery.

"We shan't be stopping off there, shall we?" I asked with perfect British diction. While I waited for the Sopwiths' applause to die down, I pictured a horde of aunts and uncles waiting at the port to grab me and send me back to Long Island, thereby preventing me from becoming a traitor to my race. Irishmen never use words like thereby.

"No, Tommy, first Liverpool and then we'll hug the coast straight for Weymouth, where I'll have to turn *Endeavour* back over to His Majesty's Naval Service."

The yacht was requisitioned for war use. The Sopwiths also had a ship like the *Titanic*, which they'd once sailed all the way to the Galapagos Islands off the coast of Equator. But Lord Sopwith hated Hitler so much he let the Royal Navy have both of them. The navy'd only leant back *Endeavour* so's Lord Sopwith could sail over to New York for a secret meeting with Roosevelt. At the president's place up in Hyde Park, they'd discussed the future armament of the U.S. Army Air Force. Big stuff. This was all hush-hush and I'd been sworn to secrecy.

Using the spyglass, I gazed at the green hills my ma so sorely missed. I wondered what she was doing right then and if, in her wildest imagination, she pictured me looking on her homeland. Just like that I was homesick, something I shared with every soldier who'd ever crossed these waters on the way to fight for his country in a foreign war. I straightened my back, held my mop to my shoulder—as though it was a rifle—and looked as brave as I hoped to be. Inside my stomach fluttered.

Lord Sopwith, taking a pipe from his mouth and chuckling said, "At ease, sailor."

CHAPTER EIGHT

Somewhere in German-occupied Europe

THE HEEL OF A KNEE-HIGH black jackboot is pressed to a man's chest—a man who has only a moment ago been thrown to the floor. Viewed from ground level, a Gestapo agent is a terrifying sight.

The man on the floor doesn't recognize the Gestapo agent, who has concealed his eyes with dark glasses. The agent's nose is broken and there are cuts to his face, but the man on the floor did not inflict these injuries. He hadn't seen the Gestapo agent coming. There was no chance for self-defense.

The Gestapo agent's long black leather trench coat is opened, revealing a previously concealed service revolver, resting in a holster.

The man on the ground wiggles, hoping to get loose, but his hands and feet are bound making it impossible. The Gestapo agent removes his revolver and the man on the floor tries to scream; but there is a gag in his mouth.

The man on the ground has no idea what is happening, or why it is that this Gestapo agent has targeted him for execution. His boots flail in the air, aiming for the Gestapo agent's crotch, but miss; his steel helmet comes off his head and rolls across the hardwood floor, crashing into the leg of a metal desk. This is unfortunate, to say the least.

On the side of the helmet is the insignia of the SS—the one that resembles two thunderbolts. His insignia is the last thing the SS Waffen troop leader—or rather, *Truppführer*—sees before he is shot in the head.

CHAPTER NINE

I WAS PINNED INTO THE CABIN of a flat bed truck—stuck in the middle, straddling the gearbox. O'Reilly was gripping my elbow so I couldn't escape. The truck driver was keeping me from making an exit from the driver's side. The ship's crew loaded steamer trunks into the back of the truck. Lord Sopwith stood beside us smoking a pipe, while Lady Sopwith directed the crew, making sure the trunks containing her dresses got loaded right side up.

"Sorry about this, my boy," said Lord Sopwith, who was the first to thwart my escape from the boat once we'd docked in Weymouth. "Just rang up an old schoolmate—works at the American Embassy. Hum—so it's decided you'd best stick with Lady Sopwith and I until we can put our heads together and work out a plan to get you home. It's either that, or I turn you over to the customs police. More comfortable with us, what?"

"We can't have you wandering about the English countryside, Tommy," said Lady Sopwith, who had a soft spot for me. "There are ruffians everywhere."

"The chaps at the embassy will sort it all out. Meantime, best we keep an eye," said Lord Sopwith wiping dust from his wire-frame glasses.

"His lordship means *I'll* be keeping an eye on you," whispered O'Reilly as he tightened his grip on my elbow.

"You traitor. You...Benedict Arnold!" I knew that got him where it hurt.

Lord Sopwith looked slack-jawed at *Endeavour*, docked at the pier, like he'd never see her again. "Straight to Hampshire," he said, hitting the hood of the truck. "It will be good to be home again, O'Reilly." Walking over to a Rolls Royce, he waited for the chauffeur to open the door. Then he jumped into the back seat, next to his wife.

I was a prisoner. That much was clear. The Sopwiths, as much as I liked them, were now my mortal enemies. They stood between me and rescuing my brother Jack. I would have to devise a plan of escape, and quickly, if I didn't want to be carted back to East Hempstead.

As we began driving, I tried to imagine the Sopwith place—picturing an ancient castle with a moat around the perimeter, filled with vicious, man-eating alligators. I might drown trying to swim across a moat, but the alligators I'd handle with my slingshot, using rocks as ammunition. There would be tall, stone fortress walls, built to keep people out—but in my case, in. This posed no obstacle whatsoever for an expert climber, so long as he didn't remember his fear of heights. There would be turrets with narrow slits for windows, designed to be just wide enough to point a bow and arrow, and if I was lucky, wide enough for a kid to squeeze through. I sucked in my stomach.

It was the dungeon I feared most. This is where O'Reilly would want to keep me—chained to a wall and fed on bread and water until the embassy people came to get me. Born a little earlier, I might've learned the art of escape directly from Harry Houdini, because he'd lived in New York too. Unfortunately, he'd died in 1926 and was buried along with his top secrets. I have to admit my training was lacking in this one area. All I had was my sister Mary's nail file.

I looked over to O'Reilly and he glared back at me with a sinister gleam in his eye. When I stared back with a wild look, he growled under his breath.

As we drove through the English countryside, I began to see signs of war for the first time. There were people in uniform everywhere I looked, even girls. It's true that men were beginning to join up in America, and I'd recently seen some in their spanking-new army uniforms. But here, half the population was ready to take on the Nazis. Adolf Hitler better not dare put a toe in England. Once we got stopped at a crossroad and forced to wait ages as a convoy of army vehicles a mile long passed in front of us. The rumble shook the ground.

We passed through a small village, which was damaged when a bomb dropped smack in the middle of the town square, knocking down a large monument. I saw what was left of a bronze statue of a mounted horseman. Aside from knocking the bronze man from his horse, the bomb blew out the windows of the tavern across the street. You looked straight through them window frames and saw men sitting at long wooden tables, laughing and drinking beer, as though nothing had happened. There was a red phone booth knocked over and the phone must still of worked because a lady was bent over and was speaking into the receiver.

"Fortunately, most of us were in church that morning and no one was hurt," said the driver. "No one but Lord Wellington, that is." He chuckled when he said "Lord Wellington."

"He weren't liked around here, were he?" I said, not certain if I'd said it proper. The Sopwiths were in the Rolls, so it didn't much matter.

"Lord Wellington? Why, we English worship the man. He's a national hero. Put an end to Napoleon Bonaparte at Waterloo, didn't he?"

Oh, that Lord Wellington—the statue.

"Have many German bombs dropped around here?" I asked, electrified that I was now in the thick of it.

"Not bad around these parts, laddy. Now, London is a different kettle of fish. Up in London they're getting a pounding, no doubt about it. 40,000 souls perished in the Blitz, most of them Londoners—that's more than in this whole parish."

I tried to picture 40,000 souls but it was impossible not to think about their bodies too: bloody and blown up, missing limbs, crushed faces. I had to shake my head violently to get the picture to leave. Meanwhile, the driver kept on talking:

"In London people are spending more time sleeping in the Tube stations than comfortable in their own beds. My sister had to send her four boys down to stay with the wife and me, and we've our hands full, what with them running around and mucking about. I'll be glad when this blooming war is finished and we send 'em packing."

I asked how far it was to London. I'd be making my way there to find Daphne and enlist her help.

"Couple hours drive, is all," said the driver. "That's where Jerry wants to drop the bombs. I think when one falls around here, it's just slipped out early. No one's taken deliberate aim at Wellington in, I'd say, nearly 125 years."

I knew he was making a joke and expected me to laugh. But the picture of those 40,000 bodies snuck back into my head and my laugh came out like a sneeze.

"God bless," he said.

We followed the Rolls as it turned off a main road and down a narrow lane lined with old trees that got planted perfectly spaced from one another. The branches joined up over the road, forming a leafy tunnel. It reminded me of the Midtown Tunnel, the one that now connected Long Island to the city.

"Warfield Hall, the seat of Lord and Lady Sopwith," said O'Reilly, pointing his nose 38 degrees northwest. My fertile imagination had done me dirty, because perched up on a hill was a house like the ones they got up on the north shore of Long Island—houses so big they give them names instead of numbers. There was one like it in Westbury, built by a fella named Phipps, who sold the steel beams we Irish lugged up to the top of skyscrapers and welded into place. Warfield Hall didn't resemble a castle one bit and probably had no dungeon. Funny, but I was a little disappointed.

We pulled up to the front of the house and Lord Sopwith exited the Rolls, coming alongside the truck to give his instructions to O'Reilly. "We can't lose our young charge, and so as long as he's our houseguest, perhaps he shall enjoy spending his days in the library." He asked O'Reilly to step out of the truck so they could have a word in private. Then looking in my direction, he said in a whisper, "Might be best to lock him in, what?"

"With pleasure, my lord," said O'Reilly.

Looking at me Lord Sopwith said, "You do like to read, I noticed. Might want to try your hand at Wordsworth. Or Coleridge."

Realizing an escape from a library would be a cinch, I looked as cheery as possible. "Oh, I'm a regular bookworm, sir."

"Well then, that's settled. Just don't eat any of my first editions." With that, he leapt up the stairs, taking three at a time. Dignified, they call it.

As it turned out, I was wrong about an easy getaway, because the library windows faced out to the front drive. Dead center the chauffeur worked away waxing and polishing the Rolls, with all that chrome. A gardener trimmed the topiary lining a circular driveway. It's time consuming keeping shrubs from looking shrubby, especially with a hand clipper. *If only he had a gas-powered version*, I thought—he'd be done and gone in a fraction of the time. My dilemma came down to gas rationing. It looked like I wasn't going anywhere until sundown.

I eyed the windows and seen that the sashes were easy to open, so I just twiddled my thumbs waiting for darkness to set it. Then I found a book I'd always wanted to read: *Robinson Crusoe*. Found it smack in the middle of a section labeled "Romantic Poets," where it shouldn't of been. I settled myself in a wing-backed chair next to one of the windows. The room was warm and stuffy and I dozed off. A maid, not much older than me, woke me as she fumbled a tray into the library. On the tray was a stack of sandwiches which, funny enough, contained nothing but paper-thin slices of cucumbers. And just the thing I needed to take my mind off of my troubles: tiny cakes, each individually iced and decorated—filled with strawberry jam. Steam rose from a pot of tea. I poured some into a cup, but when I found only one sugar cube in the sugar bowl, I decided to pass. *Rationing again,* I thought. What I wanted was a soda, anyways.

When the maid returned to take the tray, she looked at the empty plates. "You've got an appetite on you, I'd say." She was real Irish, as it turns out. Maybe I'd make her my accomplice.

"You know I'm in the library against my will, don't you?"

"So I take it. I'm instructed to keep the door locked."

"Any chance you'd be a doll and forget to lock up on your way out?" I said, faking an Irish accent. I winked. Hopefully that buttered her up.

"Don't be daft! I'd lose my place and end up on the dole. And besides, they're good to me here. Mrs. Balson is teaching me how to cook and bake. Matter of fact, it was me what made the very cakes you scarfed down. Pretty soon I'll be advancing to soufflés and molded aspic. And I'm getting the inside scoop on housekeeping, too. Mrs. Balson, she's getting on. Why, if she holds out long enough to train me up proper, she's promised to recommend me to take her position. So there you have it: I'm going places and I'll not have you interfering."

"What about that O'Reilly? You don't mind taking orders from a tyrant?"

"Mr. Seamus O'Reilly? He's a pussycat. Takes a while for him to warm up to a body, that's all. His bark is a lot worse than his bite."

"Pussycats don't bark," I said. She grabbed the tray away, even though there were still a few cake crumbs I wanted to eat. As she left, she slammed the door and made a noisy job locking up.

I was let out of the library for supper but roughhoused down to the servant's quarters by O'Reilly, who clutched my elbow the whole way. Mrs. Balson turned out to be a grey-haired lady who—by the look of her—enjoyed eating as much as cooking. A mutton stew bubbled away on the stove. I got a whiff of bread baking in the oven. And there was a nice apple pie cooling on a rack by the sideboard. It had one of them basket weave tops only professional bakers know how to do up.

"I'm ever so glad to have a child in the house again," said Mrs. Balson. "Been quiet since our little Sopwith pup went off to America."

The grub was good, and I shoveled it into my mouth.

I didn't know what the future would bring but imagined times of hunger and near starvation. And I'd escape out of a wide-open window and not have to squeeze myself out of a slit in a castle wall. I could afford the extra padding.

"How ever will I get by with my rations? Why, this boy is like to eat us out of house and home, Mr. O'Reilly!" said Mrs. Balson.

"Don't trouble yourself, Mrs. Balson. We'll soon have him off our hands."

"Is that so?" she said.

"It's my understanding that someone is on the way from the orphanage to fetch him. He'll be incarcerated there until his parents come and retrieve him...that's if they ever do."

I froze in place, with a fork full of mutton stew held mid-way between the plate and my jaw. I shifted my eyes between O'Reilly and Mrs. Balson.

"Get on! Her ladyship'd never allow that to happen and you know it. Those appalling orphan farms—and now when they're so over-crowded with war orphans. Her ladyship wept all the way through *Oliver Twist*. Shook up she was. She'd never!"

Turning to me she said, "Tommy, you'll find that book in the library, tearstains all over it. It's Charles Dickens wrote it."

Then she turned her shoulder to O'Reilly and huffed.

CHAPTER TEN

The next day, I joined Lord and Lady for tea on the patio, where I was able to get the lay of the land. What a shock it was to see the English Channel right there in the backyard. With a decent spyglass, I might've seen France.

Sandwiches got put on the table, this time containing nothing but thin slices of hard-boiled egg and weeds. Lady Sopwith called it watercress but it seemed like weeds to me, and it took a dozen to fill my stomach. What made the job extra hard was that I was made to hold them with only my index and third fingers.

"I do hope, Tommy," said Lady Sopwith, "that this isn't all too trying for you. It's admirable you want to rescue your brother, but you must see it's quite impractical. Good to trust such things to the trained professionals. No doubt, Britain has many secret agents undercover all over Europe. Surely finding a missing RAF pilot is tops on their list of priorities, and—"

"Now Phyllis, remember loose lips sink ships, what?" said Lord Sopwith.

Lady Sopwith turned to me and winked.

Lord Sopwith gazed out at the Channel. "I say, fine

day to be out on the water. Tomorrow it's back to the drawing board for me, I'm afraid. No sense being cooped up in the library, Tommy. How would you fancy joining me? I've got a jolly fine powerboat. Maybe we'll get in a swim."

"That's a swell idea." I was sure glad for the chance to get outside even if it *did* include swimming.

The boat was a sleek racing boat. I watched as Lord Sopwith added fuel from a gas can he took from a boat-house. We boarded and he made sure I buckled my seat-belt. "She has a top speed of nearly 52 knots," he said, as he pulled back the throttle and we jolted away from the slip. A knot is a nautical mile, I came to learn.

We anchored the boat in a quiet cove and I jumped right into the water and floated on my back. Lord Sopwith took a Cuban cigar from his pocket and lit it. Meanwhile, I did some quick math in my head and when I got back into the boat I said, "So that means a boat like this crosses the Channel in half an hour!"

"Hypothetically, I suppose," he said, getting ready to jump in the water himself. "Although, one would want to go a bit slower."

"Have you ever crossed the Channel in a boat?"

"Many times, young man. Many times. Of course, I'd prefer to cross in something larger than this." He looked in the direction of France. His eyes got watery. Then he told me that in '40, when there were more than 300,000 men to evacuate from France in advance of the approaching Germans, and very little time to do it, he sailed over in *Endeavour.* "Every seaworthy vessel in England was employed in that operation—anything that could float. Sad day it was too, with the Nazis getting ready to goose-step into Paris and under the *Arc de Triomphe.* Bloody, awful mess."

"I hate all Germans," I said. "Except for Mr. and Mrs. Fisch, my neighbors."

"Well, I suggest you temper your feelings," said Lord Sopwith. "There are plenty of good Germans, some dear friends of mine, who are conflicted about what's happened to their country. Some are actively working against Hitler. Don't be so quick to judge, young man."

An hour on the water and I was beginning to look like a lobster—I have Irish skin with freckles—so I was glad when Lord Sopwith said it was time we head back.

As we hiked up to the house, I watched Lord Sopwith's every move. I made small talk as I followed him into the house, the whole time asking questions about boats and fishing: fly-fishing, tackle and fishing lures, which way salmon ran—upstream or down? Lord Sopwith answered my questions without suspecting my real objectives. My trick worked. I saw him put the speedboat key on a bookshelf in his study.

"What do you say we clean up before dinner, Tommy? Won't do to join Mrs. Balson's table smelling like a fish, old boy."

"No, sir, wouldn't do at all," I said.

CHAPTER ELEVEN

SO FAR, MY PLANS TO ESCAPE got thwarted at every turn. I'd been in England almost a week. Darkness made for the perfect escape from the library but, every night after supper, I was locked in a windowless attic room.

It didn't look like a prison cell—Mrs. Balson made sure of that. She directed the chauffeur and the footman to carry up a nice feather bed and a side table with a good reading lamp. I was allowed to remove whatever books I wanted from the library, as long as they weren't illuminated manuscripts. So for a while I made the best of it.

It was while reading *A Christmas Carol* by Charles Dickens that an idea struck me like lightening. It was the Christmas theme done it: if fatso Santa could come down a chimney, couldn't a beanpole go up one? That very night I dragged my duffel bag up the chimney, broke the chimney cap with a hammer, and was out onto the roof. Like Tarzan, I swung down the ivy vines covering the front of the house. Didn't need a rope or nothing.

During my survey of the property I'd noticed, in the distance, train tracks coming to and from a village. The train, I figured, would take me to London. So I made straightaway for the village. With any luck, there would still be a train coming through that night. If not, there would be one first thing in the morning—hopefully, before anybody discovered I'd bolted.

Far from the village, I heard a steam whistle. I ran so fast, it caused a painful stitch in my side and my heart was beating like the drum in a marching band. I got to the station in the nick of time. The signboard over the platform said London. The doors to the cars were already shut and the train was beginning to pull away. I jumped onto a stair ledge and held tight to a handrail. As the train gained speed, I clung onto it for dear life. "Whoopee!" I yelled, as the conductor blew the steam horn and the train entered a tunnel. The sad thing was that my baseball cap flew off my head, lost forever.

I peered into the window and spied on the passengers inside a train cabin. It was dark outside and it was sort of like looking into a fishbowl. On one side sat a lady and a kid, on the other side, a man. The grown-ups were having a knockdown-dragout fight and didn't notice that a boy was hanging from the side of the train. I watched in horror as the lady poked the man with a knitting needle—the man didn't even flinch. Only their little girl was aware of me. Her nose was pressed to the window, her tongue slobbering the glass. I did likewise and crossed my eyes.

The train came into another station, slowing enough for me to crawl into the window. The man and his wife kept rocketing insults as I leapt past, into a long corridor. The little girl ran after me, and I said, "Scram!" When she kept on following me, I whirled around and turned my eyelids inside out so that I looked like a zombie. This did the trick: she burst into tears and ran back to her folks. I was free to look into each cabin until I found one that was empty. I stashed my duffel bag under one bench and myself under the opposite bench.

Two men entered the cabin a few minutes later. Even though I only seen their shoes, socks, and trouser hems, I knew both had on uniforms: one army and one Royal Air Force. The soldier asked for a cigarette, which he called a *fag*.

"Might as well call it a coffin-nail," said the airman.

After a couple minutes silence, I smelled smoke— or as Lady Sopwith would say, *smelt* smoke. It was hard not to start coughing. They struck up a conversation and the army fella called the RAF man a lucky devil. "I wanted RAF, but turns out I'm blind as a bat. Didn't even realize it until my physical, that's the funny part. Up until then, I thought the world was a blurry place."

"Got eyes like a cat," said the airman, taking a long and loud drag off his cigarette. "Runs in the family. My father was a sharpshooter in the Great War." He said he was a rear gunner on a Bristol Blenheim and he'd flown twenty missions during the Battle of Britain and he'd shot down a dozen Messerschmitts. At least.

"What I wouldn't do to trade places with you," said the army man. "The only thing I'm flying is a desk in a windowless office in London—sending rations from one warehouse to another. Takes a brave man."

"Well, if it makes you feel any better, there's been

plenty of nights over France I've dreamed about a desk job like that. And now that we're making missions to Germany, well—"

"Awfully good of you to say. Where are you headed now?"

"I'll switch trains at Waterloo for Victoria. I'm stationed down at RAF Rochford in Southend-on-Sea."

Southend-on-Sea! I'd heard that name before. I'd found it on a map and circled it with a red crayon. Used a ruler to figure out exactly how far it was from Hempstead, New York: 3,549 miles, as a bird flies. Then I'd taped the English map to one wall and a New York map to the other. I stuck one of Mary's pins in the Hempstead dot and one in the Southend-on-Sea dot. A black thread connected the two places and I had to duck every time I got into bed. I was so surprised to hear the mention of the place that I hit my head on the underside of the bench seat. This was an opportunity too good to miss. I jimmied out from under the bench.

"Blimey!" said the soldier.

"For crying out loud," said the airman.

I brushed off my trousers and extended my hand to the airman. Taking a firm grip, we introduced ourselves. I warned him that I'd have to jump back under the seat when the conductor came to collect the tickets, but that it was vitally important we speak.

"Fire away," he said. I got right to the point, asking him if he'd heard of my brother, who'd been stationed at RAF Rochford in Southend-on-Sea. I described my brother to a tea. "Mooney?" he said, looking up at the ceiling and exhaling rings of smoke. "I believe not. I do know one chap with the Eagles though, name of Oscar Coen. He's with the 71ˢᵗ. He'd know your brother Jack, without a doubt."

I told him it was crucial I meet this Oscar Coen. Before the airman answered, the cabin door began to slide open and a conductor bellowed, "Tickets!" The airman stood to block the conductor's view as I slid back under the bench.

After handing over their tickets, I heard the door slide shut again and the airman put the latch on. "Coast is clear, old bean." I slid out from under the bench, just as he was closing the curtains. He got right back on track: "Oscar Coen—Well, you're in luck. It happens that my best girl and his are thick as thieves. Happy to give you Sally's number—just ring her up. But why not simply phone your brother Jack?"

"Jack's missing somewheres in Belgium, is why," I said. "I want to know what my brother might be up against over there. You know—get the lay of the land."

"Reconnaissance is what it's called," said the soldier. "Recon for short."

"You think this Oscar fella might help with recon?"

"Oscar? Most assuredly," said the airman. "Why, Oscar was downed as well. Missing for almost two months and everyone assumed he was dead. I hadn't a minute with Sally the whole time. She was off comforting Oscar's sweetheart. Luckily for me, one day he waltzed into the ops building at North Weald. Like nothing had happened. Said to the sergeant on desk duty, 'Did ya miss me?'

I blurted: "He should'a said, did *you* miss me."

The airman slapped my back. "Right you are!" Then he rubbed his chin trying to remember where he'd left off.

Suddenly I had a vision of myself in a nun's habit, the kind that's jet black from head to toe. My lower lip started wobbling. Wasn't right that I'd corrected a war hero, flying ace, and original Eagle Squadron pilot. And when he wasn't even there to defend himself. There was one way to make up for my blunder, so I said, "What happened after Oscar said, did *ya* miss me."

The airman snapped his index against the fourth and picked up where he left off. "Turned out that during a raid over France, debris from an ammo train Oscar'd fired on hit his Spitfire, forcing him to bail out. Not a scratch on him. Good thing for Oscar the French Resistance got to him ahead of the Gestapo. They smuggled the old boy to Spain and from there he took a boat back to England. If anyone can help you, it's Oscar." He stopped short, combed his fingers through his moustache and said, "What are you—like eleven years old?"

"Practically thirteen," I said.

Consulting his watch, he wanted to know if my mum knew that I was out this late. His watch was a fine military issue chronograph, the kind with three dials, but I didn't even think about taking it. "Oh, sure," I said. "I'm traveling home from my grandma's. Ma will be waiting for me at the station."

"And your granny neglected to give you train fare?"

asked the soldier.

Before I could stop it, a story about using the money for a comic book slipped out. Hopefully the soldier wouldn't want specifics. The English probably had different superheroes than us Americans, ones that spoke properly and drove Rolls Royces. After all, Superman was fighting for Truth, Justice, and The American Way. He worked for the *Daily Planet*, which every kid knew was really the *Daily News*. And where's else was Metropolis but New York City? But maybe in the English version Superman fought for Truth, Justice, and The *English* Way. Maybe English kids thought that Metropolis stood for London. And the problem didn't stop there: Flash Gordon graduated from Yale, a college in Connecticut. But maybe in the English version be graduated from somewheres else. Eton.

"Well, that's fine then," said the airman. He put his left ankle on his right knee, leaned his elbow on the armrest, and sank back into the seat.

I pleaded for Sally's phone number, getting my knees dirty to drive home the point. He put her exchange and number on the back of his ticket stub and handed it to me with a wink, "Promise me you won't ask her out on a date." I held up three fingers: the Boy Scout pledge.

People began piling into the corridor as the train pulled into a terminal big as Penn Station, only you couldn't get a Nathan's Famous hotdog here; and that's what I always looked forward to on trips into New York City. I figured this was Waterloo Station, London. My plan was to head straight to Daphne's address. Before I left East Hempstead, I had the bright idea to write Jack's fiancée, informing her of my imminent arrival.

She'd be expecting me.

CHAPTER TWELVE

FINDING DAPHNE'S PLACE was more trouble than I counted on. First off, I made the mistake of thinking London was the same as Manhattan. New York City is a cinch to navigate, what with most streets numbered and running the whole length of the island. Everything that runs width-wise is divided into east and west, and even some of them streets got numbered and called avenues. All you need to know is the names of a few streets: Park, Lex, and Madison. If you have that down, and your numbers, it's impossible to get lost.

Well, maybe not impossible. Once we'd all gone in to see the Ringling Bros. and Barnum & Bailey Circus and I got a hankering for one of them huge pretzels with rock salt that are sold from carts. I slipped out during the stupid dog act, because I hate dogs—especially when they dress them up and make them walk around on their back legs. I didn't pay enough attention—my slip-up— and once I ate the pretzel, I was shocked to find I didn't know my way back. This was when I was younger and scared easy. But before terror could grip me, Jack showed up, grinning and bending his index finger. It was that pretzel's fault we missed the trapeze act, which was the whole reason for coming in the first place.

London was different, one huge maze. Every little street had a new name and there didn't seem to be a connection between them. On Long Island, neighborhoods are organized with a theme. If you're looking for Maple Street, for example, and you happened on Pine Street, you're getting hot. But in London, Maple Street might be next to Woodpecker Street, which might be next to Daffodil Road. I got frustrated walking in circles—getting farther and farther from Waterloo Station but probably no closer to Daphne.

I didn't want to stop and ask for directions, because I couldn't trust anyone. Ma always warned me not to talk to strangers in the city and not to take candy from them when they tried to lure you into their car—even if they were waving Tootsie-Rolls. Besides, it was now near midnight. A kid walking around by himself might raise a red flag—like he'd run-away from home or something like that. The world is full of do-gooders who would want to drag him to the nearest police station.

My stomach began to growl and I realized I was starving. Just then, my nostrils got filled with the mouth-watering smell of French-fries. I followed my nose and took a seat on a stool in front of a food booth. The cook behind the counter said, "What'll it be, guv'nah?" I had a little trouble making out what he'd said.

"French-fries, sir."

The man laughed and said, "Yank, huh?"

Now, why he'd think that? I wondered. "Been a

86

Brooklyn Dodger fan my entire life," I said. Too bad I didn't have a baseball cap to prove it.

"That's a good one!"

A beautiful plate of French fries was slap down in front of me, gleaming with hot grease—the way I liked them. "'Av some fish to go with 'em chips?"

"No thank you, sir, but I will have some ketchup."

"Vinegar."

"Pass," I said, and tucked into the plate of fries, happy as a clam in a shell. I finished in no time flat and asked for another order.

"Don't yer mum feed you at home?"

"Oh yes, sir. But she's Irish and we get our potatoes either baked, boiled, or mashed." Lifting a fry, I said, "This is the way to get your potatoes, if you ask me."

The cook watched me wolf down the second serving. "At explains it," he said. "The Irish can't cook for nothing. Me wife is Irish, so I should know." He draped a dishtowel over his arm. "Truth be told, we English aren't exactly masters of the culinary arts. I'd say what you 'ave in front of you is the very summit of our skills: fish and chips—that is if you'd 'ad the fish. Now, you didn't hear me saying it—but the French, they're the ones know what's what." He pointed at my empty plate, rallying, "They don't 'ave fish and chips like that in Germany. Keeps us going, it does."

"You got Coca-Cola?" I asked.

"Tea. No sugar, I'm afraid. There's a war on, if you 'aven't noticed."

"I'll pass."

Just as I finished the last fry, an ear-piercing siren went off and the cook began to shut up his booth. He said, "Better come along, lad," and we headed with a wave of people to a staircase in the middle of the sidewalk and began stepping down into a chute. I heard airplanes coming closer, and the sound was like a swarm of buzzing bees. Any second and a bomb could fall on our heads, but everybody was being polite: After you—No please, after you—Pardon me. This never would've happened in New York—there'd be a stampede right off the bat. But when the sound of German bomber engines got right overhead, some people began pushing. One lady stumbled, breaking the heel off her shoe. My new friend, the cook, helped her up. I held onto his apron for dear life.

We entered a train station identical to the New York City Subway. I took the subway loads of times with my parents, when we'd go to visit an uncle who lived up in the Bronx. In New York only hobo's sleep down in the subway. Here in London, there were hundreds of ordinary people making their beds for the night. It was like a crazy sleep over party.

"Might as well get comfy," said the cook, who found an empty space along the wall and invited me to sit. "We could be here a while."

I overheard one lady say to another, "Bloody Hitler. I hope someone drops a bomb on his head tonight."

"Now, wouldn't that be lovely, dearie," said her friend.

After a few minutes I heard a whistling sound

above and the first bomb hit nearby. The lights in the station flickered on and off. Dust floated in the air, and people huddled closer together.

My heart was thumping. Nothing as exciting had ever happened in East Hempstead, not since the Revolutionary War, anyway. At first I was glad to be in London and in the thick of it, and not just hearing about the war on *The Voice of America*—thousands of miles from the real action. Then a bomb dropped close—almost a direct hit—and it shook the whole place so bad, tiles fell off the walls. Right then I would've given anything to be a thousand miles away, listening to *The Voice of America*. I wouldn't of even complained about the boring parts, like "A Word From Our Sponsor," followed by a advert for cold cream.

I'll confess that I even screamed a few times, which wasn't something English people did, them already used to the war. But they sure looked terrified, same bug eyes as me. Soon though, the explosions started sounding more distant. The tension loosened and everybody got chatty with one another. I figured this was a good time to find the men's room but, when I stood up, my legs were shaking so bad I had to sit down again or fall over.

"My sister's place got leveled in the Blitz," said a lady on our left, to no one in particular. "She was sitting on the loo, you understand, and when the bomb hit everything around her crumbled—including the wall facing the street. There she was, with her knickers pulled down around her ankles, for all and sundry to see. She's still not recovered from the shame of it."

"I've got one to top that," said a man seated to our right.

"Let's hear it," said the cook. "We need a little entertaining down here."

"You see—me wife, she were having her bath when the house was hit. She ran straight out the front door, starkers, she were. She's a looker too. Had nothing on but her wedding ring. A bloke comes strolling along, looks down at her ring and says, 'Nice day to you, ma'am. Tips his hat and continues on. A real gent."

BOOM, BOOM, came the sounds above us. I scooted closer to the cook, who put his arm around my shoulder. Ma's rosary beads would've come in handy then.

"That's the one good to come out of all this," said the lady, when the ruckus died down. She was wearing a hat with a parrot feather stuck from the side. "Seeing people rise to the occasion, pulling together and acting decent."

"'ear, 'ear," said the cook. "Makes you proud to be an Englishman." All the people around us made sounds or nods of agreeing.

The man to the right continued his story where he'd left off. "Me wife took a bath in her swimsuit for a month afterwards. Now she never gets in the bath, not unless she's got her robe right near by."

"No wonder," said the lady. "I'll start doing that myself."

Another bomb dropped close by and the lights went out. It got quiet then, quiet enough that I heard a lady weeping and her husband saying, "Lost our boy in the Blitz, we did. Hard to be reminded, not that we forget for a second." My friend the cook heard it too, and squeezed my hand.

"The boy died?" I whispered.

"Seems so," said the cook, all choked up. I got choked up too, so I didn't say anything more.

The lights came back on, and a lady with the feather cap reached into her string bag and pulled out a package, "Biscuits, anyone?" I was the first to volunteer when I realized she was offering us cookies. The man with the naked wife pulled out a thermos and offered us all tea.

"Lovely!" said the lady. Her happy-grunts, as she sipped tea from the thermos cap, made me want some myself. I dunked a cookie into the tea and it wasn't half bad. She opened up a blanket and made a place for me to lie down. "Poor little thing," she said. "We'll find your mummy in the morning. For now you're safe with us, duck."

I crashed fast asleep, as bombs rained down above us. This much hair-raising tuckered a fella out. I dreamed about fireworks on the Fourth of July. When I got to the grand finale, another siren blared and woke me. The lady with the parrot feather cap said, "That'll be the all-clear. Time to be getting home to make breakfast for the hubby."

That reminded me that I'd never paid for my French fries the night before. I reached into my pocket and removed my stack of dollar bills and reminded the cook that I owe him for the fries.

"Ah, forget it. They're on the 'ouse," he said and

pointed to my dollar bills. "Besides, what would I do with that? We've got King George on our notes, not George Washington." I hadn't thought of that.

"Tell your mum to trade those in for you at her bank," said the lady. "That or the black market."

"Where's that?" I asked.

"It's not where, it's *whom*," said the cook.

"Criminals," said the lady. "People making a profit off of our misfortunes. They'll sell you a pair of nylons for a 1000% mark up."

"I don't want nylons," I said.

"Lucky you." She pointed out the line she had drawn up the back of her bare leg. "Barclays, stick to that." She rose and patted down her wrinkled dress, and then reached out her hand to me and said, "Come now, let's help get you home."

I took Daphne's letter out of my back pocket, unfolded it, and handed the envelope to the lady. I told them it was the address where I was staying but wasn't sure how to get there. It wasn't really a lie because I figured that Daphne would put me up. The cook, the lady with the feather hat, and the man with the naked wife, all leaned in to examine the address. They had a tug-of-war for the envelope and a corner tore from the thin blue airmail paper.

"Leytonstone. That would be in the East End," said the cook.

The man snapped his finger. "Hop on here and after three stops switch for the Central Line at Tottenham Court Station—then ride Central all the way to the

Leytonstone tube station."

Just as he said that, a train pulled into the station and we said our good-byes. When the lady bent down to hug me, the feather in her hat almost took out my eye. As we parted, the cook put a coin into my hand. "That will cover your fare."

"I'll come back for the fish some day, I promise." I was serious too.

"And a double order of chips," he said, smiling.

I boarded the train and it pulled away from the station. Before we entered the tunnel, I turned to look out the window. My three new friends were waving wildly to me from the platform. Spending the night in a subway station, while the Nazis pound you from above, and death can come at any minute, makes you feel warm and fuzzy toward people.

CHAPTER THIRTEEN

Arriving at the Leytonstone Station, first thing I done was to check the clock above the ticket seller's booth: the hands pointed to seven. It was the weekend, so with any luck Daphne was asleep in her bed. She was 17 or 18-years-old and probably still lived with her folks. I couldn't just ring the bell and announce myself, not with grown-ups around. I'd have to concoct a cover story.

No one had collected the fare for the subway ride and I still had the English coin in my pocket: the one with a picture of a king. As I exited the station, I heard a lady call out, "Bouquet for your sweetheart! A dozen posies for a bob!"

I stepped to the lady, holding out my coin. "Is this a bob?"

"Right you are," she said.

"Then I'll have a dozen posies, please." She handed me a bouquet of blue flowers with yellow centers. They had no smell, but what could I expect for a bob?

"Got a sweetie, have you?"

"Can you point me to this street?" I showed her the

envelope. Wadley Road, I was happy to learn, was a hop, skip, and a jump from the station.

I would've gotten to Daphne's faster if it weren't for being distracted by bombed out buildings where people sifted through rubble looking for their worldly possessions. I found an alarm clock for one lady and a kettle for another. An air raid warden chased me out of a bombed out house where I'd joined the search for a missing grandmother. Then I spent an hour helping two kids find their cat. Spotted it hiding out in a crushed wardrobe with its fur sticking out like a porcupine. After I rescued the cat, an ambulance driver applied Mercurochrome to my scratch wounds and brought me to a canteen for a cup of tea, which she said would do wonders for my rattled nerves. (See, I was still shook up about the missing grandmother.) Then I came to a cordoned off street. I saw the damage with my own eyes, and it didn't look too bad: a hole in the roof was all. But then a man said it was a UXB. I asked him to explain.

Unexploded Bomb, that's what the letters stood for.

That bomb crashed right through the roof and was sitting somewheres in the house waiting to blow. A crowd of fools stood by the barrier gawking but, as soon as I got the explanation, I flew from that place like my pants were on fire. Then I had to figure a new path to Daphne's house.

My heart was pounding soon as I spotted the right house. I double-checked the envelope. The house was an attached two-story stucco number, like a Brooklyn brownstone. There was a flower garden in front. I could've saved the bob.

I opened an iron gate, which led me up a short walkway to Daphne's door. I thought to myself, *Jack's opened this same gate. Jack's walked down this same path. Jack's rung this same bell.*

A mother-type cracked the door open after three slams of a brass doorknocker. "Delivery for Miss Daphne," I said, holding up the wilted flowers.

"Now, who could they be from I wonder?" said the lady. "Best you come in, luv." As I wiped my feet on the doormat, she whipped her head backwards and called out, "Daphne! There's a delivery for you!" She pointed me to a bench padded with needlepoint letters that spelled HOME. Getting there, I tripped over shoes, boots, and umbrellas. Meanwhile, the lady vanished. I could've been a robber.

My eyelids began drifting south. I was half-asleep when I heard footsteps on the staircase above. I shook myself awake and looked up at the landing. For a second I thought I must be dreaming.

Her skin was like real butter, not margarine. Lips as luminous as a candied apple. Her hair was like hot fudge. Her face reminded me of an icon of the Virgin Mary that hung above our mantel. Except she was wearing a pink quilted robe over matching slippers, with pompoms near where her pink lacquered toenails stuck out. She floated down the stairs like a hot air balloon or a zeppelin, not that I'm calling her a blimp, you understand. It was just that her feet didn't seem to touch the ground. And I'd bet a year's worth of Cracker Jack prizes she was 34-18-34. No wonder Jack was head over heels. I was pretty sure they didn't make them like that in Ireland.

"Daphne?" I said with a stammer.

"That's me," she said, taking the flowers and putting them to her nose. "Who could be sending me flowers, cheeky devil?" She looked me in the eye. "There's no card?"

I whispered, "Daphne. It's Tommy Mooney."

"Why would Jack's brother be sending me flowers?" Then she turned white as a ghost. "Good grief! Oh no! Jack!"

Woops! She figured somebody was sending her the kind of flowers people send to funerals. Condolences, they're called—they only ever mean one thing. I said, "Daphne, you don't get it. It's me, Tommy Mooney." I smiled wide and pointed to myself.

"Jeepers Creepers! Tommy? What on earth?" She took in a big gulp of air and then froze in place holding her breath. If she didn't take in oxygen soon, she was going to pass out.

"Look," I said. "Can we talk somewheres private?"

Grabbing my hand, she pulled me up the staircase and into her bedroom, locking the door behind us. She still looked like a deer caught in the headlights. I looked around the room and seen a photograph of my brother Jack, propped up on the side table near her bed. It was one I'd never laid eyes on before. Jack looked more grown-up than I remembered him. Daphne noticed my eyes riveted on the photograph. She lifted the frame and placed it in my hands gently, like it was an egg.

Without warning I started blubbering like a newborn who'd had his rear-end slapped. Once it started, there was no stopping—I could hardly breathe and began hiccupping. Snot flowed from my nose. My shoulders shook and I began to feel dizzy. I hadn't cried that hard since the time I crashed into a milk truck and dislocated my collarbone, totaling my brand new pedal car.

Made a spectacle of myself, that's all I'll say. Maybe it was seeing this new photo of Jack. Or being with the fiancée. Maybe it was missing my ma and being so far from home. Or maybe it was that the whole neighborhood might blow at any second.

Daphne took my hand and sat me next to her on the bed. She put her arm around my shoulder and handed me a lacy handkerchief. She said softly, "Come on now. Jack will come back to us. We have to believe that."

When I went on sniffling, she pulled up my chin with her index finger. "Come now. Stiff upper lip."

"Daphne, we have to find Jack. It's up to us."

"Of course we will, Tommy," she said, patting my hand. "Of course we will find Jack."

So that's when Daphne first agreed to come to German-occupied Belgium with me. Although later on she tried to wiggle out of it—said she'd only been trying to *humor* me, was how she put it. No way I was letting her out—a promise is a promise. Our fates were now tangled up like shoelaces—two bodies destined for the same place.

Belgium.

CHAPTER FOURTEEN

WHILE I WAITED IN DAPHNE'S BEDROOM, she dressed in the hall bathroom and then went downstairs to her folks, who expected her to eat breakfast with them. I decided to stay clear of the grown-ups, skipping breakfast to do it. Meanwhile, I took a look around her room, going to her bookshelf first. You tell a lot about a person by what they read. You just had to look at my sister Mary's bookshelf to know she was a dope.

I'd never heard of most of the books on Daphne's shelf: some broad named Jane and a few writers all from the same family, Brontë, made up the bulk of her book collection. I flipped some pages and saw loads of thee, thou, and thines. A fella could learn a lot about English reading Daphne's books. She spoke like a princess; if I borrowed her books I'd be talking like Prince Charming before long. But a couple of Daphne's books were in a foreign language, most likely French. Then again, it might a been Gaelic. She also liked Shakespeare, which figured. Americans have Dick and Jane; English folks have Romeo and Juliet. The rest were art books, some as heavy as the illustrated Bible that sat in our family parlor.

Next I took a quick peek into her top dresser drawer hoping to find chocolate, only to slam it shut when I realized what a blunder I'd made. The drawer contained nothing but brassieres and underpants.

Safer to look at her wall decorations, which were mostly pencil drawings and watercolors. Most of the drawings were of my brother and the likeness was dead-ringer. Filling one wall was a half finished painting of a girl standing in front of some sort of a piano. Once I went with my older sister Nancy to the Metropolitan Museum of Art. I'd gone to look at the mummies and treasures of the ancient world but my sister forced me to look at the paintings too. Daphne's painting looked like something that might hang in a city museum once it was finished. Under the painting was a coffee table piled with half-squeezed tubes of paint, paintbrushes, and coffee cans full of turpentine. It made the room smell like art class.

By and by Daphne returned to the room and looked relieved. "They've left for Hyde Park," she said.

"The Roosevelt place upstate?"

"The London park, silly. It's like your Central Park. I talked my parents into taking a picnic lunch and they plan to go rowing on the Serpentine, so with a bit of luck they shan't return until tea time."

I followed her downstairs and into the kitchen, and she motioned for me to sit on the kitchen counter. She asked if I was hungry. "We're out of eggs, but I'll make you a burger," she said, waving a spatula in the air. "Jack taught me how."

"A hamburger for breakfast!" I thought, *No wonder Jack fell for her.*

"Do you like it with fried onions, like your brother?" She tossed an onion up in the air, twirled around and grabbed it from behind. "These are as rare as pomegranates."

I thought to myself: *Was there ever a sweller girl in the world?* She diced up some onion and using the spatula like a tennis racket, aimed each piece into a frying pan. She didn't miss once. I thought, *My God, she's super!*

"It's so peculiar," Daphne said, as she examined my ears, "but you bear an uncanny resemblance to Jack." She thought this was "smashing," said it made her feel happy for the first time since he went missing. She opened the icebox and peered in. "Mayonnaise? Tomato sauce? Marmite?"

"Gee, you're nice," I said, trying hard not to sound gushing.

As I ate my burger, she told me about her getting a letter from my ma, and how I'd made everybody worried sick. There was a five-state bulletin out to find my kidnappers and bring them to justice. Daphne insisted we get on the horn to Ma and let her know I was safe. Her folks were going to faint when the bill came for a transatlantic call, but she said it couldn't be helped. We went to the parlor where they kept the phone. Daphne had to untangle the cord that was attached to a wall. Meanwhile, I took a look around the room. They had some nice furniture, the kind with feather cushions, but otherwise it was a regular kind of house, nothing too fancy.

Except for a table set in the corner of the room. The goods on that table might be worth something: family photographs, framed in silver. What I needed was a magnet to see if the metal were real or not. Instead I looked for the telltale number stamped on genuine sterling: .925—that's what you wanted. The first frame I lifted was silver plated, not worth the picture it came with. Then my eye fell on a candlestick: more like a candelabra it was. On the base were the three magic numbers. The thing was heavy, too, with places for nine candles. I'd seen one before. "My German teacher's got one like this," I said.

"A menorah?"

I had no idea what a menorah was but I didn't want to look dumb, so I said: "Right-O."

"It's for Hanukkah," she said, helping me out of a spot.

"I know what Hanukkah is: the Jewish version of Christmas."

Daphne laughed. "Not exactly. But you're right: the two holiday's often fall at the same time in December."

To let her know I was grown-up, I said, "I know Santa Claus is made up."

She hammed it up like an actress in a silent movie. "Oh my stars! Tell me it's not true!" Then she got serious. "I'm only half Jewish. My father's Anglican."

"What's an Anglican?"

Then Daphne let the bomb drop. Turned out Anglicans were the ones who broke off from the Holy Roman Catholic Church during the Reformation. I'd learned about them in catechism class, only the priest called them Episcopalians. And while messing with my sister Mary's report on Henry VIII, I found out that it was them who martyred Sir Thomas More, an actual saint. Ma was going to flip when she found out Jack was marrying a heretic.

Daphne showed me her profile; it sure was perfect. "Can't you see the resemblance to Pauline Goddard?" she said. "She's also half Jewish/half Anglican."

"The dame in *Pot o' Gold* with Jimmy Stewart?"

"That's right. It means we get gifts at Hanukkah and more on Christmas. I've already warned Jack to be prepared."

Daphne sat on the sofa and placed the phone on her lap, lifting the receiver and pressing down a few times until she got a dial tone. She used a pencil to dial, sticking the eraser side in the "O" slot so she wouldn't chip her nail polish. I let her know a call wasn't necessary, because the American Embassy was already in touch with Ma.

"American Embassy? They're involved?"

"Yes, and they'll be on to the fact I've flown the coop and start hunting for me, so we can't dawdle." My plan, I told her, was to return to Warfield Hall, borrow the speedboat and get over to Belgium before they picked up my trail.

"We?" Daphne coughed. She placed the phone on a coffee table. "We? I'm not doing any such thing. Are you mad? There's a war raging over in Belgium. People are having bombs dropped on their heads everyday."

"As far as I can tell, people are getting bombs dropped on their heads every day here too, so where's the difference?"

She stared at me like a dare.

"Look," I said, "Jack might be wounded and need our help."

She started biting her nails. Then she told me about training to be a nurse, which she was failing at miserably. She gave me some examples and I winced. She was as bad at nursing as I was at English. Next I mentioned that Jack might be in a German prison camp and need our help to escape. This was the one possibility worried me the most. It was always in the news about gangsters trying to break out of prison but they never succeeded. Not if they were on Alcatraz Island, anyways. Sharks ate one of them convicts.

"I've heard horror stories about those camps," she said. She inhaled and her eyes misted. I needed to divert a crisis.

"Forget I said that. He's not in a camp, Daphne. Jack's too clever to let the Nazis get him." She wiped her face with the sleeve of her blouse, sniffled and blew her nose with her hankie. "But he might have amnesia," I said. "That happens when you get a bump to the head, which almost always happens in a plane crash."

(I'd got this idea from a film preview. The flick was called *Random Harvest*. It looked awful sappy, but I didn't tell Daphne that. It starred Ronald Colman, a soldier in the Great War who gets a bump on the head and suffers amnesia. Before the war he was married to Greer Garson—the love of his life—but after the bump, he doesn't know her from Adam. If it could happen to Ronald Colman, it could've happened to Jack.)

"Heaven forbid," she said. "What if Jack is wandering around Europe right now, not even knowing his name, nor whence he came, nor who he belonged to. I can't bear the thought. Why, he might not even remember he's engaged to be…" She stopped short. She was a girl with a vivid imagination, which was now working to my advantage. I decided to help her along, suggesting that maybe Jack could find a French bombshell to help him remember who he was.

"Where did you say that powerboat was?" she asked.

"Southampton," I said. "We take the train from Waterloo Station. I know how to get there on the subway."

"You mean The Tube?"

"Yeah, that."

"And this fellow, Lord…"

"Sopwith."

"He's going to lend a 12-year-old boy and an 18-year-old girl his speedboat to take over the English Channel to Nazi-occupied Belgium?" I kept my mouth shut, but I must've had a guilty look on my face because she said, "My God Tommy, you aren't thinking of nicking a boat from a peer of the realm?"

I explained that there was no such thing as stealing in matters like this. In a military operation it's called *commandeering.* Daphne looked at me, her mouth crooked. So I tried something else. "It's a long swim. Possible though. Why, in 1926 a mother—"

"Forget swimming, Tommy. I've never learned properly. I can only dog paddle, and you can't dog paddle from England to Belgium."

We were both speechless, each trying hard to think up a plan. Then Daphne suggested we ask one of Jack's mates to fly us over. I reminded her that they all flew Spitfires and it was a tight squeeze for even one pilot. Jack had wrote—I mean *written*—to us about a friend of his who tried to take his girlfriend up with him and crashed the plane while taxiing. That got me thinking maybe we could parachute in. I asked her if she was acquainted with any bomber pilots.

"Jump from an airplane? I would die of fright before my feet hit the ground."

"Than the speedboat seems like our only option," I said.

"I suppose it is better than jumping from 10,000 feet, I'll grant you that. But what about German U-Boats?"

"The speedboat goes almost 52 knots per hour. That's faster than a torpedo, put it that way."

"How much faster?"

"Fast enough."

"Well, then. It's all settled." She patted my arm. I'd convinced her, and then some.

That's when my conscience snuck up on me. Maybe it was her eyelashes done it, so long and curly. Or maybe her eyeballs, whiter than golf balls. Could've been that her finger was rubbing at the ticklish underside of my arm. Funny enough, my conscience spoke in a combination of voices: Jack and Mr. Fisch. It said: *What are you doing risking her life?* After all my scheming, I had to warn her. I started the sentence with a moan, followed by: "What about the despicable Nazi agenda?"

"Which one?"

"The Jewish one," I said, figuring this was the end to all my plans and that I'd never see Jack this side of purgatory.

"Oh." She fixed her eyes on my head like it was a crystal ball. They moved around in the sockets, squinting one second and flashing open the next. She made little grunts and sighs, sad then angry. "It's not as though we're going to Germany," she said.

"Nooooo, never!"

But then I remembered Hitler's own words and how they'd made me tremble, how they'd given me nightmares. And I remembered Lord Sopwith telling me about Belgian refugees and "unspeakable acts of cruelty." And what else? *Horrible inhumanities.* Maybe I was making a big mistake dragging Daphne to occupied Europe. Heck—maybe it was a big mistake dragging myself there. All the gung-ho was seeping out of me, getting replaced with worries. To be honest, I half wanted someone to talk me out of going. Like the time I stood on the high board getting ready to dive and Jack suggested I practice at the poolside first. Oh, the relief! And here was my chance—maybe my last chance to turn back. Helping me along was Jack's voice, whispering in my ears: *Tell her already!*

I stammered, "But in Belgium there's unspeak—"

Daphne pressed her index finger to my lips. "Shush," she said. "Your point is well taken, Tommy. But I shan't worry the future, for it may turn out well yet."

Just like Jack—always looking for the bright side of a new moon.

CHAPTER FIFTEEN

WE HID OUT BEHIND A BUSH in front of the Sopwith's mansion. The bush was trimmed into the shape of a shoehorn, which made for the perfect cover from both the front and sides.

"How much longer must we wait?" said Daphne, yawning.

The lights were still on in Lord Sopwith's study. Lord Sopwith was an aviation pioneer. When people were still in horse and buggies, he was making fighter planes. He was working on an ultra aerodynamic propeller. I knew because I'd sneaked a peek at the blueprints. If he succeeded, the whole course of the war might change: British fighter pilots would move faster through air. His lordship had a million projects like that.

Maybe he was working on a time machine—probably with H. G. Wells himself, who happened to be an Englishman too. We could all get in and jump forward a few years and the war would be over.

I learned about supersonic jets in a *Flash Gordon* comic book. If anybody was going to make that happen, it would be Sir Thomas Octave Murdoch Sopwith. He might be working on one of them aviation breakthroughs right now, while we waited to borrow his speedboat key.

"I'll be back in a minute," Daphne said, "I have to use the loo." I had no idea what a loo was and asked her to explain. "I suppose I'll have to give you English lessons," she said pinching my cheek. "You are as bad as Jack."

"What? Jack doesn't talk like a New Yorker anymore?"

"Good gracious, he most certainly does. The man is stubborn as a mule." She paused and had a dreamy look in her eye—lovestruck is what you call it. "He says that if I dare try to correct his language again, he'll teach our first-born to speak like a Bronx cab driver." She started wiggling. "And for future reference: a loo is a WC." Before I could ask what WC stood for, she'd ducked behind a giant flowerpot.

Meanwhile, I kept a sharp eye on the house. All the windows had blackout curtains, making it near impossible to tell which rooms were lit. I watched as the lights in an upstairs bedroom were switched on and the blackout curtains shut up afterwards. For a split second I'd spotted the silhouette of Lord Sopwith in an upstairs bedroom window. I was positive it was him by the outline of a cigar in his mouth. By the time Daphne returned I was sure all the lights downstairs were turned off.

"Time to move," I said. "You'd better stay here and keep watch, while I go inside and nab the key." I looked at her to see if she approved of my plan.

"Fine by me," she said. "What shall I tell the constable when he arrives?"

I leapfrogged to the nearest bush and then from bush to bush until I was positioned right under the study window. One of the windows was left wide open. Good thing for the Sopwiths I wasn't a real burglar. Within no time, I was coming back out of the study window, powerboat key in my blue jeans pocket next to my two lucky marbles.

We made our way to the boat dock, where the powerboat bobbed merrily on the water. I found a full gas can in the boathouse and put this in the back seat. Daphne gave me her hand and I helped her aboard. She had a pink suitcase along for the trip, and I passed this to her, along with my duffel bag. Then I untied the rope and took my place behind the wheel.

"Jack learned me how to drive," I said, letting my grammar slip, what with all the excitement. I should a said *taught*. Daphne didn't correct me though, that's how sweet a girl she was. Or maybe it was because she was as scared as a rabbit being chased by a poacher. She dug her fingernails into the leather dash.

"Jack drives exactly as he flies, pushing 400 miles an hour," she said. "Please don't try any of his stunts with this speedboat. You know I can't swim."

I calmed her, making out that I'd driven miles and miles down Route 66. To tell true, I'd sat on Jack's lap as he helped me steer the car down the block and back. "This thing is much easier to drive than a Ford pick-up," I said, with a lazy-fare shrug. When I gulped it felt like a walnut was stuck in my throat.

I handed over my compass and asked Daphne to be the navigator. It was simple: all we had to do was hug the coast going east until we reached the tip of England.

"We shall look for the white cliffs of Dover," said Daphne. "They'll be brilliant in this moonlight, and from there we cross over to Calais. That's the route the ferry took before the war. I've done the crossing many times—once spending an enchanted semester in Paris, at art school."

"Check," I said. "After we see them white cliffs we cross over the Channel going southeast. Then we hug the coast of France until we reach Belgium. That's going to be the tricky part, 'cause if we overshoot our target, we'll end up in Germany."

She studied the compass nervously, with her nose pressed against the glass. I turned the key and the boat hummed to life. The gas gauge needle was almost to the full mark. I looked out the windshield and realized I was sitting a little low in the seat and didn't have very good visibility. I asked Daphne if she minded I use her suitcase as a booster. "Be my guest," she said, helping me place it on my seat.

Astronomy is one of my best subjects. I looked up at the moon and seen that it was a waning gibbous—the days following a full moon—and it was a cloudless night. We'd be able to see fine with the headlights off. "Hold onto your hat," I said, pulling back the throttle as we moved clear of the dock.

We were out of the waterway and into open water when Daphne cried out that we were being followed.

Sure enough there was a big boat speeding up to ours. I should've made a run for it then. But in my confusion I slowed, giving the other boat time enough to pull up next to us. From a megaphone came, "Halt immediately!" Painted on the side of the boat was H M COAST GUARD.

"They're English, thank God," said Daphne. "Let me do the talking. But keep your hand on the throttle and be ready to go full board when I give the signal."

She stood up on her seat and waved. She smiled big and her pearly white teeth gleamed in the moonlight. Her hair blew in the wind. Her skirt flew dangerously above her knees. I heard whistling coming from the other boat deck.

"Hello there!" she shouted.

"Well, hello there to you, miss," said the man on the megaphone, deepening his voice.

"Everything's tip-top here, officer. No need to concern yourselves."

"There's a curfew on, luv. You need to come in to the shore."

"Right you are! Tally Ho!" Daphne flopped in her seat and motioned me to give the boat full-throttle. I done as she said and we left them behind in a spray of water. The odometer hit 47 knots an hour. Soon the Coast Guard boat was far behind. Daphne put her hand to her heart. "Brilliant. But if they'd been German—"

"In that case, let me do the talking," I said. "I might not be pretty as you, but I *Sprechen* the *Deutsch*."

"I'll stop worrying then." Daphne laughed. We

both were enjoying our narrow escape. She shouted, "Ripping!"

"Ripping!" I repeated, taking my hands from the wheel and thrusting them into the air in triumph. We sped away, the wind whipping our hair and the taste of salt in our mouths.

A couple hours later on we came to the white cliffs and pointed the boat at France. The water became scary choppy and we was both wet before long. I began to feel seasick as we got rocked back and forth by swells, and I'm sure I must've looked like a fresh picked pea, but I didn't let on to Daphne. I was glad when the wind died down, the sea calmed a bit, and my stomach settled.

Daphne began to hark back to happier days, telling me that she'd been to Paris loads of times—not bragging, just stating the facts. She had a great aunt who lived in Paris. The aunt was a spinster who never had children of her own, so she'd sort of adopted Daphne. Her aunt Dalia was English, but moved to France years ago to be a food critic. Daphne licked her lips and said, "Oh, I've eaten scrummy food in Paris! Chefs pull out all the stops when my aunt steps through the door."

"Even though she criticizes the food?" I asked.

"You're funny. But seriously, we're all worried about my aunt. I wish she'd come back to England before the German invasion. We haven't gotten so much as a post-card since. And we've begun hearing terrible rumors."

I asked her what kind of rumors, but she didn't want to talk about it, saying that it wasn't a good idea to feed your fears.

"Maybe we'll give your aunt a lift on the way home."

"Paris is very far from Belgium," she said. And by the way she pronounced Paris, I knew she missed the place. "*Paree* is my favorite city on earth. I'd always thought I'd spend my honeymoon there, but by the time I met Jack the Nazis had taken the country. We're going to have to settle for Brighton and that's hardly the same. The Nazis have probably replaced Coq Au Vin with weinersnitchel and Champagne with beer."

"Jack likes beer though," I said, and Daphne laughed.

"There's nothing I'd like more than to be sitting right now with Jack in a nice cozy pub." She was silent for a minute and then said: "All those lovely paintings at the Louvre. What's to become of them? Do you know that Hitler is a frustrated artist? Turned down for art school. That's what this war is all about. He's getting back."

I'd never heard that theory before, not even from Edward R. Murrow on the nightly radio news. It was an interesting angle. "Fascinating," I said.

Daphne's face was in shadow, but her voice was lit with fire. "He's getting back at all the lovely and gifted people: at the artists and scientists, the philosophers and poets, the musicians and composers. Why, this war is a very battle for everything lovely in the world. That terrible man would snuff it all out if he had his way."

Right then I made out white sand along the distant shore, which I figured must be France. In my months of planning I'd never thought further than this point. I didn't want to let on, so I said: "I've got my ideas but let's hear yours first."

Daphne said the first step was to find Jack's airplane. She'd heard he went down somewhere along the train line between Oostende and Bruges. Once we located the Spitfire, we'd have a better idea where to go from there. It made sense to me. "Jack's boot prints might lead us to him," I said. "Same thing happened in *The Adventure of the Beryl Coronet*." She patted my knee, impressed that I'd read Sherlock Holmes. Her plan was to ask around with the locals and also get in touch with the Belgian Resistance. It wasn't a bad plan, as plans went, but it had obvious flaws. Weren't the Resistance hiding out underground? Wouldn't they be hard to find? These—plus all my other worries, big and small—came pouring out.

"Let's take one step at a time," she said, "find Jack's airplane and go from there. 'Keep calm and carry on,' *that's* the slogan."

I'd seen the slogan myself, glued with flour paste to every brick wall in London. But most were torn by shrapnel, peeled and faded. Other posters showed Nazis snatching little children; warned mothers to get their kids out of bomb-riddled London; reminded people to carry their gas masks. Sort of worked against the calm message, didn't it?

Nearing the shore, I let the throttle slack and the boat go quiet. We got silent and I seen we both was jittery. Daphne pointed southwest. "I recognize this. That's the ferry station. Oh, it used to be lovely to come over."

"I've never met a Nazi, have you?"

"Never," she said, "and I'd hoped never to."

"Over there," I said, pointing to the shore, "are real live Nazis. They're eating food that ain't theirs and sleeping in beds that aren't theirs."

"Speaking of which," said Daphne, "I'm awfully knackered. It's near dawn and we haven't eaten a bite or slept a wink. I know a pensione in Calais where they serve wonderful crêpes."

"I think we'd better press on to Belgium, Daphne, don't you? We can't take the chance of getting caught in France."

She got my point. I gave the boat more throttle and we continued along the coast, staying far enough out so we wouldn't be seen from the shore. Daphne asked how we'd know when we reached Belgium and I told her: "I've studied the maps some. The next large town we see should be Dunkirk—that's still in France. The next city will be Oostende, about 30 miles along. That's where we need to land. Shouldn't be too hard to find."

We travelled slow, looking for a build-up of lights along the shoreline, signaling a city. Problem was, there were very few lights on anywhere, and so we owed everything to the glow from the moon and my phenomenal night vision. Finally we came to a place that looked like a large town and Daphne pointed and said, "Dunkirk." I tried calculating our speed and the time it would take to travel another 30 miles, only my mathematical skills came up short.

An hour later, we came to another large town.

"Oostende," I said. "Let's bring the boat in while

it's still dark." I turned the wheel and we headed toward the shore. We spotted other boats—some fishing boats, some small sport crafts, and a few sailboats. Several capsized. What troubled us was that along one stretch of the shore we seen German submarines, maybe six of them, all above water. Even worse, we made out the silhouettes of rifle-toting soldiers patrolling the docks. Also along the coast we sighted huge artillery guns, mounted on concrete bunkers and pointed to the sea. And us.

"Good God Tommy," said Daphne. "Did we bring any weapons?"

"A slingshot, a boomerang, darts, and a bow and arrow. Back in East Hempstead it seemed like quite an arsenal."

"Well, bugger it all. I'm a pretty good archer. Give me the bow and arrow."

I riffled through my duffel bag and handed them to her. She held the bow to her eye, strung the arrow, squinted, and took aim. She released the tension and said, "It will have to do."

As we came closer to the shore, we saw in the moonlight that buildings along the waterfront were blown to smithereens, some were piles of rubble.

Daphne looked teary. "The place has suffered worse than London during the Blitz. One wouldn't think it possible."

"Jack's been here," I said proudly. But she corrected me. From what she heard tell, the Germans did most of this damage when they'd invaded Belgium.

"Jack and the RAF target German military posts:

depots, train lines, factories and the like. They don't want to do any more harm to the Belgians, poor wretches."

My eye caught something moving in the water. *What the red devil?*

Daphne looked over the side of the boat too, and we watched a periscope rise out of the water. "We'd better make for shore," she said, wide-awake.

I pointed the speedboat away from the submarines, to a stretch of dimly lit coastline. We pulled alongside a wooden dock and I killed the engine. "This is it," I said. "No second thoughts?"

She yawned. "A trifle late for that. We ought to find a place to rest. We'll be able to think clearly once we've slept a bit."

Taking Daphne's hand, I helped her climb onto the dock. As my sneakers stepped onto solid land, I prayed for the first time in many months. Then I crossed myself. If my ma could've seen me then—boy oh boy—she'd be jumping for joy.

CHAPTER SIXTEEN

Somewhere else in occupied Europe

TWO MEN STAND AT A STREET CORNER. One is wearing the uniform of an SS Waffen *Truppführer*, the other is a Frenchman in plain clothes. They watch a café that stands across the street—a small cobblestoned backstreet without much traffic. It's night and the two men are sheltered inside the entrance way to an apartment building, because it's raining, and also because they don't wish to be observed.

The Frenchman removes a pair of binoculars from his satchel and hands them to the Truppführer. "Can you see him? The one seated near the door to the kitchen."

"Yes, and you're right. The spitting image."

"You wanted a way out of your situation, well— there it is."

The Truppführer adjusts the focus to get an even clearer view. The man in his sights is tall with dark hair, square chin with a cleft, an almost perfect nose.

"He comes every night," says the Frenchman. "About the same time. He's a creature of habit, always orders a ham and cheese baguette and a glass of wine. Always flirts with the waitress—bragging about his prowess, suggesting she invite him back to her place. So far, unsuccessfully."

The Truppführer focuses the binoculars on the waitress. "Understandable," he says. "And after his dinner, where next? Is there a pattern?"

"Like I said, he's a creature of habit. From here he'll go to a bar around the corner. On a weeknight, it's not very crowded. He stays some nights at a townhouse in the 16th."

"Still, it's a bit crazy," says the Truppführer. "And not without risks."

"It's your call. All I'm saying is, I don't mind helping to see the man off to his Maker. That's what I'm here for. I'll help with that part, the rest will be up to you."

"So perhaps the SS will be paying him a visit tomorrow night." He laughs. "Now point the way to this bar, and I'll happily buy you a drink."

CHAPTER SEVENTEEN

I TRAILED DAPHNE AS WE WALKED along a road that ran perpendicular to the sea, taking us into the center of Oostende. Stepping around fallen bricks and mortar, we tried to stay under the awnings of shops, hug the storefronts, and make ourselves invisible. Lucky thing the streetlamps weren't turned on—some of them had the glass blown out. So the streets were dark, but the sky was bright with the beams of searchlights. Reminded me of a newsreel I'd seen: premiere night for a Hollywood film.

We heard sound from above—the roar of engines, as a whole squadron of bombers passed over. Daphne said, "They're likely headed for Berlin and good luck to them." All we could see was black silhouettes against the coal sky. Like bats they were. Artillery fire rattled the buildings and sent white tracers arching through the sky. One bullet found its mark. My hands covered my eyes and I had to peek through my fingers. Flames shot from the bomber wing and I seen it was a B-17. The plane just kept flying south and we lost sight of it. I hoped the Americans had parachutes; or better yet, a fire extinguisher.

I said: "I'm not scared, not me." Then I spun around in circles, desperate for a hiding place. Bravery, I realized, has to be built up: same as triceps or tooth plaque. It's the one thing you can't train for.

Daphne grabbed my hand and said, "Poor thing— you're shaking like a leaf." She put her mouth to my ear: "There's probably a curfew and so I suggest we see about a room. I'm not quite ready to have my first encounter with a Nazi. After I've slept—maybe."

We came to a wreck of a hotel. Part of the front was knocked down and we could've just stepped right in and robbed the place blind. Daphne ringed a bell and within a minute a candle came floating toward us, revealing a dusty lobby and an old man dressed in his nightshirt and a stocking cap. He unlocked the door and ushered us inside. "*Bienvenue!*" he said, not at all angry that we woke him up at an ungodly hour. Daphne talked to him in French. The innkeeper took us up a narrow staircase and then down a dim hallway. Flicking a switch on in one room, he said, "*Toilettee.*" Daphne didn't need to translate. Less than an hour in Belgium and I was already making progress with the language.

He showed us to a small room with two narrow beds. Daphne said, "*Parfait,*" and took the key. She put the chain on the door lock and threw herself onto the bed, bouncing up in the air and laughing nervously. "I took the least expensive room they had. And breakfast is included. It's served at eight but, since it's nearly five, he's making an exception for us and we may have it whenever we want. He's awfully sweet. Said we could check out late and he'll accept payment in French francs. They're left over from my last trip to Paris." She patted her stomach. "My, I'm famished. By any chance do you have food in that haversack of yours?"

I looked through my duffel bag and found half a pack of lifesavers. "You can have them all," I said, handing her the package.

She picked lint off of the top lifesaver. "Let's split them," she said. "You can have the greens and yellows, if I can have the reds and oranges."

Daphne went to wash up, and I decided it was high time for me to bone up on the Nazi agenda. So I found *Mein Kampf*, spit on the cover, and started where I'd left off. Halfway down the page, Hitler's talking about how he found his "true calling" by reading a book about the Franco-Prussian War of 1870. He wrote: *From then on, I became more and more enthusiastic over anything connected with war.* And this was when he was ten!

I stopped reading and started pondering. For sure, I didn't want to end up like Hitler. I made a pledge right then and there to never be enthusiastic again. About war, anyway. I found a pencil and my spiral-bound stenographer's notebook and started making a list:

THINGS TO NOT BE ENTHUSIASTIC ABOUT:

Franco-Prussian War of 1870

The Great War

Our war

Mein Kampf

Bombs

Sappy movies

Mary

OKAY TO BE ENTHUSIASTIC ABOUT:

King Tut

Baseball cards

Buried treasure

Huckleberry Finn

Spitfires

Firecrackers

Daphne

Coney Island

Summer break

Christmas

Diamonds

Movies (as long as they're not sappy.)

Comics.

Jack

The list was getting lopsided. And blurry. The pencil and notebook dropped from my hand. Next thing I knew, the sun was shining in my face from an open window. Daphne sat perched on the ledge, taking in the view. I wanted to dive back under the covers, but just then my stomach rumbled. I said, "Where did you say breakfast was?"

"Downstairs off the reception area, or what's left of it," she said. "I've already had mine and, I warn you, it's nothing to write home about. My aunt Dalia would pan the place. 'No stars,' she'd say."

"I don't care. I could eat a cow."

"You'll wish it was beef. I suspect they are serving dog. Dog sausage and week-old baguette, washed down with tepid tea. And did you know that we of the Jewish persuasion aren't permitted to eat dog? Or was that cat meat?" She started biting her nails, worried that she'd broke a rule. Like when us Catholics commit one of the seven deadly sins. "Well, never you mind," she said finally. "That's the extent of the menu. I nearly broke a molar on the baguette, it was that hard."

"Tea," I said, moaning. I got out of bed, hitched up my blue jeans, and ran my fingers through my hair so it stood up off my head. Meanwhile Daphne kept rambling on.

"—I *really* ought to have paid more attention, the few times my grandmother took me along to shul. But then she passed away, dear thing—and my mother, you see, she had *assimilated*."

"Mind dumbing that down? It's still early. I don't

even have my sneakers on yet."

"It's not early, by the way." She consulted her wrist-watch. "It's nearly noon. And what I mean by assimilated, is that my mother is *non-practicing*. Some might call it *Reform*, but she's barely even that: Hanukkah gifts at Christmas, a spinning top for Passover—that's about the extent of it. But now, with things as they stand, I feel it's important to be more connected with my Jewish roots."

Non-practicing. That much I got and told her so. New York was loaded with non-practicing Catholics and I aimed to become one myself. But honestly, why she'd want to be more Jewish when Hitler was hunting them down—well—that part I didn't get. But I just shrugged. It was too early in the morning for theology.

And she wasn't kidding about the breakfast menu. It left plenty of room for the imagination to run wild: sunny-side up eggs with ketchup, sausage links, Florida orange juice, Kellogg corn flakes with sugar on top, French fries and more ketchup. Waffles, maple syrup and whipped cream topped pancakes. I swallowed the stale roll and dog sausage and cussed the Nazis.

Daphne said: "Had I realized, I'd have saved you my left-overs." Then she gulped down my tea, even though she'd complained about it earlier—English through and through. She put down the teacup and said, "Now what?" Looking at me hopefully.

I didn't want to let her down, so I said: "Tell me everything you know about Jack's crash, so's I can fine-tune my ideas."

Daphne began telling me about the day Jack's plane went down:

"Sel Edner came to see me the day after Jack went missing. Came all the way from Essex to London with permission from their commander, Squadron Leader Hugh Kennard. They'd both received wedding invitations the very same morning Jack went missing." She got choked up and had to stop and to pull herself together. "—Sel and Jack were together on a rhubarb the morning of the 16th of June. You know what a rhubarb is, don't you?"

"It's when two Spitfires go out on a mission together."

"Right you are. Well, they were strafing a German supply train and Jack flew low to get a good shot, peppering the hell-O out of the train.

"Then an anti-aircraft gun fired on Sel's plane and his radio was smashed. He gained altitude and was flying above the clouds, trying to radio Jack but getting no reply. At first, he assumed it was the radio at fault, and that Jack would follow him out. But crossing over the Channel there was no sign of Jack. Sel turned back and that's when he—he—he saw Jack's Spitfire on the ground.

"Sel was to be Jack's best man, you know." She stopped and took a deep breath, "I mean he *shall* be Jack's best man." I handed my napkin over, but she managed to hold herself together long enough to tell me about Sel mentioning that Jack's Spitfire was north of a train depot, right alongside rail tracks about 12 miles between here and Bruges."

I reached into my duffel bag and pulled out a map of Belgium. I'd cut it out of an encyclopedia, along with the whole section that covered the country. I made a pinhole using one of my darts. "That puts him right about here. Should we try and take the train?"

"Let me find the innkeeper and see about schedules," she said, and got up from the table. I waited and studied the map. A few minutes later, Daphne returned. "I am happy to report that the trains are running a tad behind schedule. Apparently the tracks have received heavy damage from the American forces."

"Think of that," I said, all proud. "But where does that leave us? Maybe we borrow a car?"

She shook her head. "Tommy, for one thing, I can't drive. And a 12-year-old behind the wheel of a car will be a trifle conspicuous in broad daylight."

I asked if she could ride a bike.

CHAPTER EIGHTEEN

WE FOUND A BIKE RACK, jammed full and we had our pick. Most of them were rust buckets and belonged to locals, with wicker baskets strapped to the handlebars. But two bicycles—new paint jobs—had tin carrying cases hanging from the top tubes, stamped all over with gothic letters. And nubby tires. A helmet rested on one of the back racks, looking like a horseshoe crab with a swastika decal pasted to its shell. Daphne said we'd better take the German bikes because they were chained together with one flimsy lock. She took a hairpin from her bun.

"Teach me," I said.

"Not now." She swiped at the helmet, toppling it to the ground. Then she attached her suitcase to the back rack, hitched up her skirt, and mounted the bike. "Okay—maybe in exchange for jitterbug lessons," she said.

I figured she wanted to boogie-woogie the American way, seeing that Jack was an expert. Most English girls only know how to waltz. I opened my mouth to say something about the Triple Step Whoosh but got stuck on the word triple.

Holy Mother of God.

A genuine Nazi was coming straight at us. And there I stood gaping at him. It wasn't like when you see them in a Hollywood movie: this one was living and breathing and in Technicolor—although he was mostly wearing black. Everything in me said run. But I didn't want to look like a coward in front of Daphne, so I got ready to spit at him. Then I realized there was a fine line between bravery and foolery, and I didn't want to cross it. Daphne didn't move an inch, but somehow I ended up standing behind her.

"*Bonjour, Fraulein,*" he said, using a combination of French and German. He was looking at Daphne in a way that would've had Jack letting loose all his cannons on the guy—he didn't even notice we were stealing bicycles from the Wehrmacht. Daphne growled. Obviously, he didn't get the message, because he stood there with a lamebrain grin on his face.

She whispered into my ear, "Let's push off before I make a frightful scene."

As we pedaled away, I yelled back in German, "*Drecksau!*" Mr. Fisch, my German tutor, used the expression whenever he talked about Adolph Hitler, and I was hoping to make use of the word myself—dirty pig, it meant. My heart raced like a hot-rod. The Nazi shouted something after us, but I couldn't make out the words.

Daphne yelled like a cheerleader, "*Am Yisrael Chai!*"

For the first time, I wondered if truly brave people ever got scared. Well, the obvious answer was no.

I'd have to ask Jack when I found him—him being the bravest person I knew. Then I got to thinking about a time the school bully called me a chicken-liver when I wouldn't jump from a cliff into a watering hole. Two words, stinging like a wasp. About a month later that same bully smashed his head and was still in a coma. So maybe being scared was a good thing sometimes. Maybe I'd be a little more scared next time I opened by mouth to cuss a German. What if he'd had a motorcycle or a machine gun?

We slowed down after a few minutes and Daphne stopped to ask for directions. Soon we turned down a road marked with a bullet-riddled sign reading: Bruges, 26K. By and by we got out of the city, traveling into farm country. The air smelled like fresh-cut grass and cow dung and was a nice change from the dust of war-torn Oostende.

"What's the meaning of *Am Yisrael Hi?*" I asked.

"The people of Israel are alive…I think. It's one of the few Hebrew sayings that I can remember." She started racking her brain, and then she belted out a song. Boy, she had a voice good enough for the radio, even if she did stumble over a few of them hard to pronounce words. "I've got some of it tangled, I'm afraid," she said.

"Sounded swell to me." I shouted, "*Am Yisrael Hi!*"

Daphne laughed. "One thing I *do* know is that you must give it a hard aitch."

I tried again and she said I sounded like a Bar Mitzvah boy, which I took to be a complement.

After a couple of miles, we reached a roadblock. We

pulled the bicycles behind a farm building, to give us time to discuss options. We watched as German soldiers stopped a farm truck and made a farmer and his wife get out of the vehicle. They were checking identity papers. The only thing identifying me was a handwritten tag my ma had sewed into the collar of my jacket.

"There are only two of them," I said. "We could take 'em out easily." It sounded brave, but the pitch of my voice was like a girl's.

"What, with your boomerang?" said Daphne. "They're carrying rifles."

I used a sailor word, then added: "We'll have to ditch the bikes and hoof it, detour through the fields of corn."

We waded through the stalks of corn: ripe and juicy and smelling of sunshine. Daphne ripped off two corn-cobs, handing one over to me. She pulled back the silky husk and sunk her teeth into the kernels, spraying juice in the air. "Mind you," she said, "I'd have preferred it cooked and with a little butter and sea salt, but I'm not complaining."

"No, mind *you*," I said, "I'd of preferred mine from a Cracker Jack's box."

We continued making a huge arc around the check-point, coming out onto a dirt farm path that ran along the side of the paved road. Only a strip of corn stalks hid us from view. I stopped to find my compass and get our bearings. Belgium was a tiny country and I didn't want to stumble over the German boarder by mistake.

"Don't worry," said Daphne, "if we get lost, we're

more likely to end up in the Netherlands." She put her suitcase down and examined her hand. "Ouch. I'm getting blisters already." I offered to carry her suitcase in exchange for my duffel bag. She swung the duffel over her shoulder and kept on walking. "You're same as your brother: gallant."

I was beaming. "What do you have in here anyway?"

"Bits and bobs."

"Bits and bobs of lead?"

"You can't expect a woman to travel as light as a boy. Our needs are greater."

"I'll say," was all I said. We continued walking in silence, enjoying the fresh air and sunshine, almost forgetting we was in a war. Every blue moon a farm truck passed along the road, sometimes a horse-drawn cart. Then a high-school boy on a bicycle passed by us going in the opposite direction. He jingled his handlebar bell and pointed his finger in warning. That's when we heard loud rumbling: a convoy of German army trucks. We ducked behind a bale of hay. They were headed in the direction of Oostende. I said, "If we had some explosives, we could do some damage."

"I take it there aren't any in this duffel I'm carrying? Please say it's so."

"Nothing to do the trick. Only a few packs of firecrackers."

"Well, that *is* a relief."

We waited for the convoy to pass and then took a hard look at our situation. We'd come to a mowed field, with not enough hay bales to shield us from view. Daphne said it was time we used our thumbs. We'd wait for a farm truck heading toward Bruges, and in the meantime rest our feet. I was already dead-tired from carrying her suitcase and was the first to sit down. Daphne took off her shoes and rubbed her feet. More German trucks passed by, a couple of old-folks on bicycles, a horse and plow. Then, in slow motion, a black car pulled to the side of the road, not twenty feet from our hiding place.

A Mercedes Benz 260D with the top rolled down.

Mounted to the hood were more of them little Nazi flags so popular around these parts: red with those menacing swastikas in the center. The driver exited the car and then rushed to the passenger door. A Gestapo agent stepped out of the car. He was wearing a long black, double-breasted, belted trench coat, and a fedora. The driver clicked his heels and stood at attention. The Gestapo agent paused for a minute taking in the view, the whole time hunting around in his pockets for a cigarette case.

He started walking our way. We ducked lower. Hay crushed under his feet, closer and closer. He sat on a bale three down from ours, took off his hat, and leaned his face to the sun like he was sunbathing. Daphne touched her finger to my lips. Meanwhile the driver had removed a can from the trunk and was filling the tank with gasoline. The Gestapo agent screamed, "*Beeile dich!*" It must've meant hurry up because the driver started moving faster, spilling gasoline on the ground by mistake. The G-Man lit a cigarette and I started to get worried, what with all the hay and gasoline on the ground. If a fire started we'd have to run, then we'd be captured. My heart pounded in my chest and I broke out in a cold sweat. I looked over to Daphne, who was biting her nails.

After two long drags, the German ground the tip of the cigarette against a rock, sticking the butt into his trouser pocket. I exhaled as he walked back to the car. Daphne loosened her grip on my hand. We listened to the Mercedes purr to life and head on down the road.

"Ruddy hell-O," she said, looking at her chewed up nails.

"You'll find a nail file in my duffel bag."

"My, my, you have come prepared."

"It's for escapes."

"We should have used it on him," she said, sparks coming from her eyes. "Plunged it right into his hard heart."

"Next chance we get," I said half-hearted.

As she manicured her nails, I kept watch for a Belgian vehicle. Finally, a pick-up truck lumbered into view, loaded with so many potatoes that the muffler dragged against the road and the tires were almost flat. Diesel smoke billowed from the tail pipe, making the air black. The truck needed an oil change. I said we'd better wait until something better came along. Daphne said we weren't in the position to be picky and ran to the road with her thumb stuck out. The truck came to a jerky stop and she motioned for me to hop in first.

"*Parlez-vous français?*" said Daphne, once the truck got rolling again. I knew from my study of the encyclopedia that in this minuscule country Belgians spoke four different languages: French, Dutch, Flemish, and German. So I wasn't surprised when the old farmer answered her in a language neither of us knew.

"*Ich leiber Deutsch zusprechen,*" I said, hoping he spoke German.

"*Ja Wohl, I sprechen Deutsch,*" he answered.

Daphne stiffened beside me. I told her not to panic, that I had everything under control. I was about to use a trick question. (Like asking a kid if he thought my sister Mary was smart. If he answered back *yes*, then I'd know he was an idiot.) So I took a deep breath and asked the farmer if he'd seen the Gestapo around, already knowing the answer. Besides, it was one of the only complete sentences I knew in German.

"*Schmutzigen Schweine!*" said the farmer. Just another way of saying *Drecksau.* He started mumbled under his breath. Garlic breath.

I turned to Daphne, explaining why we could trust the farmer. Then, substituting the words I knew for the ones I need, I laid out our situation. He looked confused but then said, "*Amerikaner und Engländerin?!*" A troubled look took over his face: knotted eyebrows, pinched lips, dilated pupils. We weren't safe, he explained; we shouldn't be wandering around Belgium hitching rides with any Tom, Dick, or Harry; he warned us not to trust anyone, not even a Belgian. He talked too fast for me to catch everything, but the gist was: lucky for us he came along when he did.

I turned my head to Daphne, my grammar a little screwy as I translated back to English. "He wants that we should come back to his farm. He doesn't want to leave us on the side of the road. What do you think?"

"He *seems* sweet," she said, eyeing the farmer. "Perhaps we should take up his offer. And besides, my nerves are frazzled."

I gave the A-Okay hand signal. The farmer shifted into second gear and put his foot to the floor without picking up much speed. We moved forward in jerking motions and the glove box kept popping open and hitting Daphne in the kneecaps. Ten minutes later and we pulled up to a farmhouse with the farmer honking his horn.

CHAPTER NINETEEN

A LADY STEPPED OUT OF THE DOOR, wiping her apron. She reminded me of my ma and I felt safe. The farmer hurried us into the house and talked to his wife. Meanwhile, I scoped out the place. The ceiling was low and the windows small; most of the light came from the open door. Pots and pans hung above a fireplace and inside— where the fire goes—was a hook with a big-bellied pot.

The lady's eyes flew open as she listened to her farmer husband. She kept on saying, "*O je! O je,*" which I figured meant, "Oh dear! Oh dear!" She told us to take a seat at the kitchen table and sliced us each a chunk of homemade bread. She set down a jar of raspberry preserves and took a towel off of a plate, revealing all sorts of hard cheeses. She made us eat off of her best china, which she kept propped up on a side cabinet. I never wanted to leave this house.

Then I remembered our mission. I tried to explain about Jack's plane going down in Belgium. I used pantomime, my hand like an airplane crashing into the table. *Absturz, absturz,* I kept saying, exactly like I'd been taught. Still—they couldn't understand what I was getting at. I said to Daphne: "I learned my German from a real German. They must speak a dialect and can't understand the real deal."

She rolled her eyes.

The farmer got up to leave the house, and we heard his truck start up and jerk away from the farm. His wife made a rolling motion with her hand, telling us to keep on eating. I was happy to oblige and so was Daphne. The farmer's wife put her elbows on the wooden tabletop. Her hands cradled her chin—from it sprouted several hairs. "*O je! O je!*" she said like a broken record.

The farmer returned with another man, this one with black hair and a long thin face. He was also wearing overalls, but his steel glasses—with rims small as a Liberty Half-Dollar—made him look like a druggist. "My cousin tells me you are American?" he said, to our relief in English. "May I ask what is your business in Belgium?"

"Should we trust him?" I asked Daphne.

"You can trust me," he said. "But can *we* trust you? That is the question." Turning to the farmer and his wife, he rattled off something in Dutch. Then he turned back to me. "Where in America are you from, may I ask?"

"East Hempstead, New York," I said, laying on the Long Island nasal. It was times like these you had to forget Shakespeare.

"And what is the tallest building in New York?"

The conversation was taking a funny turn, but I played along: "Empire State Build-din."

"And if you were to take an elevator to the top of

the Empire State Building, what would you find?"

Everybody knew the answer: an observation deck. To get up there you take an elevator that makes your stomach fall to your shoes. The observation deck is so high up that if you tossed a penny and it hit somebody on the street below, it flattened them like a pancake. They had them viewer machines and for a nickel you could see Ellis Island, where my ma and da were inspected for diseases before they could be Americans. Jack said the elevator down was the same effect as stalling an airplane.

"And if you look from this observation deck to the west, what do you see?"

I got my bearings and then said, "Jersey?"

Daphne interrupted, "Jersey is in England! Everyone knows that."

He said, "He's answered correctly. We have family living in Hoboken. I've been to visit them."

"Oh," I said, getting it. "You had to test me to see I ain't a German agent."

"Exactly. Have you heard of the Hitler Youth? They turn little children into monsters, train them up to be good little snitches and bullies. It would be exactly like the Germans to use children to expose the Resistance."

I pointed out that there'd been hordes of German tourists visiting New York City before the war. They came to sightsee and eat them hotdogs and knishes street vendors sold from carts. Also hot chestnuts. And they all went to the Empire State Building. Some of those Germans could've gone on to become Nazi spies.

"You make a good point." Rubbing his chin, he

asked, "Who won the World Series last year?"

I looked down at my shoes, shaking my head as I answered the question. "Tragically, the New York Yankees. Monday, October 6, 1941: *A date that will live in infamy.* Ebbets Field, Brooklyn. The Yankees were up against the greatest team ever was: the Brooklyn Dodgers. Joe DiMaggio tried to sucker-punch Whit Wyatt: the umps split up the fight. Against all odds, the Yankees took this last game in the series: 4-1." I looked into his eyes. "And how do I know this, you might ask? Well, I'll tell you. I was in the bleachers with my da. Seen the disaster unfold before my very eyes."

My interrogator turned back to the farmer and his wife and they talked between themselves. He looked at me smiling. "You have passed the test. Now tell us your mission."

First I wanted to know why he hadn't tested Daphne. "That won't be necessary," he said laughing. "She has an honest face." I wondered what that said about mine.

Daphne spoke up, explaining everything. Then she said, "And if we don't find Jack soon, the RAF will presume him dead."

A cold shiver went down my spine. "What do you mean *presume dead?*"

"I'm sorry," she said. "I know that comes as a shock." She explained that a week ago she'd talked with Lieutenant Kennard, Jack's commander, and learned that RAF Command would make a pronouncement if Jack didn't show up soon. It was just a military formality, she said, "utter twaddle." Even Kennard figured the same because there wasn't a shred of evidence to prove that Jack died in the crash.

My lower lip began to wobble. The farmer's wife said, "*O je!*"

Daphne flung her arms around me. "Don't you think I'd know if Jack were dead? He's my soul mate. I'd know."

"That means the RAF will stop looking for him," I said.

"Well, pudding head, why do you think I'm here?"

My interrogator cleared his throat. He was in touch with somebody in the Resistance, he said. It was one of their chief aims to rescue downed Allied airmen before the Gestapo arrived to investigate a crash. He promised to ask his friend if there was any information about Jack. I asked if we could come along and meet the friend.

"That won't be possible," he said. "These people are taking huge risks—to both themselves and to their families. Their identities must be carefully guarded. I know about this man because, well…that's as much as I should say. It is far better if you wait here with the DeQuicks. My cousin is a good man, as is his wife. They'll see that you are well cared for. But you must keep to yourselves. Don't even speak with the neighboring farmers. Understood?"

Daphne wanted to know were he lived and what his name was, but he brushed off her question and said, "It could take some time to get information, so you must be patient. I will return as soon as I have news. Or better yet, I'll send a coded message. Again—don't stray from this farmhouse. You will endanger these good people by doing so."

Mrs. DeQuick handed Daphne a kerosene lantern and escorted us to a stone barn with a thatched roof. I understood her say she'd be back shortly, bringing along some items—the details were lost in translation. She pointed up to a hayloft and we climbed a ladder. I always liked sleeping in barns.

"I think we should pull the ladder up," said Daphne. "In case the wrong people come." Knowing what sort of people she meant, I jumped to help her.

She set her suitcase on a bale of hay, took a small key from a string around her neck and opened the two small locks. I watched in amazement as she took one thing after another out of the small suitcase, arranging them like she was decorating a house and was planning to be there for a while. Out came a mirror, which she hung from a peg on the wall. Out came a silver hair-brush and comb set. Out came dresses. One was a long evening gown beaded with red sequins.

"You dragged a getup like that on a rescue mission?" I asked, dumbfounded.

"A mission to rescue my fiancé, so yes, indeed I did." She found a few hangers made of pink padded satin and hung the dresses from a rafter, saying, "They need a good pressing but this will have to do." She reached back into the case and retrieved a pair of red high-heeled shoes. They were also studded with red sequins.

"They look like Dorothy's shoes in *The Wizard of Oz*!" I said.

"Maybe Jack will appear if I click my heels and say a wish."

I asked what else she took along and she reached back into the case, removing the framed portrait of my brother Jack in his RAF flight uniform: the same photograph that had me weeping before. Now it had the opposite effect. I asked to take a look and she handed me the frame. "What's all that stuff strapped to him?"

"That—" She pointed to his flight helmet and the cord that ran from it, "—is what attaches to his radio. And that,"—she pointed to his back—"is a parachute."

"So maybe he bailed out?"

"In theory yes, although Sel Edner thought not. Jack was flying low when Sel saw him last; and then next thing, his plane was on the ground. We can't rule it out entirely. Sel was hidden in the clouds and might not have seen Jack gain enough altitude for a bail out. Still, it's unlikely. If the Spitfire had crashed from a higher altitude there'd have been an explosion, and thankfully there wasn't."

I pointed to something strung around Jack's upper body.

"That is a holster," she said. "And inside, my good man, is his service pistol."

"You mean Jack had a weapon on him when he crashed?"

"A .45 caliber Enfield, to be exact. Pretty deadly when fired at close range. I know, because he once aimed it at a bloke who was being fresh with me. I'd just met Jack. It was then I knew he was sweet on me. I'd never had a fellow defend me with his life before."

"Did he kill the guy?" I asked, wide-eyed.

"Of course not. The blighter got the message immediately, apologized and made a hasty exit." She laughed remembering the scene. "Turned out the gun wasn't loaded."

She placed the frame on a bale of hay between us. Pointing to one side, she indicated her quarters and to the other side, mine. I followed her lead and arranged my weapons on a bale in my space. I wanted them close at hand. Daphne hooted as she registered what was in my duffel. "Laugh now," I said.

"Fight the Germans with toys, why don't we?"

Before long, Mrs. DeQuick called from below, "Yoo-hoo!" We lowered the ladder and climbed down.

Daphne took a tray, saying, "What a sweetheart." She gave Mrs. DeQuick a peck on the cheek and the farmer's wife giggled. She gave us each a feather pillow and a blanket, which she'd carried under her pudgy arms. "*Merci Beaucoup*," said Daphne. It meant, "Thanks a million."

Mrs. DeQuick understood some French because she answered, "*Vous êtes les bienvenus*," which I figured meant, "Nothing to it." She left the barn, pulling a sliding door closed behind her.

On the tray sat two clay mugs of warmed milk, and something wrapped in foil. Daphne held it up and said, "Could it be, I wonder?" She gently peeled back the wrapper, revealing a piece of chocolate. "Do you have any idea how precious this is? The Belgians are world famous for their chocolate, but that's yet another thing Adolph Hitler has messed with."

"He's changed the chocolate recipe?" There was no end to the man's tomfoolery.

"No, silly. There's a chocolate shortage because of the war. This is worth its weight in gold." She broke the piece in half and placed her portion in her mouth, making happy sounds. "You realize, don't you, that if they're going to keep feeding us, we'll have to earn our keep."

Chores. I thought I'd escaped all that when I left East Hempstead.

"Come now," she said. "I'll teach you to milk a cow. It's something I learned staying at my cousin's farm in Hampshire on school holidays. It's jolly fun. You just pull the cow's teat."

We climbed back up to the loft, raised the ladder again and got ready for bed. Daphne brushed her hair until I thought it might fall out. Then she removed a paperback from her suitcase. She dimmed the lantern and moved it closer to her bale bed.

"Do you have a book I could borrow?" I said, sitting there in the shadows. I held up the only book I'd taken along, *Mein Kampf.* "This book gives me nightmares if I read it before bedtime."

Daphne's head whipped my way, making her hair fly. "That's an evil book! You oughtn't be reading it," she said, tearing the book from my hand. She ripped it in half and threw it against the wall with a fastball pitch. "That wicked man calls us dirty Jews and says we smell bad."

Her eyes were swimming, shiny in the lantern light. A tear ran down her cheek and hung like an icicle from her trembling plump lip. Knowing that Daphne was one of the people Hitler was out to get gave me a bad feeling too: like at the end of summer or a wasp sting or chalk screeching on a chalkboard. She blinked and her long black eyelashes grew wet and heavy. It was terrible to see her hurt like that and to think it was part my fault. So I scooted over and put my arms around her. She smelled real good if you ask me, like flowers. I hugged her tighter.

She pushed me away. "Don't get fresh," she said, trying to laugh.

"So can I borrow a book?" I said, backing into the shadow so she wouldn't see me blushing.

"Help yourself." She sniffled and pointed at her suitcase, giving me permission to take a peek. Well—*golly*—no wonder that suitcase was so heavy. She'd brought a whole library. I glanced at the titles, which were mostly in French. She must've noticed my perplexing because she said: "I didn't bring many English books, afraid that we'd be searched—only *Pride and Prejudice* and *Romeo and Juliet*, which I'm fairly certain even the Germans read in the original language."

"Why didn't you bring *Richard III?*" I said, digging my heels into the hay. "I'm not reading *Romeo and Juliet.*"

"You're so like Jack, it's terrifying. His idea of a romance is *Riders of the Purple Sage.*" She fluttered her eyelashes and puckered her lips. "And yet, your brother is one of the most passionate men ever lived."

"Well, I ain't."

She said that since my English was so "atrocious," I might as well try one of her French novels. I was about to poo-poo that idea when she mentioned that there was a particular one she'd brought along, specially for me. I riffled through the stack of books, franticly trying to make out the titles. Then I lifted *Les Trois Mousquetaires* triumphantly.

"That's the one," she said, winking.

I didn't mind that the book was in French; it was an illustrated edition of *The Three Musketeers*. Gee, it was nice of her to think of me!

After that, we both settled down happily, with our noses each pressed to a book and taking in the fantastic smell of aged paper.

CHAPTER TWENTY

WHEN I WOKE UP THE NEXT MORNING, Daphne was kneeling at a small window, taking aim with my bow and arrow. Before I could speak, she turned to me, let the arrow go slack, and put her index finger to her mouth signaling me to keep my mouth shut. She swung around, getting positioned to shoot. I flew to her side and looked out the window. Parked in the center of a clearing between buildings was a German army truck, and standing by it were two soldiers with rifles slung on their shoulders. Mrs. DeQuick was pointing to a building far from the one we was in. She looked nervous. One of the soldiers shouted something at her and she wobbled into the building. The two Germans followed behind.

"Should we go down and defend her?" I asked.

Daphne bit her lower lip and said, "I'm not sure what to do."

The question was answered for us, when Mrs. DeQuick exited the building. Behind her came the two Germans, straining as they each carried a steel milk canister to the truck. The one got into the driver's seat and started the engine, as the other finished lifting crates of potatoes into the back before shutting the tailgate. *Commandeering.* I waved my hand like a magician conjuring a spell. "May they forevermore eat potatoes boiled and never get a French fry."

Once the truck left the yard, we went down to the farmer's wife. By the time we joined her, she was sitting on the edge of a well. She reached into her apron pocket, retrieving a letter and used it to fan her face. In a jumble of languages, she explained that the Germans sent somebody at the same time every week—like clockwork—to take provisions, which they never paid for. She'd forgotten all about them, what with all the excitement of our arrival.

She held the letter far from her, like an old lady who needs glasses. I noticed it had no return address, and she explained that it was slid under the door and that her husband believed it was a message from the cousin. She slipped and let out that his name was Antoine. She opened it and removed a slip of paper, looking puzzled. Shrugging her shoulders, she handed it to me. It was a receipt.

"She says she's never been to this bookshop," said Daphne.

I studied the receipt and seen it was made out for the purchase of a book called, *Der Rote Baron.* "The Red Baron!" I shouted.

Daphne started biting her nails. The Red Baron was the German fighter ace from the Great War who had crashed and died. *Maybe not the best choice for a code name,* I thought. The receipt was dated 29/9/42. I tried to figure out the code but was baffled until Daphne pointed out that, in Europe, the day and month were flopped backwards.

"Than it only means one thing," I said. "We got to meet somebody on September 29th."

"The day after tomorrow." Daphne pointed to scribble below the title of the book. It read: *04-40*. "Look here. That's military time for 4:40 in the morning. Brilliant. And I suppose the meeting is to take place at this bookshop."

Mrs. DeQuick invited us into the house and dished up a hearty breakfast.

"It must be nice to be a farmer," said Daphne. "Ever since the war began we hardly ever get fresh eggs in London. We're lucky if we get them hard-boiled and from a tin." I looked at my egg—drippy in the center and fried, just like I liked them.

For the rest of the day: chores. Daphne gave me the lowdown on how to milk a cow and I showed her how to hoe potatoes, something we Irish can do in our sleep.

The next day we prepared for our *rendezvous*. The farmer drew a map for us, showing exactly how to get to the small village where we would find the bookshop. It was three or four miles away and we'd have to walk. Belgian vehicles were only permitted to travel during daylight and we couldn't ask the farmer to break the curfew.

We left when the moon was low in the sky. The map took us down several dirt paths and avoided the main paved roads. I was half asleep and we weren't in the mood for chitchat. The only thing I said was, "Daphne, if you keep biting them nails, you won't have fingers."

After about an hour we came to the village and found the bookshop. Inside the door window hung a sign that read, *Geschlossen, Fermé,* and *Gesloten.* Closed any which way you said it. Looking at her wristwatch, Daphne said, "We're a tad early."

We sat on a bench with a view of the bookshop and waited. At 4:40 the sign in the window flipped over; now it read: *Ouvrir.* "Here we go," whispered Daphne, and we stepped up to the unlit shop.

When we knocked on the door, a lady opened it. I said, "*Der rote Baron?*"

"*Ja,*" she said, peeking a look outside to be sure no one was spying on us. She flipped the sign back to "closed." We followed her past bookcases and into a back room, where she turned on a light. "I speak English," she said.

"Do you have news of my fiancé, Lieutenant Mooney?" asked Daphne, holding my hand and digging her fingernails into my palm.

"Let's wait for my colleague." She carried over two chairs and welcomed us to sit. I watched as she reached into her pocket for a hankie but noticed that she didn't use it. A minute or so passed and a back door opened. A man entered the room, removing his hat. His face looked like an undertaker's.

He and the lady also took seats, their two chairs facing ours, our knees almost bumping. The man spoke Dutch and the lady translated.

"I'm afraid that we are the bearers of bad news," she said. Daphne began to cry and my own eyes went drip, drip. "On the morning of June 16, a Spitfire went down near the village of Nieuwege, very close to the rail line. Unfortunately, the Germans arrived ahead of us. Our people watched as German soldiers removed the body of the pilot."

"Body?" said Daphne.

"Yes. The pilot was killed in the crash. I'm very, very sorry." She handed Daphne the hankie and placed her hand on Daphne's knee. I pushed back my sadness, because I knew this must be harder for a fiancée than a brother, and I wanted to be strong for her. A fiancée is practically a wife and mother. Only I wasn't feeling strong. My muscles had all gone to mush, especially the ones in my lungs and heart. My stomach did cartwheels.

"Are you all right?" said the lady, shaking my arm. "Let me get you some water."

I asked if there was a number on the plane. I was hoping it was another plane we were talking about and not Jack's. The lady translated my question for the man. Numbers and letters in Dutch are like numbers in German. "Oh," was all I could get out. The number on Jack's plane was W3841. We was talking about his Spitfire. I asked them to point us to my brother's plane.

"Do you really want to see that?" asked the lady. Daphne shook her head *yes* and then bit her lip until it was bleeding.

The lady listened to the man, then said, "He's saying that it won't be safe for you. You'd have to pass near a train depot and a warehouse where the Germans store munitions. The area is heavily guarded. It's not wise for you to go there. In fact, my colleague refuses to say where the aircraft is located." The man shook his head *no,* and said something I didn't catch. The lady explained: "He's withholding this information for your own good."

I didn't press, because she already gave away that the airplane was near a village called Nieuwege. It couldn't be too hard to find.

The man had something more to say. The lady spoke: "My colleague doesn't have exact information but says the Germans have begun taking British pilots—those killed in action—to Dunkirk for internment."

Dunkirk. I knew exactly where that was: France.

The man spoke again and the lady said, "He offers his condolences and wants you to know that the Belgian people are grateful for the sacrifice made by your brother. He asks that you offer our heartfelt sympathy to your family." When she said this, I thought of my ma. It was going to be me who'd break the news to her.

The two Belgians stood, and we done the same. "Is there anything more we can do for you?" asked the lady, "Any other way we might be of help?"

There wasn't. Daphne thanked them and then we went to leave.

"If you change your mind, find me at this shop."

We left the bookshop and stood in the middle of the street. My knees felt wobbly and my head started to spin. It was still dark, but the sky was beginning to lighten and we could hear birds begin to sing their morning songs. Daphne continued to stand in the middle of the street. I didn't want to leave her side, not even for a split second.

Right then, all I wanted was to go home to Long Island. When I said this, Daphne didn't say a peep. She just stood in the road and stared into space. What she finally said was, "I don't believe it." I figured she was saying something like, *This is so horrible* or *I'm in shock.* But what she was saying was she still believed Jack was alive. "He's out there somewhere, I feel it. And I'm not about to give up hope."

I wanted to say, *But all the evidence says different.*

A milk truck veered around us. The driver honked his horn a few times. On the fifth honk, just when the bumper was a few feet from crushing me, I flashed to a time not too long ago: I was sitting in a butt-torturing pew at St. Brendan's, waiting for the moment they'd pass the collection plate. To tell you true, I was bored stiff and wanting to get home and head for the woods behind the house and climb a few oak trees, or maybe build a tree house. It didn't matter what. Anything was better than sitting in that tomb of a church listening to the priest drone on. He was talking about three things—the three most important things in the world. One of them was *hope.* I remember that part because the priest yelled the word and it jolted me awake. I wasn't all too happy about it at the time.

Something else was actually the *most* important thing—bigger even than hope. But hope was up there on the list—number two or three—bigger than marshmallows, bigger than gold and jewels, and bigger than four-leaf clovers—even though that was the Irish symbol of hope, come to think of it.

I felt around in my back pocket for the card my grandma sent me—only three leaves left.

But maybe Daphne was on to something. *Hope* is what got me this far—all the way to Belgium. It made everything tick up until now and without it I was high-tailing it to some harbor in Spain, looking for a boat out of Europe, or swimming home if I had to. I'd be back in East Hempstead—in the room I'd shared with Jack—bawling my eyes out and taking flak from Mary besides.

I was scared out of my mind then, and so was Daphne—biting her nails again. She looked into my eyes and I seen she was fighting the same thing: the thing that wasn't hope, the thing that was give-up.

"Where do—we go—from here?" she asked, swallowing sobs.

I looked at the card, thinking I'd have to find a clover and rubber cement.

"We stick to the plan," I said. "Find that Spitfire. And then we find Jack."

CHAPTER TWENTY-ONE

WE WENT ON WILD-GOOSE CHASES, one to a downed Hawker Typhoon. "This is an airplane Lord Sopwith's company designed," I said, as we surveyed the smashed aircraft. I climbed onto the wing and into the cockpit. It was my first time sitting in a real fighter plane.

"Get out of there," Daphne said, rapid-fire.

I took the throttle in my hands, closed my eyes and imagined myself soring in the clouds—chased by a whole squadron of the German Luftwaffe. I did a few flips and rolls and came up behind them. Every one of my shots landed in their fuel tanks. The sky was bright with explosions. Daphne yelled, "Thomas Robert Mooney! You get out of that plane this instant," which was all that saved the Luftwaffe from total destruction.

Someone pointed us to another RAF plane but this one was a bomber. I climbed in and entered the fuselage, a little terrified of what I might find. I was scared stiff there'd be stiffs in the plane, still strapped to their seats. I looked around for parachutes and only found one. The place smelled of burnt metal and rubber.

The reward for my courage came when I spotted a

packet of letters, tied with a ribbon. The pink envelopes were addressed to a Sergeant Howard Hunter. I put the packet to my nose and found the letters still stunk of perfume. I put them into my jacket pocket.

After three days of searching, I was ready to call it quits. I was putting on a good face for Daphne's sake, because I'd gotten her into this mess. But trying to be hopeful, all the daylong, was almost impossible. Hope was like the surf at Jones Beach: you felt good when it crashed on you, but it was near impossible to keep your feet planted in the sand and not fall on your backside when the tide rolled out.

That's when we ran into Antoine again, selling potatoes at an outdoor market—the very potatoes I'd hoed. We filled him in on our search and he said, "I've been asking around myself and I've learned that there's a Spitfire not far from here. I've seen it with my own eyes. The problem is that you must pass close to a place that is heavily guarded by the Germans. It can only be done at night, and even then—"

Daphne knitted her hands together and said, "Please, Monsieur DeQuick—if that is your name."

"Promise you'll take care," he said, after weighing the situation as well as a few spuds that he placed on a scale and then into a customer's string bag. "I can take you part of the distance on my way home and give you directions from there. There's no rush, because you really must wait until dark." He pointed us to two little three-legged stools and yelled into the crowd, "*Pomme de terre! Pomme de terre!*"

Hours later and we were lying in the back of a horse drawn cart, covered with hay. Antoine DeQuick called to us when we reached a crossroad and then he pointed in the direction we should go. "Good luck to you both," he offered. "And if you have any trouble, backtrack to the green barn. Beside the barn, on the north side, is a small hatch leading to a root cellar. It's very hard to spot. I know where it is because this is where my friend keeps the beer he brews."

The sun was still high in the sky, but it was nippy and you knew that fall was coming. Leaves on trees were turning red and orange and yellow. We only talked to remind each other of the directions. They were written on my palm. "There's the stone barn with a thatched roof, where we turn to the left," I said.

"Now let's look for the small path leading from that well," said Daphne.

"There's the silo we are looking for."

A few minutes later and Daphne pointed a finger. "The green barn."

"Bingo." I looked from my palm to a rock wall and the gate we had to pass through. We stood frozen and I said, "Shush," putting a finger to my mouth. Both of us cupped our ears and listened to the sound of a coming train. We moved on to a whitewashed wall. Daphne crouched behind the wall and I took a peek over the other side. Just as Antoine said, there was a warehouse and on top sat a heavy artillery gun pointed toward the sky.

Beside the warehouse stood a train depot—used by the Germans to load and unload munitions. A few outbuildings must've served as barracks. There was a train stopped on the track—the one we just heard. A handful of farmers worked the field between the depot and where we hid. I spotted two German soldiers at the entrance of a fenced area, each toting rifles and standing stiff as ironing boards. One held onto a leash attached to a German Shepherd. Another soldier had some other kind of gigantic dog.

We were both petrified of dogs. I figured the Nazis trained their dogs to pick up the scent of Englishmen or Americans—just like the Swiss trained their Saint Bernard's to sniff out skiers with broken legs. Daphne doused herself every morning with the perfume Jack got her last Valentine's Day. He'd bought it in London and that had me worried.

Once we got to the train depot, all we had to do was follow the track north. In less than a half-mile we'd come upon the Spitfire. We'd have to wait until the cover of darkness to make our way down the tracks, since the gun post on the roof would have a view of our path.

Daphne unwrapped a hunk of Mrs. DeQuick's cheese and the remains of a loaf of bread. With my mouth full, I mumbled, "If this ain't it, I think we need to go home. All these downed British planes make me think we might be losing the war."

"Don't be such a bloody pessimist," she snapped. "And would you *please* stop saying ain't!"

She'd never spoke mean to me and it stung. Stung

like a scorpion. I felt pretty lonely just then—like the last man on earth. It was Daphne who looked upset though. She sniffled, took my hand in hers and rubbed circles in my palm. "I'm sorry little brother. Don't mind me. The truth is, I love your grammatical foibles because they remind me of Jack."

The wind cut through my jacket, the flannel one I'd left home with when it was still summer. A gust blew a tear right off of Daphne's rosy cheek. I knew she was cold also, because her teeth chattered. She was wearing a light cotton dress. I removed my jacket and handed it to her. She rewarded me with a quick kiss on the forehead. "That's much better, Thomas. You are a such a gentle-men."

She'd called me Thomas. I liked it because it sounded grown-up. I didn't mind being called Tommy either, the nickname for a British soldier.

We waited so long my leg fell asleep. Now the sun was set and the moon was getting higher in the sky. Luckily, it was the phase where there's a sliver of light—a waning crescent it's called. I peeked over the wall and seen that the farmers had gone home. The gate into the German base was shut and the two soldiers were nowhere in sight. The locomotive hissed out steam and moved from the station, headed to Oostende. Everything was quiet in the immediate area. There was the faint sound of artillery fire—*ack-ack*, it's called—at least a quarter-mile away to the south. Hopefully the Germans had all gone to bed. I hurried back to Daphne and said, "C'mon. Time to move."

We both ran like racehorses to a position behind a small storage shack that stood a few feet from the track. We had a new angle on the fenced in area, where we spotted several soldiers. All of them wide awake. They were singing Nazi songs. I could tell.

"My God, I think they're rat arsed!" said Daphne.

"Drunk as skunks."

I took another peek and seen they were each holding a beer bottle and passing around something that looked like a gallon of whiskey. One was tipsy, stumbled, and fell. "Shazam!" I said. The Germans were too drunk to notice us, but it was the dogs I was worried about. I forced a terrifying image from my mind.

We made a dash down the track. Daphne stumbled to her knees. Her suitcase went flying and hit the ground with a thud, opening and spilling everything on the ground. I helped her up and we both hurried to gather her belongings and stuff them back in the suitcase. "You're not hitting the bottle yourself, are you?" I whispered to Daphne, and she laughed for the first time that day.

"No, Thomas. I tripped on a rail."

I found a huge bottle of perfume in the grass—the perfume Jack gave to her. "Yardley English Lavender," she said when I handed it back. "What would I do without it? The fragrance reminds me of Jack."

"I'd of thought Jack smells more like monkey grease."

After I recovered from a pinch in the arm, we made our way down the track. A half-mile or so and I saw in the distance a lopsided Spitfire: wing bent and broke. It made me think of a bird that had fallen from its nest. As we got near to the airplane, I read the numbers painted on the side of the fuselage.

My brother's plane.

A cloud moved above, casting us in pitch darkness. We were now far from the depot and invisible to the Germans.

"I'm going up first to take a look." Daphne stepped onto the wing, stood on her tippy toes and leaned into the cockpit. I wanted to give her a few minutes alone, so I stood by the propeller, which was smashed to pieces. I was waiting for the sound of weeping or screaming or some other girlish reaction. Instead I heard her say, "Oh, thank God!"

I scrambled onto the wing and she made room for me to look with her into Jack's cockpit. There was nothing there to be happy about. "Can you see what I see?" she said.

"I can't see much of anything." I jumped back down to my duffel bag, grabbing my flashlight. Back up on the wing, I switched it on and examined the control panel. It was a grim sight to be sure, but Daphne remained jolly-like. Covering the seat and some of the gadgets was the ominous sight of dried blood. My heart lurched. I felt faint. Daphne began giggling. I figured she'd lost her mind.

"You don't get it, do you?" she said.

"Can't you see what's here?" I asked, bug-eyed with fear.

"It's not what's *here*, Thomas. It's what's *not* here."

I said, soft as possible, "We already knew the Germans came and removed Jack's body. The man from the Resistance said so—remember?" I put my arm around her shoulder.

She pointed to an empty spot on the top right side of the dash, above the boost gauge. I was sure then she had lost her marbles. "Look carefully," she said.

I shined my flashlight onto the spot and wondered what the heck she was talking about. Then I got it. "There was something taped there," I said looking her in the eye. I stared back at the spot, to a square made of transparent adhesive tape on the dash. "What was taped there?"

"A very flattering snapshot of yours truly."

"Was it always there?"

"Jack said it was his lucky charm. He would have never left England without it being firmly in place."

"Which means...?"

"That obviously Jack *removed* the photograph. And a dead man can't do that. Proof positive that Jack survived the crash."

"Hmm," I said, thinking of the flip side. I had my doubts, but I was afraid to speak them. For one thing, there were a lot of lonely men in the area and any one of them might want that photograph. Men everywhere put pin-ups on their walls. As a matter of fact, I had one of Judy Garland hung in my bedroom and Jack had one of Rita Hayward on the opposite wall. Daphne's photo might be hanging above a Nazi's bed. The idea of it made my stomach turn.

Right then I figured Jack for dead and was about to say so. But I decided to find a gentler way to get Daphne to give up the search. I pointed to a haystack. "Even if Jack is alive, it will be like finding a needle in a haystack. Jack would be hiding out in disguise. Why, we might pass him on the street and not recognize him."

When I seen she wasn't being moved, I changed my tactic, trying to sound chipper: "This is great! We can go home with good news for Ma. We've done what we set out to do." (This is what people call *humoring*, even though there was nothing humorous about the situation.)

She stamped her foot on the wing. "We set out to *rescue* Jack. I always knew he was alive. Proving him alive was never the mission."

"Fair enough. Then where do we go from here?"

She slammed her hand on the Plexiglas hatch window. "Dunkirk!"

I had an awful feeling about where this was leading, and it looked like it was going to require a shovel.

CHAPTER TWENTY-TWO

WE SAT ON THE WING QUIET-LIKE, letting things sink in. Neither of us wanted to leave Jack's Spitfire. I was feeling sorry for myself. Jack was my only brother and there'd be no one to take his place. Ma said, "I'm finished" the day I was born. My whole life was sprawled out in front of me: lonesome, that's what it amounted to. Being the only boy in a family of girls is worse than being an only child. And on top of it, Jack was my best friend. I'd never find another one like him. Daphne was okay, but she was a girl. And I doubt she'd want to move to New York without Jack.

There was supposed to be a better ending—a tickertape parade down Broadway, me sitting next to Jack in an open-top sedan, Roosevelt in the front seat.

I tried to think if I could've done something different: beg Jack not to sign up, tie him to a kitchen chair, slip him a Mickey Finn. Any which way I turned the thing around, the story had the same ending: Jack going off and getting himself killed. I couldn't shake the feeling that it was somehow my fault. Brothers are supposed to look out for each other.

I looked over at Daphne, afraid maybe she was

thinking the same thing, blaming me. Her eyes were fixed on the moon, her face ghost-white in its light. She looked angry all right. "You mad at me?" I said.

She looked me straight in the eye. "Why would I be mad at you, silly? It's Hitler and his lot I'm angry with. He's the cause of all this sorrow." She roped her arm around my bicep and we got on the same frequency, her thoughts winning over mine.

It really *did* help to blame Hitler.

My brother was probably dead and Hitler was going to get away with it, by the look of things. Meanwhile, just down the track, Germans were celebrating. They didn't give two hoots that they'd ruined my life. The whole set up was rotten.

My eyes wandered down the train track ending up at the German military installation, not half a mile from us. On top of that warehouse was the same artillery gun that shot my brother from the sky.

If things went much further, the Nazis would be goose-stepping into London in no time flat. And from there it was a short boat ride over to the old country. I had grandparents in Ireland, and even though I'd never met them, they were still kin. Next thing you know, Long Island. I'd be sitting at Ebbets Field with Nazi Stormtroopers in the box seats, cheering for the Yankees.

The rhythm of Daphne's breathing worked like a hypnotist's pocket watch. My eyes started to droop and my head got fuzzy with sleep and fell to her shoulder. Daphne's cheek rested on my head and her soft hair covered my face like a blanket.

ACK-ACK-ACK, ACK-ACK-ACK, came the racket of artillery shells exploding in the sky. We jolted awake. Two fighter planes roared over our heads, banked and turned back toward the German base. Ideas began flowing like the Mississippi River. Make that the Nile. "So," I said, "would you do anything to stop the Nazis from taking over the world?"

"Of course, Thomas. Anything."

"Then I'll need the perfume."

"Oh dear, not that."

I explained the general outline of my plan and Daphne added some nice touches. She handed over the bottle, first dabbing a little perfume behind each ear.

We needed a diversion. I figured we'd use a box of firecrackers. It worked to get me onto *Endeavour*. Daphne didn't think it was a good idea to waste them in that way. "I've got it!" she said, leaping from the Spitfire wing and lifting her suitcase. "It's time I got into uniform. Don't peek until I say you can."

When she gave me the signal, I turned and looked down to her—and what a sight it was! I whistled like a sailor. Daphne pulled on a pair of long satin gloves, which reached above her elbows. Jean Harlow would be rolling over in her grave she'd be so jealous.

We went over the plan again. I gave her a handful of darts, which she concealed in a small red satin purse. She asked for the slingshot too. I slung my duffel bag over my shoulder and clutched Daphne's suitcase in my left hand. I wished it were blue, not pink. *At a time like this*, I thought, exhaling everything in my lungs.

We made our way back down the tracks, hiding behind the shack again. I circled around to the front of the depot, approaching the opening of the fence and the guard post. A drunken soldier saw me coming and stumbled to the gate. I raised my right arm in the air and shouted, "*HEIL!*"

The soldier tried to wave his arm in the air but was still holding a beer bottle.

A dog growled.

"I've come to find my brother," I announced in German, and if I spoke it with a heavy Long Island accent, he was too drunk to notice.

"*Ihr Bruder?*" he asked. Your brother?

"My brother, the major. I've come all the way from Dusseldorf to visit him. He's expecting me." I lifted Daphne's pink suitcase to make my point. The soldier waved me in, while taking a gulp of beer.

Right on cue, Daphne made her entrance. She stepped into a circle of light made by a small floodlight above the gatepost. The light bounced off the sequins on her red evening gown. She was sparkling like the Christmas tree at Rockefeller Center. She said, "*Bonsoir*," and the soldier's jaw dropped. He forgot all about me.

As I made my way into the complex, men called to one another. An entire battalion headed to the gate. Daphne had good aim, but I had better act fast. I bolted for the warehouse. No one stopped me. No one was there to try.

The place was full of wood crates. Some were

opened and I seen ammo cartridges—the kind they loaded into the anti-aircraft guns. I didn't know if this would work, but it was worth a try. Dumping the contents of my duffel bag onto the cement floor, I got to work. Opening Daphne's suitcase, I retrieved the bottle of Yardley English Lavender and poured some on my duffel bag. I placed this by a crate of ammo. I splashed perfume on the wood crates in the immediate vicinity. On top of the duffel bag, I stacked books, opening the pages so that the paper was exposed—pages and pages of old and dry paper. The books got doused with more perfume.

Jane would appreciate that.

Shakespeare would write a sonnet.

And the three musketeers would invite me to be the fourth.

Then I topped the pile with the two halves of *Mein Kampf*, the one book that wanted burning.

I dragged another stack of ammunition close to the first pile, so the two stacks of boxes were a foot or so apart, my kindling between them. Using box tops, I added to the firewood. I placed a few packages of firecrackers alongside the books. My summers at Boy Scout camp were about to pay off. "Forgive me Howard," I said, setting the packet of pink love letters on top of *Romeo and Juliet*.

Now I stood, adrenaline pumping through my veins. A firecracker was in one hand, in the other a box of matches. I lit the box of matches first and then the firecracker. I had it from experience—there wasn't much time before the flare ran down the short piece of string and the firecracker exploded. Heat singed my fingers as I tossed the flaming matchbox and firecracker at the stack of books.

BANG!

I waited until flames began licking the ammunition. I grabbed my bow and arrows and stuck the framed photograph under my arm. Flight Lieutenant John Joseph Mooney of the 121st American Eagle Squadron was coming with us.

Not wanting to draw attention, I ambled back to the gate. When I got close, I seen Daphne was firing rocks with my slingshot. She had a good eye. More than one soldier was feeling it.

By now the racket coming from the warehouse was like the sound of a fireworks show at Coney Island. The soldiers swiveled their faces to the building. One looked our way and begged to Daphne in French, "*Ne vont pas!*" which I later on learned means: *Please don't go.*

A piercing siren went off, and my ears begun to ring. A spotlight swung around catching us in its range. A screeching noise came from a loudspeaker. Then came German words I didn't understand, but were pronounced like swearwords.

Daphne removed her high-heeled shoes and we bolted in the direction of the green barn we'd walked past earlier in the day.

And then, in one glorious explosion—heard as far as Berlin, I'm sure—the whole kit and caboodle blew. I wondered if there was TNT stored in the warehouse.

Nazis used the stuff to make the bombs that were destroying London.

A bullet whistled past my right ear. We ran to a field of corn stalks and picked up our speed, running between two rows, hoping to block the view of sharpshooters. A gigantic dog ran behind us, threatening to catch up at any second. I couldn't help but scream, "Ma!" The dog bit into the hem of Daphne's dress, but she managed to loosen herself and keep going.

By the time we reached the green barn, the dog was ten steps behind. I hurried to find a trap door, as Daphne fended herself off by waving a pitchfork she'd found propped against the barn wall. I located the door to the root cellar—the one used to ferment beer. I turned to grab Daphne. She was now standing still, gulping in oxygen, her arms resting on the pitchfork handle. The dog sat in front of her—wagging its tail happily—tongue hanging out loose and spittle dripping from its mouth.

"If I'm not mistaken, he's an Airedale," said Daphne, wiping her sweaty brow. "Essentially, large British terrier. Why, I do believe he's decided to return to the fold."

All three of us stepped down into the dark space, me using the flashlight, which was still sticking in my blue jeans pocket. Daphne and me sat with our backs resting against a keg of beer. The dog laid down at Daphne's feet, licking her toes.

The place smelled like a pub. Besides beer, the root cellar contained mason jars full of canned vegetables and fruit and also loads of tin cans. Somebody was hiding the stash from thieving Nazis. Using my pocketknife, I opened a can of beans and noticed that my hands were shaking. Daphne opened a jar of stewed tomatoes and said, "What a fright that was," letting out a long sigh.

I shrugged my shoulders and steadied my hands by digging them into the dog's fur. I coughed from deep down in my lungs, hacked up phlegm and spit on the ground, hoping to seem macho.

Daphne found a jar of poached pears. The dog licked the jar clean. "What shall we call him, Thomas?"

"How about Franklin, after FDR?"

"How about Winston?"

"How do we know he's a he?" I asked.

Daphne lifted the dog's tail. "I think we shall call her Marlene. After Marlene Dietrich, of course. She's also German but working for our side." Daphne patted Marlene on the head and said, "Poor Marlene. You should have seen how those German soldiers treated her. I might not be a dog-lover. But when I saw one of them kick her, it took everything in me to not start screaming."

I patted Marlene on the head even though I didn't like dogs and preferred cats. "We'll take care of you, girl," I said. Marlene licked my nose, then circled up in a ball and went to sleep.

Some time later on I woke to the sound of the rusty hatch door being opened. I grabbed my bow and arrow, expecting to have to defend Daphne. Marlene let loose a fearsome growl, barked, and bared her teeth menacingly.

"Are you in there, Joe DiMaggio?" I recognized the voice. It was Antoine, the vegetable seller.

Daphne shouted, "*FERSE*," to Marlene, who started whining. "I heard the Germans use the word when they wanted her to heel."

"Come quickly," said Antoine, taking my hand and helping me up the steps. The sun was coming up over the fields, hitting the barn side so that now it was orange instead of green. Next to it sat a car with the engine running but the headlights off. He motioned us into the boot. "Hurry, hurry!" Marlene jumped in after us.

There I was—in a stuffy trunk again—wondering where the car was heading. It was freezing in the trunk, and the dog became a bed warmer, Daphne and me pressed up against her fur. My hand was a muzzle, keeping Marlene from barking. Also keeping her from licking my face. When we stopped about an hour later, we waited for the trunk to be opened. When it did, we were inside a garage. By the rumblings coming from the outside, we knew we'd arrived in a booming metropolis.

"Brussels," said Antoine, reading my mind. "I thought it safer to hide you in the city. The Gestapo is searching for you. Apparently we have you to thank for a nice bit of sabotage."

He took a close look at Daphne, moving his eyes up and down her red sequin dress but without the least sign of rude. "We'll have to get you out of that gown and into something less memorable." He looked at Marlene and asked where she'd come from. As we followed him up an inside staircase to a flat above, we told him how the dog had switched sides.

"*Excellent!*" he said in the French way.

CHAPTER TWENTY-THREE

WE WERE INTRODUCED TO a lady old enough to be
my grandma. She was Antoine's mother, Madame De-
Quick. But she didn't look anything like the other Mrs.
DeQuick, them not being blood related, only in-laws.
This Madame DeQuick was tall and broomstick skinny. Her hair was the color of straw, like what happens
to all platinum blondes when they pass fifty. And unlike the other one, all her hair was on top of her head,
none on her chin. Even her eyebrows were plucked and
then penciled like big arches, so that it always looked
like she'd put her finger in a live socket. And there was
no sign of a husband—only a gold wedding band—so it
made sense that she was dressed in black.

"*Bonjour*," I said. "And *mercy*." Everyone laughed.

Antoine said, "You'll stay here until I sort out a better situation. My mother will dote on you, to be sure.
You are now heroes of the Resistance!"

"You're not leaving us, are you?" I said.

"Work to do, potatoes to sell," he said.

Once Antoine left, his mother went to a drawer
near her sewing machine, found a measuring tape and

began taking Daphne's measurements. She wrote the numbers on a small pad of paper with a pencil she took from her mouth. When she was finished, she reached over to a bookshelf and grabbed a stack of magazines, handing them to Daphne. I seen they were ladies' magazines.

"French *Vogue!*" Daphne was thrilled and began thumbing.

"*Choisir,*" said Madame DeQuick.

"I do believe she's offering to make me a new dress!" Daphne glued her eyes to the pages. There's nothing girls like better than picking out clothes. I spent half my life cooling my heels while my ma and sisters went dress shopping. Mary never found anything that looked good on her, which was what took so long.

The two began schmoozing about girl stuff. I left them to it and began exploring the flat. *"Haute couture!"* was the last thing I heard Daphne say before I began wandering down the hallway.

Behind the first door was the bathroom. Amazing even myself, I started up the geyser using a match placed on the top. The funny thing was that there wasn't a toilet in the room and I had to relieve myself by pointing out the open window. Soon the room was cloudy with steam so's that I didn't notice the bathtub filling until water pored over the rim. It'd been weeks since my skin touched a washcloth. The water was nice and hot. A jar of bubble soap stood next to the tub and I poured the whole thing into the water. I got naked and submerged myself—practicing deep breathing.

A few minutes later, the door opened and I screamed. In stepped Madame DeQuick, with not so much as a how'd ya do (I mean *How* Do *You Do.*) She picked my clothes off the bathroom floor and said, "*Très bon.*" She removed everything from the pockets and took the clothes away with her.

My worldly possessions were now lying on the bathroom floor: my flashlight, a slingshot, a pocketknife, a compass, a stack of American dollars, two marbles, a speedboat key, a stick of gum, and a four leaf clover. Even worse, it had only two leaves left. I'd left my bow and arrows in the living room.

I rested back to enjoy a long soak. When my fingers and toes pruned, I dried myself off and wrapped a towel around my waist. Using a tortoiseshell comb, I made a part and slicked my hair back until I looked like Clark Gable.

"Brilliant," said Daphne when she got a look at me. "The smell of soap ought to throw the Germans off your trail."

Madame DeQuick left the room, returning with a pile of clothing she wanted me to put on. They looked old-fogy and I guessed they were Antoine DeQuick's when he was a boy. She got back to work behind her sewing machine, moving the treadle pedal with her right foot. She had straight pins in her mouth. They were the kind of pins my sister Mary liked to stick in me—them ones with the little colored balls at the end.

I didn't miss Mary at all but did miss my big sister. *I need to bring Nancy home a nice French dress*, I thought—

soften the blow when I gave her the news about Jack.

"Madame DeQuick was telling me," said Daphne, "that her son taught English literature at the Université Libre de Bruxelles before the war. When the Germans occupied the city, Antoine lost his place. And all because he continued speaking out against Hitler and encouraged his students to work for the Resistance."

"And now he sells potatoes from a horse cart?"

"He was black-listed by the Nazis. His cousin needed help with the farm and offered him work."

"It's a cover, Daphne. Antoine's the one working for the Resistance," I said. " 'In touch with someone in the Resistance,' my foot. Why, I bettya he's scouting out troop movements as we speak. *Recon*, that's what it's called. How else did he know exactly where the munitions factory was? What a good cover too, carting potatoes from town to town…too bad Ireland is neutral. Why, who would'a thought?"

Daphne put her finger to her lips, reminding me to keep my trap shut. "Keep quiet or you'll give the whole show away," she said, and Lord Sopwith's voice came back to me, thundering: *Loose lips, good man, loose lips!*

I tightened my lips until my gums hurt.

Madame DeQuick said something in French, but with the pins in her mouth I couldn't make out the words.

"She's inviting us to help ourselves to anything we find in the kitchen." Daphne asked if Madame DeQuick wanted anything. Madame DeQuick mumbled something, and I thought: *I hope she doesn't swallow one of them pins.* Lady Sopwith's voice jumped into my head saying, "*Those* pins, my dear child. *Those* pins."

We found the kitchen and Daphne looked in all the cupboards, and I checked the icebox. Even a mouse would've complained. Daphne said we'd better not impose of Madame DeQuick's hospitality, even if she begged us to stay. Obviously, folks were worse off here than in London.

"You know, I still have my American dollars," I said. "Do you think they have a black market here in Brussels? I heard that's the place to switch money."

"There's a black market everywhere, Thomas. Perhaps we'll buy Madame DeQuick some Belgian chocolate, as a way of thanks!"

But for the time being we had to be happy with tinned sardines and a half-loaf of day old bread. Daphne swallowed a fish whole and then started humming, like she was trying to remember something. "What day of the week is it?" she asked.

"Beats me," I said. I spotted a calendar hanging from a thumbtack in the wall. In a split second I had it in Daphne's hands. She tapped her finger over the page, landing on a Friday square, "I was right!" she said. "We'll look for a bottle of sweet wine and two loaves of egg bread—each woven into six strands—and a pinch of salt. Then we'll need a candle, of course."

"Is this a scavenger hunt?" I said, perking up.

"No. It's for Shabbat," she said. "Tonight starts the Jewish day of rest and we'll welcome it in with a little ceremony…if I can remember how to do it. This will be our little act of resistance."

"Or we could blow something up," I said. "Gestapo headquarters, say."

"Tsk-tsk," she said. "Have you no romance in your soul? Not every act of resistance must involve explosives."

I pointed out that ours had involved *Romeo and Juliet*. But the truth was, I needed little R & R myself. I yawned. There's nothing like a hot bath to make you drowsy. Daphne had to prop me up as we walked back to the living room.

Meanwhile Madame DeQuick was making progress on the dress. Daphne said: "It's going to be a copy of a Coco Chanel!" Then she asked me the obvious question: "By the way, I suppose that you saved nothing of mine from the suitcase—nothing but the photograph of Jack?"

"I'm sorry. I had to get out of there light. And besides, I used a lot of your stuff for kindling."

"My brassieres?"

I felt my face flush. "Never!" I said. "You didn't expect me to go running out of there holding ladies' things? I'd of been the laughing stock of the Third Reich."

"I suppose," she said. "I am glad you thought to save Jack's picture, at least."

She glanced down at her finger and then held a tiny diamond ring up to the light. I hadn't noticed the engagement ring until then, which was odd. "Nice ring," I said.

"It's art deco."

"Maybe we hock it."

She held her hand behind her back and growled. Then she turned her eyes back to Madame DeQuick, who was now holding up the dress and instructing Daphne to try it on. "Could you please give me some privacy, Thomas?" she said.

CHAPTER TWENTY-FOUR

AFTER CATCHING A SECOND WIND, I decided it was time for some recon of my own. Back I went to the staircase, down to the garage and through a door to the street. Too bad I didn't still have my baseball cap. Or my sunglasses—left in my duffel bag, I'm sorry to say. I lifted the collar of my shirt.

Wandering a few blocks, I looked in shop windows, glad for a change of scenery. That is, until I noticed a boarded up shop with the word *Jude* and a Jewish star painted sloppy over the window glass. Through a crack the size of a baseball, I saw a mannequin with no head, a broken sewing machine, and bolts of fabric thrown on the floor. A German soldier stepped over and said, "*Geschlossen.*" What'd he take me for, an idiot? I could see for myself that the place was closed.

Around the corner I stumbled on a flea market. People sold junk: tables with three legs, chairs without seats, rusty weathervanes, and moth chewed blankets. One old man sold corncob pipes and it made me miss my guardian, even though Lord Sopwith's pipes were made of ebony. Then something in a shop window grabbed my eye.

It was a toy biplane made of wood and metal and was super-realistic. Jack learned to fly in a biplane just like it. When I entered the shop a bell tinkled above the door. A bald man stepped out from behind a curtain in the back, and when I pointed to the airplane in his window, he said, *"Oui, jeune homme!"*

Reaching inside the window display, he handed me the biplane. I was surprised at how light it felt in my hands. With the right wind, it might fly. The shopkeeper reached over and found a tiny tag attached to the wing strut.

Already, I was desperate to have the airplane, because it would make a swell gift for my brother...if Jack was still alive. For a split second I thought about my brother, dead with blood covering his broken body, with more blood running out of his nose. My imagination was doing me dirty. I looked at the airplane and forced my mind to switch to a picture of me handing the biplane to Jack, him alive and well. I reached into my back pocket and removed the stack of American dollars I'd been carrying since leaving East Hempstead. When the shopkeeper saw the stack, his pupils widened.

"Will this be enough?" I said, worried because antiques cost more than spanking new things, which never did made sense.

The shopkeeper spun the hour hand on a fake clock sign, locked the door and pulled down a blind. I followed him behind the curtain and into a windowless room with a desk and shelves filled with more toys. And mechanical banks: a lion eating a franc from a tamer's hand, a cricket player batting centimes, Jonah the Prophet feeding coins to a whale.

Sitting me down in a chair, the shopkeeper shook his head and wagged a finger. I held the airplane in one hand, my dollars in the other. "Please," I said. *"S'il vous plait."* And in case that wasn't enough, *"Dankeschön."* He calmed down and took a seat behind the desk—all the time keeping his eyes fixed on me. After removing his spectacles, he detached a keychain from his belt. Opening a locked drawer below his desk, he removed a tray of money and counted out Belgian francs. He pulled a ten-spot from my stack but left me the rest. I bolted out the door.

With my Belgian change I'd do Daphne's shopping and bring back a treat for Madame DeQuick. Strolling down the street, I passed a bakery, a shoemaker, and the kind of store that sells rubber bands, paperclips, and notebooks. Belgian children lined up to buy school supplies. Down an alleyway, a sign dangled from a hook: *Chocolaterie.* The window display was bare, but I stepped inside and asked for a Whitman's Sampler, the world's best box of chocolates: caramel, cashew clusters, maple fudge, marshmallow, and toffee. Plus cherry cordials soaked in brandy—which only grown-ups are allowed to eat. The shop girl looked at me like I had two heads, then handed me a bar labeled *Congobar*—the Belgian version of a plain ol' Hershey bar.

Four things left on the shopping list.

An hour later and I'd about given up. Until I spied a saltshaker sitting on an outdoor café table, next to an uncorked bottle of red wine and a basket of fresh baked rolls, eggless unfortunately. I waited until the Wehrmacht officer got up to use the men's room—probably to wash his blood stained hands—before swooping in and grabbing a candle out of a jelly jar, too. My conscience was squeaky clean, because in the window was a poster: *Juden nicht erwunscht*—Jews not welcomed. Served them right.

Daphne would be in a tizzy seeing me missing and so I made a beeline back to the flat, getting lost once when I turned at the wrong place and found myself in front of Nazi headquarters. I turned tail when I caught sight of the giant swastika flag hanging from a balcony. Holding my new biplane high above me, I flew back to the flat, battling the Red Baron the whole way.

Daphne was still absorbed in her magazine, without a clue that I'd been gone. When I walked into the parlor, she looked at my airplane puzzled-like. A blow-by-blow of my adventure threw her in a snit, but I calmed her with the chocolate bar. With a smile back on her face, she twirled around in a circle and said: "What do you think? Delicious, no?"

"You sure do look *chichi*," I said.

"This is the latest from Paris. Madame DeQuick had the black crepe wool left over. She's a professional seamstress. It's otherwise impossible to obtain fine wool nowadays, simply impossible." She held out the sleeve of her dress for me to feel. "It's stylish, feminine luxury that will never go out of style."

She'd been reading too many magazines.

Daphne admired herself in the mirror. She strutted across the room like a Hollywood actress about to get handed an Oscar. Then she pointed to her head. "Madame DeQuick is giving me this hat, shoes, and bag. As well as—other—unmentionables. It means so much to me…as they belong to her daughter." Daphne lowered her voice. "She was taken away by the Gestapo—a student leader for the Resistance. Caught handing out anti-Nazi literature on campus—pamphlets printed clandestinely using the university printing press. You see, she worked there in the evenings and that's how the Gestapo put two and two together."

"Saints alive," I said, shaken. Something had to be done and fast. First I needed to know where the Nazis were holding the daughter. *Mother of God*, I thought, but tried to act calm. Because I'd just seen Nazi headquarters and it looked like a fortress if ever there was one. And I knew zero about breakouts.

"They haven't a clue where she is," said Daphne, sad enough to cry.

Right then a bang shook the building and I dived under the couch, sure it was a bomb. Daphne hollered with laughter. Lightening flashed through the windows. A second thunderclap and it started raining. Madame DeQuick got up to close the windows. From my position on the floor, I spotted *Les Aventures de Tintin* in a magazine rack. But as good as them cartoons were, they had to wake me for supper.

After the Jewish ceremony, Daphne didn't want to turn on the lights. I figured she was angling for a candlelight supper. More romantic. I'd just opened my mouth to protest when suddenly the electric clock stopped ticking and the fan made a wheezing sound and went dead. I jiggled the light switch every which way before giving up. So in the end, Daphne got her cockamamie wish. And claimed the whole thing was an *Act of God*. Even after Madame DeQuick explained that power cuts were becoming nightly occurrences in Brussels.

In the flickering light we ate the kind of meal you get stranded on a deserted island, and then Madame DeQuick and Daphne began yapping away in French.

In the pitch dark, I felt my way to a bed.

CHAPTER TWENTY-FIVE

THE CITY RACKET WOKE ME early the next morning. Candle wax coated the kitchen table, along with breadcrumbs. Sitting in the parlor was a pretty lady on the sofa next to Madame DeQuick, her legs twisted daintily at the ankles. She wore flat mannish lace-ups, scuffed up and needing polish. Antoine sat cattycorner to her, dressed in a suit and tie, and with all the dirt scrubbed out from under his fingernails. Daphne was drinking something I figured was tea. They all stood to greet me.

"Would you like some?" asked Antoine, pointing to the coffeepot. "There's no coffee available, but we have this substitute—a mixture of chicory. It's more of a laxative than anything." Taking another sip, he made a sour face.

"*Shabbat Shalom*, Thomas," said Daphne pouring herself another cup.

"Let me introduce you to Dédée," said Antoine.

Her real name was Andrée Eugénie Adrienne De Jongh, but I didn't learn that until much later. I took her hand and kissed it, because I felt like I was in the presence of royalty. She wasn't dressed fancy or anything;

it was the exact opposite. She was wearing a plain grey skirt and a white button down blouse—nothing that stood out in a crowd, which was what she was going for.

"Dédée may be able to help get you out of this predicament," said Antoine.

"You did a daring thing," said Dédée. She laughed and her whole face lit up like on a billboard for toothpaste. "Now the Gestapo is hunting for you, and so I'm here to arrange a way to get you out of Belgium."

"We've yet to find my fiancé," said Daphne.

"So I understand from Antoine," said Dédée. "That's why I've gotten involved. It's my job to help downed RAF pilots get back to England."

"Dédée is being modest," said Antoine. "To date she's helped dozens of pilots evade capture and return home. It started last year when a Scottish airman was stranded in Belgium. Dédée managed, single handedly, to get him to the British Consulate in Bilbao, Spain."

"Not single handedly, Antoine."

She launched into the story: with the help of a Basque guide, they'd made it over the treacherous Pyrenees Mountains. Slipping on ice, snow up to their belt loops. Without that guide it would've been impossible; they'd now be laying dead in a crevasse. Dédée arrived in Bilbao, Spain with frostbitten fingers and chapped lips. The diplomats at the British Consulate were shocked to see them and "jolly" glad to have their airman back. Dédée couldn't wait to turn around and do it all over again.

Daphne asked what she'd done before the war. Art

student was the answer. "Good training for this sort of work," said Dédée laughing. "I suppose illusion and creativity is something I'm skilled at."

"I'm an art student also!" said Daphne.

"I'm going to arrange to have you sent from here to Paris and then from there to the South of France, where you'll make your way over the Pyrenees Mountains and into free Spain. From Spain you will be taken to a boat and then—*voilà*—you will be home to England. We've done this many times. By now we have the route carefully arranged. We call it the Comet Line."

"We aren't prepared to go home," said Daphne. "We came to find Jack. If you can't help us find him, then we plan to go to Dunkirk."

I said: "That's were the Resistance people at the bookstore said we should look for his—his grave."

"Daphne, my dear," said Dédée, "we are certain that your fiancé perished in the crash. Our agents saw the Germans remove his body from the airplane. It's time to go home to the comfort of your families and mourn." Dédée took both Daphne's hands in hers, but Daphne looked down at the floor saying nothing.

"Your lives are in danger," said Antoine. "We can't let you fall into the hands of the Gestapo."

"Daphne's half Jewish," I said. "Like Pauline Goddard, the actress."

"*Quoi!*" said Dédée, and for the first time she looked terrified. "All the more reason for you to leave immediately."

"Without delay," said Antoine, throwing up his

hands. "If caught, you'll be executed. Or wish you'd been."

"*O je,*" I said, looking at Daphne with Oliver Twist eyes.

She loosening Dédée's grip on her hands and hugging them to her body like a stubborn child. "I intend to go to Dunkirk before jumping to conclusions. I'm quite determined, quite settled in the matter." She said this with gusto, then whispered, "Otherwise, I'll always wonder."

"Think of the boy, if not yourself," said Antoine, pointing his chin to me. "Think what's best for *him*."

I snuggled close to Daphne. She grabbed me to her and we hugged. I wanted to say, I'll protect you, don't worry, but I'd lost all my nerve with that word *executed*.

"I'll arrange everything for your evacuation," said Dédée. "Antoine will let you know when to be ready to leave. It could take a few days to organize everything. In the meantime you'd best remain here. I'll arrange for a driver to pick you up. I have one in mind. He's very dependable and you need fear nothing." Dédée kissed Daphne on both cheeks as Antoine and her got up to leave.

Marlene leaned her chin on Daphne's knee, gazed up toward her—ears lowered, eyes droopy—and sighed.

A couple days later on, Daphne woke me while it was still dark. She was wearing her new black suit with a hat pinned to her head and a black lace veil covering her eyes. When she lifted the veil, I seen she'd been crying.

She gripped a valise Madame DeQuick must've leant her. She placed it on the floor and sat on the edge of my bed.

"Thomas, I need to go to Dunkirk, but you shan't come with me."

"You're leaving me?" I was waking up fast and sat up in the bed, throwing off the covers even though the room was cold.

"Darling, I'd feel dreadful if something were to happen to you. I think what Madame DeQuick was telling me about her daughter, and then sleeping in the girl's bed—well—it's made me realize how foolish I'd been to let you come to Belgium. You go to Paris and I'll meet you there in a few days. We'll have a grand time with my aunt Dalia, eating like kings. Then we'll go to Spain together."

"What will happen if you're catched?"

"You mean, *caught*? Can't you see I'll be safer going alone? The Gestapo is looking for a boy and a young woman traveling together. And besides, your mother would never forgive me if I let you take any more risks." She tickled my chin, "Do you know how important it is for a bride to have a mother-in-law on her side?"

"But—" That's all I could get out, because my head was all in a tangle. I looked into her eyes and saw stubborn determination. "How will you find me in Paris?"

"Don't worry. I'll come back here first and I'm sure they'll take me to you. Now give your future sister-in-law a hug and a kiss, and then go back to sleep."

She rushed out of the room. I jumped out of bed

and reached for my clothes, meaning to follow her. I'd left them on the floor next to the bed when I undressed, but everything was gone. It was the oldest trick in the book. Lying there was my biplane, bow and arrow, a key, a marble, a two-leaf clover, and a stick of gum. It wasn't going to be easy to find where she hid my clothes. At least she took the slingshot. Also, one of my good-luck marbles—or maybe it had rolled away. I hoped it was in her pocket.

I couldn't go back to sleep and laid awake thinking. It was my own fault Daphne was going off without me. If anything, I'd been like a pebble in her shoe, always talking about giving up. *You dumb cluck!* I thought.

Madame DeQuick came to wake me and I explained about Daphne leaving for Dunkirk. She looked worried and said, "*Impossible,*" shaking her head. She gave back my blue jeans and the rest of my clothes. They'd hung out to dry in the back garden all this time. We found Antoine's old clothing stuffed under the kitchen sink.

Marlene was sore as me when she realized Daphne was gone.

CHAPTER TWENTY-SIX

IT WAS TOUGH DRAGGING MYSELF out of bed the morning the driver came to take me to Paris. Daphne still hadn't come back. For all I knew, she was in a Nazi prison camp with no one to help break her out. Madame DeQuick stopped me from flying to the rescue. At night I'd had dreams where I heard Daphne crying somewheres way far in the distance, but I couldn't never get to her. It was enough to drive me bonkers.

And I was headed home to East Hempstead without my brother. A long journey stretched ahead of me, with nothing to look forward to except maybe seeing the Eiffel Tower—not much of a consolation prize, if you asked me.

Marlene had to live with Madame DeQuick. My ma was allergic to dogs, so if I took her back to East Hempstead she'd end up at the pound. Madame De-Quick was happy to have a pet. At least she wouldn't be lonely—maybe the only good thing to come out of the whole deal.

The driver arrived in a Renault four door and opened a rear door for me to get in. When I asked, he let me sit up front next to him. I was glad to see he could speak some English. "Will you be taking me all the way to Paris?" I asked.

"No, *petite monsieur*, only to Mons, near the border of France. Another agent will meet us and you will continue with him. *Comprendre?*" I watched as he opened the glove box and reached in, removing a pistol, which he placed between us on the seat. "To be safe," he said. "And by the way, my name is Paul-Henri and I'm your uncle if anyone should ask."

"So, I guess that means your name isn't really Paul-Henri?"

The man laughed when I said this. "You are very swift."

"And from Mons, who will take me to Paris?"

"We are to meet a man at the train station in Mons. He'll be carrying a box of bonbons. That's all I know."

"Do I get to eat the bonbons?" Bonbons were sweets: chocolates usually filled with nuts or maraschino cherries. I have a passion for maraschino cherries. Our contact would look like he was waiting for his girlfriend—enough throw the Nazis off.

We drove through the congested streets of central Brussels, some so narrow the Renault barely fit between parked cars. Our side mirror scraped the paint off of a blue car, but we didn't stop. I reached out and rubbed the blue paint off, so's there'd be no evidence. Paul-Henri poked me with his elbow as a way of thanks. We came to wider streets with less traffic and Paul-Henri relaxed and began whistling a tune I didn't recognize. Something snappy like what a high school marching band might play at a Fourth of July parade.

"What is it?" I asked.

" '*The Internationale.*' It's a Russian song."

"Are you Russian?"

"No, Belgian." He kept on whistling the tune. I wondered why he was singing a Russian song if he weren't Russian.

Soon we got rolling through countryside spotted with windmills and fields like green patchwork quilts. Paul-Henri reached behind the seat and found a paper bag, placing it in my lap. "I'd forgotten," he said. "This is from Dédée."

I opened the bag and seen it contained a coloring book and a package of crayons. Also, a book of crossword puzzles with the clues all in Dutch. At the bottom of the bag I found an oval tin with a picture of a skinny queen on the lid. Inside were mints. They were called "LeReine Pastilles."

"Dédée says you can eat the mints but must save the tin until you are safely home. They are for a signal: to let people along the line know you are who you say."

"You should have said *whom*," I said, figuring he needed help with English, just like me.

"*Comprendre?*" he said, reverting to his native tongue.

I opened the mint tin and counted the mints— there were twenty. "Goody," I said, because I wanted to gobble them up.

"The coloring book is for your amusement, but the crossword puzzles will tell you where to find our people in Paris, should you be separated from your contact. Find the message and then fill in some of the blanks in the other puzzles, so that if the book is discovered, the Germans will be confused."

This, I thought, *is getting interesting.* I leafed through the crosswords and noticed one of them was halfway completed. "I can't understand none of the clues," I said. "They seem to be in Dutch. How will I complete the puzzles?"

"Be creative." He winked at me.

Within an hour we came to a crossroads. In one direction a sign pointed to Mons, in another direction, Bruges. And a third sign pointed to Lille. Under *Lille* was written *Dunkerque.* Paul-Henri turned toward Bruges. Trying to be helpful, I pointed toward Mons.

"We need to take a detour to avoid a German checkpoint," said Paul-Henri, turning down a bumpy dirt farm road. Dust came into the opened windows and I began choking. "Roll up your window," he said, "We'll be on this road for a spell."

It was getting stuffy in the car, and I was glad when we got to a paved road and I could let down my window again and breathe in the fresh country air. Soon we arrived in Mons and pulled in front of a train station, which looked identical to the capital building in Washington, D.C. "Wait here in the car," he said.

I watched him mounting the stairs to the station, looking in all directions for a sign of our contact. I wished I'd given him the LeReine mint pastilles, but it was too late.

I took a peek at the crossword puzzles, killing time. Reading from top to bottom, one down spelled, GERMAIN. Six across spelled SAINT. The A met up with the one in GERMAIN. I'd never heard of a saint by that name. Over to the other side, there was a word PRES, meeting up with DES, but I didn't understand the Dutch clue. I was baffled; it was all too cryptic. Until I got to the bottom right side of the puzzle: thirty-three down was a date—1927. The clue was "Charles Lindbergh." I had that figured out straight away. 1927 was the year Lindbergh made his famous flight from Long Island to Paris.

I gave up on the crossword, took out a crayon, and began working in my coloring book. The theme was automobiles of the 1930's. While filling in a Lagonda Motors Ltd Drophead Coupe with a bright purple crayon—highlighting the trim with canary yellow—I heard a car backfire. I looked out the window but didn't see a moving car anywheres near ours. Then I heard the backfire again. This time I stiffened, because it sounded like a gunshot.

Two men came running down the steps from the station. The metal taps on the soles of their boots made loud stomping noises. One was wearing a long raincoat. The other was dressed in a pinstripe business suit with big shoulders. The sun flared off something metal and shiny sticking out of his front pocket. Both their faces had the expressions you see in Hollywood pictures—on mobsters right after they've bumped off a bit player. The two men jumped into a car and raced away. I began to get a queasy feeling in my stomach.

I needed to use a men's room, on top of everything. So I exited the car taking my things with me. I mounted the stairs in slow motion. As I got near the platform, there was the commotion of people running away from the ticket window—some screaming and wildly waving their hands. One lady fainted into her husband's arms. The man calling himself Paul-Henri was laid out on the ground, and blood spilled from a head wound onto the tile floor. It was a good thing Daphne wasn't there to see it.

I turned my back to the wall and pretended to take a leak, but the whole time I kept one eye on the scene of the crime. I didn't feel scared because I seen the two killers leave the station. Not at first, anyway. But then I began to shake. It started in my knees and before long the shake moved up to my hands. I had to sit down against the wall. Meanwhile, people started moving away from Paul-Henri's body. Everyone knew he was dead—dead as a doornail. Too bad, because he was one of the good guys.

It didn't seem right to leave Paul-Henri. So I stood up, with some trouble, and walked over to where he was laying. My head was so light I had to sit down again, right there in the middle of the station. Paul-Henri's hand was stretched out, like he wanted someone to hold it, but I was scared to touch a dead body. And his eyes were still opened, only they looked like marbles, not real eyes.

My ears stopped working for some reason. Sort of like when you drive down a mountain too fast. Tears tried to escape from my eyes, only I wouldn't let them. It helped not to blink, or even to move one muscle. I kept staring at a polka dot on his tie, even though right above it was a gold tiepin with a diamond chip. It was like that blue polka dot was the whole planet earth. I felt wet where my hands were folded in my lap and reached up to my face to brush away tears. But my face was dry. I looked down and was mortified. I hadn't done that since kindergarten.

Bells started ringing and at first I thought they were in my head. Then someone shouted, "Ambulance!"

Better beat it before the cops show up.

Everybody was onto the fact that the police were in cahoots with the Nazis. And my fingerprints were all over Paul-Henri's car, footprints too. When a train pulled into the station, I jumped onto it and bolted for the lavatory. I was shook-up from seeing a dead body for only the second time in my life. The other time was at my great-great-aunt Sinéad's wake but that didn't count because she was ninety-seven and died of old age.

When somebody began banging on the lavatory door, I slid the lock back and cracked the door open. A man shoved the door in, forcing me to stumble against a steel sink. I was afraid he was Gestapo but it was only a plain German soldier who had to go—bad. I got out of his way and left him to it.

I rushed down the corridor and into a sleeper car,

thinking that was a good place to hide. Most of the cabins were closed with red velvet curtains and I peeked behind a few. There was Nazis in every cabin: one was kissing his girlfriend who yelled something at me in French. I ducked into an empty berth and hid out behind a cushion. Telephone poles and barns whizzed by, all in a blur and making my head spin. A conductor came down the aisle but, luckily, he didn't stop to ask for tickets. He shouted, ""LILLE! LILLE!"

I remembered seeing Lille written on a road sign when Paul-Henri turned toward Bruges, headed the back way to Mons. *Wait a minute*, I said to my brain, because something was coming to it. The sign read Lille/Dunkerque. That must be French for Dunkirk.

I was headed to Dunkirk. Where my brother Jack was buried. And maybe where I'd find Daphne.

I took out my coloring book and started filling in a Triumph Dolomite Roadster but had trouble staying inside the lines, what with my hand still shaking. Had to put the crayon down and stare out the window counting telephone poles instead. Meanwhile, I was fighting tears. And I won't say who won.

CHAPTER TWENTY-SEVEN

Somewhere in German-occupied France

A STONE'S THROW FROM LE BOURGET AIRPORT, there's a bar that's a favorite with the Luftwaffe. If you were to enter on this night in September 1942, if you were to pass by the few patrons, nervously sipping bourbon and white wine, if you were to enter the men's toilet and look into the last stall, this is what you'd find:

You'd discover a man, late-twenties or early-thirties. Hatless, hair close cropped, and wearing the rumpled uniform of the SS: brown shirt and black tie askew, the shirt untucked. The buttons on his black trousers are undone. On the right arm is a red band with a swastika. The band has come loose and is dangling from his shirt.

His tall black boots are, by the way, spit-shined—resembling patent leather. This is incongruous with his otherwise slovenly appearance. The man is passed out, presumably drunk.

Outside the stall, another man studies himself in the mirror. Touching his nose, he examines the areas under his eyes, which are healing nicely after a recent mishap. He straightens his tie; attached to it is an iron cross. He buttons his dress jacket: it's black and made of wool. Slung on his arm is a long black greatcoat, suited to the changing weather.

He has second thoughts and unbuttons the jacket to remove a thick billfold from the inside breast pocket. Admiring the fine leather, he opens it and smiles. There are Reichsmarks that Parisians will have to accept. Even better, there is also a thick stack of French francs. He will eat well tonight. It's payday for pilot officers of the German Luftwaffe.

He removes a black and white photograph, sighing as he looks at it.

In the billfold are also identity papers, marked with the same iron cross that adorns his throat: *Flieg-er-Stabsingemieur* Hans Dorfmann. He looks at his reflection in the mirror and then at the photograph.

He locates a single key in his overcoat pocket. On the keychain is written an address in the 16th arrondisse-ment: an upscale neighborhood, undoubtedly the apart-ment of a "relocated" Jewish family. Bile rises up in his throat, but he calms himself and straightens his officer's cap.

Taking a wedge out from under the door, he opens it and exits the men's toilet. Everyone in the smoky bar is quiet and a hush falls over the room. The band, playing *Nuit et Jour* by Cole Porter, slow the pace and the drum-mer misses a beat. A couple dancing near his path break apart and move out of his way. The patrons pretend to ignore him, but he feels them watching his every move.

Walking up to the bar, he asks for a whiskey in broken French—single malt-scotch. The bartender acts quickly, ignoring other patrons—pouring a small amount into a glass and waiting for the Luftwaffe officer's approval before pouring more.

Finally, the Luftwaffe officer walks out of the bar and everyone lets out a sigh of relief. One man spits on the floor in the direction the officer has gone. The night proceeds on a merrier note. The drummer finds his beat. The couple resume their dance, holding each other a little more tightly.

The officer pauses on the sidewalk and removes a pack of cigarettes from his overcoat. A woman—two sheets to the wind—stumbles toward him and strikes a match, offering him a light. He pats his pockets and finds he's misplaced his match case. The woman makes a suggestion but is waved away dismissively.

He vanishes into the night, gone to make trouble elsewhere.

CHAPTER TWENTY-EIGHT

THE DUNKIRK TRAIN STATION swarmed with Nazis. I exited the station without making eye contact with anyone, looking down at shiny black boots and balloon-thigh trousers. I avoided Germans but bumped into a pillar.

A café, with a revolving door from the station lobby, had pastries in the glass window. You'd of thought I'd have no appetite after what happened to Paul-Henri. It wasn't the case: I was hungrier than ever. There was a cinnamon bun in the window that sure looked good, but maybe it was wrong to eat? A fly landed on the bun and even that didn't squelch my appetite. Then I remembered that after my great-great-aunt Sinéad's wake, everyone went to her house and ate up a storm.

A chunky waitress motioned me to a booth with red-leather seats, and I obliged her. She handed me a menu, but I pointed to my cinnamon bun and she took the menu back. "*À boire?*" she said. I figured she was asking me if I wanted to order a drink.

"Coca-Cola?" I needed one worse than ever. Everybody knows that soda settles a queasy stomach. I still wasn't over the recent calamity and wondered how long it would take.

The waitress laughed. "*Café, thé, eau minérale.*" I ordered an *eau minérale*, whatever that was. It turned out to be a soda without the syrup, but the bubblies were pretty nice, and worked like Pepto-Bismol.

"*Oh là là,*" said the waitress when I went to pay my bill with Belgian money. Europe was a funny place. It's like if a New Yorker went on a day trip to Atlantic City to try his luck, and his nickels wouldn't fit in the slot machines. She took my Belgian money though, giving me in return a few French coins.

Now I had to find the cemetery and, to be honest, it was something I was dreading. I'd been to a cemetery before, with my ma. Before Jack was born, there was another brother, but he died as a baby. It was a germ that came from Spain and killed millions of other people too. His name was Thomas Robert Mooney, Jr., same as me. That's what made the whole visit to his grave doubly creepy. See, Da wanted a son to carry on his name, and so I became Junior II.

One thing I remembered, was when we'd go to Queens to visit my little brother, Ma would pick some flowers and lay them on his grave. She'd also bring a small hand broom and clean up around the tombstone. The whole thought of it, with Ma leaning over the tombstone and running her fingers over the carved letters, made me wish I'd never come to Dunkirk. But what else could I of done? I guess I could've returned to Madame DeQuick's. But then I'd ended up on the train to Dunkirk, so it was fate took me here.

To begin with, I had to find the place where British airmen were buried. The town center was a mess. If this war didn't end soon, New York was going to look like this. The Statue of Liberty would look like a lady who'd been in a car crash. Central Park would be a battleground. The Metropolitan Museum of Art would be Gestapo headquarters—Adolf Hitler's portrait would be hanging in the grand entrance, and everyone would have to salute it before being allowed to view the mummies.

Dunkirk reminded me of building houses with Lincoln Logs and making the whole thing fall down when I was bored of playing. Only these were real houses that were knocked down.

Next to an old church I spotted a cemetery and so I entered through an iron gate and studied tombstones. Some of the people buried there died a long time before: one fella named Claude, all the way back in 1620. As far as I seen though, all of the departed were French, many with the same family names and none of them Mooney.

I spotted a redhead bent over a grave and, just like my ma, she was cleaning leaves and garbage from around a headstone. It made me feel safe to speak to her. I stood behind the lady, not wanting to bother her until she was finished with her task. She must've had eyes on the back of her head, because she turned her face in my direction. When she seen I was a boy holding a toy, she smiled large. "*Bonjour,*" I said. "*Parlez-vous anglais?*" I hoped she spoke Anglais.

"Yes, I do," she said, pulling a gardening glove off her hand and stretching it out for me to shake. She reached into her pocket and took out a cellophane wrapped pep-permint—the kind that's red and white striped. She offered it to me. I peeked out of the side of my eye and seen the grave she'd been attending was for a boy about my age who died two years before. The lady invited me to share a bench and I began pouring out my story.

When I finished with the long version, she dabbed the corner of her eye with a handkerchief and said, "You poor, poor boy. It must have been terrifying to see a man murdered right in front of you."

"Not at all," I said. A lie.

She squinted her eyes; she wasn't buying it. "You're traveling alone? A boy your age?" She looked up to heaven. "You will stay with my husband and I, and we'll help find your brother's grave. That is settled." She smiled big, and I couldn't refuse.

The redhead's name was Madame Faure, and her and a husband owned a tobacco shop that was near the city center. We walked there on foot. She introduced me to her husband, who was manning the shop, standing behind the counter. When Madame Faure repeated my story to her husband, he reached to a shelf and handed me a penny candy. I'd landed in the sweet spot.

She escorted me back outside and then up to their flat by way of an entrance on the side of the shop. She showed me to a small bedroom, once her son's. The room had wallpaper with little tin soldiers, and blue and white striped curtains. As I placed my toy biplane on the bed, she managed to look both sad and happy all at the same time. I wondered how she done that. It was getting dark now, and her husband came upstairs after closing the tobacco shop for the night. We'd stopped along the way home and picked up food for dinner, which Madame Faure cooked up in the tiny green kitchen. Mr. Faure invited me to sit in the parlor while we waited.

He lit a pipe and choked as he inhaled the first puff. "Don't ever get started!" he said to me. "Bad habit, even if it is good for business." He began straight off talking about his lost son. "His name was Jacques-Yves and he was our only child. We might have another, when my wife is ready. I hope so." He took a long draw from his pipe. "Jacques-Yves was a sweet boy. My son liked to help in the shop on Saturdays and we became inseparable. On Sundays we would all go out to the beach and on nice days have a picnic. We knew the Germans had already reached Brussels but decided to make our picnic anyway, thinking it might be the last." He rested his pipe in an ashtray. I could tell he was thinking about that day back in May 1940. "Yes—it's been no picnic since that day," he said finally.

"You don't have to tell me about your son, if it makes you sad," I said, half wishing to change the subject.

"Oh, no. My wife can't talk about it, but I'm made of stronger stuff." His whole face changed, like a father watching a telegram boy walk up to his front stoop. "We were sitting out on the sand, beside our car, when a squadron of German fighter planes flew low over us. We heard the drone of their engines. *Heading to Paris*, I thought, or maybe to attack a nearby factory. They passed over, but then one circled back and fired at us. Why, I will never know. Pure hate, that's all it could have been. I suppose it's Hitler's way of demoralizing us. Kill a few innocent children. It works—I'll tell you that."

Madame Faure came into the room and announced dinner was ready. When Monsieur Faure and me got up, he put his hand on my shoulder and shrugged. "Best to put on a good face for Madame," he whispered.

I knew that the Faures were thinking about Jacques-Yves having me there, but they did nothing to make me feel awkward. Dinner was yum. Madame Faure worked a miracle with the piddlings available at the market, and there were peppermints to follow. It was the best meal since Daphne made me a burger back in London.

Daphne.

I wondered where she was tonight and if she'd found herself a swell French family like mine. Before I went to sleep, I kneeled by the side of the bed—like my ma would want—and prayed for my best friend Daphne: that she'd stay clear of Nazis, go to bed with a full stomach, and that she'd bump into me before long.

CHAPTER TWENTY-NINE

THE NEXT DAY WE WOKE EARLY and the lady made me a nice breakfast using an egg from a chicken that lived behind the shop. I helped pick the exact egg I'd be eating. Monsieur Faure promised to ask around about the burial place of British airmen. Everybody smoked in Dunkirk and he was connected.

"Monsignor André at Église Saint-Éloi officiates burials at the cemetery," he told us when he returned to the apartment later in the day. "We know the Monsignor. He prefers my special blend. I call it *Faure's Fumer*. We can visit him tomorrow."

"Does the priest work for the Germans?" I asked.

"Heavens no," he said.

"These poor airmen—no family to see them off. So tragic," said Madame Faure, shaking her head. "It's kind of the Monsignor to see that the men are buried properly."

"I dare say it puts him in a difficult position having to deal with the Germans," said her husband.

Before dinner we left the flat and made our way to a car, parked nearby. We traveled a short distance from the town center and rolled the car to a stop across the street from the graveyard. A German military ambulance pulled up to the curb and we watched as two medics lifted a stretcher from the back and carried a covered body through the gate. Madame Faure took one look at me and said, "Deep breaths, deep breaths." A man came out of a brick building and signed papers, directing the medics into the building. We figured it served as a makeshift funeral parlor.

"It's not safe to be asking around while the Germans are here," said Monsieur Faure. He put the car into gear and began to pull away from the curb.

On the drive back to the town center, Monsieur Faure turned the radio to a news channel, but after a few minutes retuned to a music station. "Propaganda. That's all the news is these days," he said. "Sometimes we pick up *Radio Londres*, but if the Germans find you listening, it's big trouble."

That night I tossed and turned and even after counting to a hundred sheep, I was still wide-awake. I kept thinking about my brother and how there'd been no family members to see him off.

Taking my sneakers in my hand, I tiptoed across the parlor and down the stairs to the street level. Without much thinking, I headed in the direction of the cemetery—an easy enough walk. A chain with an open padlock hung from the iron gates. The metal hinges creaked as I slipped through. I creeped alongside the brick building, all too aware of the sound of gravel crunching beneath my feet. There's usually nothing more exciting than visiting a haunted graveyard at night. But not tonight. On top of everything, I forgot to bring flowers.

Then I heard noise coming from the brick building, the one that must've served as a funeral parlor. Chills went down my spine when I realized there was somebody on duty. It seemed like an odd hour to be working, though. Pressing my body against the bricks, I inched closer to the door, taking a look inside. The beam of a flashlight bounced around the room and I ducked to the ground to avoid its rays. My nose started bleeding. I fished around in my pocket with a shaky hand, searching for a hankie. In the moonlight, my blood looked black.

"I spit on you!" came a voice. "Beastly Hitler, I spit on you!"

Blood stopped dripping from my nose. I should've known Daphne would break into the building using her hairpin. When I walked through the door, she leaped back knocking over a trash basket. I heard her let out a gasp.

"Daphne, it's me," I said quietly, not wanting to scare the heebeegeebees out of her. She pointed the flashlight to my face.

"Thomas Mooney!" she said, in a pitch-perfect imitation of Sister Bridget at St Brendan's. "What on earth are you doing here? You oughtn't be in Dunkirk. You should be on your way to Paris."

"The plan changed," I said, promising to explain later. "You shouldn't be here either."

"It's all right. I've been staking out the building for

two nights now and no one shows up until morning when the caretaker comes." She had a large ledger book in her hand, which she waved in front of my face, saying it contained information about every British airman buried in the cemetery. She lit up the pages with the flashlight. I leaned in to look. Daphne's fingers traced down a list of names. On one line, information had been scribbled over, making it impossible to know what had been written. The entry right above was for a Pilot Officer James A. Noble, who died on June 15. Below was the entry for a Sergeant Stanley Mather, who died on June 17. According to the book, in all of 1942, there was no one by my brother's name taken to Dunkirk. The crossed out line made me wonder, but I kept my mouth shut.

"It could be there's another cemetery in town," I said. "Or maybe the Resistance people were wrong and he wasn't taken to Dunkirk. The Germans could've taken Jack's body anywhere."

"I think he's not buried here, simply because he's alive and well."

Here we go again, I thought, but tried hard to hold onto the idea that she might be right. "Listen, there's a priest in charge of burying RAF airmen. We can pay him a visit tomorrow." Mostly, I wanted to get out of this building before Stormtroopers stormed in. Daphne sighed but caved. Before we left, we straightened up the room so it didn't look disturbed. Then we closed the gate, locking the padlock.

By the time we reached the apartment, birds were beginning to chirp. Madame Faure answered the door in her nightgown, her long hair in two braids making her look like a schoolgirl. She put a teakettle on the stove and brought out a plate of biscuits. Daphne looked like a wreck—like she hadn't slept in years.

Monsieur Faure woke and was surprised to find a stranger in his living room, but glad when he heard it was Daphne. "You are very welcomed in our home," he said, kissing her hand. Right before she used it to stifle a yawn.

"Oh, my," said Daphne sleepily, almost in a whisper. Then her eyes riveted on a picture that hanged crooked over a steam radiator. She looked shocked, and no wonder. I'd already spotted the painting. It was like something you find in a girlie magazine; they call it the *centerfold*. (Not that I'd ever seen one.) Approaching the painting with both hands folded behind her back, Daphne said, "I know the artist!"

The Faure's came up behind her shoulders, one on each side. Six eyes looking dead-on at the painting with no shame at all. I figured that Monsieur Faure was violating the fifth deadly sin: lust.

Out of the side of my eye, I saw that Daphne was now waving her hands wildly. "I'm sure of it," she was saying, "this is Sophie Doumer's work, one of my dearest friends at art school. I was in the studio when she painted it, standing not three easels to her left, and painting from the exact model—a Russian girl named Katarina. Why, see here—there is the girl's mole!"

Madame Faure started laughing. "Sophie is my sister."

Daphne spun around so that she was staring Madame Faure in the face. "My goodness, now I see that you are practically her twin."

"Hardly," said Madame Faure. "I'm almost thirteen years older."

Daphne reached out for one of Madame Faure's braids. "Same exact color…I'd say alizarin crimson with a touch of cadmium orange."

"And gray." Madame Faure pointed out a strand twisting through the braid.

Daphne turned back to the painting. "Sophie was the most gifted of our class. I say, look at those edges—marvelous!" She ran a finger over the Russian girl's bosom, landing on a—. My cheeks grew warm.

After that, Madame Faure forced Daphne to take a nap in the spare bedroom. A bunch of French words, all meaning thank you, poured from Daphne's lips. I showed her the way.

"Oh, Thomas," she said, closing her eyes. "I missed you terribly."

CHAPTER THIRTY

LATER ON THAT DAY—once Daphne was finished with her beauty sleep—we walked to a Gothic Cathedral. Gargoyles glared down at us with their beady eyes as we passed under a stone arch and into a side entrance. The church smelled like wax and furniture polish. The sound of our footsteps ringed on the stone floor, bounced off the vaulted ceiling and disappeared into all the nooks and crannies. Underneath the floor people were actually buried. One plaque was dated 1560—so long ago, the Lenape Indians still owned Manhattan Island, and the Dutch hadn't come along yet to swindle them with glass beads.

Monsieur Faure asked a nun if we could visit with the Monsignor, and within a few minutes we got whooshed into a Bible-filled office.

A man rose from behind a colossal wood desk. One of his hands leaned on the desk and one reached for an ivory-handled cane. His face was like a prune, only friendlier. He wore a purple-trimmed black cassock with a purple sash around his waist, meaning he was in tight with the Pope. Stepping from around the desk to greet us, I noticed his cassock smelled like mothballs and frankincense.

He hugged Madame Faure, making kissing motions toward her two cheeks. That would never happen at Saint Brendan's. Not in a billion Sundays.

The Faures talked in rapid-fire French. I could catch enough to know they were telling the priest our story. When Madame Faure talked about my brother's crash in Belgium, the priest stuck his chin out, wrinkling his mouth and clicking his tongue. She mentioned my brother's name and the priest's eyes flew open and he motioned for us to take a seat.

The Monsignor turned to Daphne and said, "Madame Faure tells me you are looking for your fiancé. And your name isn't Sabine, by any chance?"

"No," said Daphne, "why ever would you think it was?"

The Monsignor cracked a smile. "There are so many airmen killed in action being brought to us, that by now, it's hard for me to remember all of their names. Your Lieutenant Mooney, however, stands out in my memory. You see, there was quite an uproar concerning that particular body."

Body. I took Daphne's hand in mine and squeezed hard.

He waited a beat, looking at Daphne the whole time. "*Oui*, mademoiselle, I remember that body very well. Gunshot wound to through the right temple."

We stared at the Monsignor dumbstruck.

His finger touched the left side of his neck. "I'm

assuming your fiancé doesn't have a small swastika tattooed on the side of his neck? Think carefully—a very crude job, a homemade tattoo. Something he received, perhaps, while intoxicated?"

My eyeballs were going to pop out of their sockets. It could be he was senile. That happened to my great-great aunt Sinéad, who before she died, insisted that I was her long-lost childhood sweetheart.

"I thought not," said the Monsignor, pulling on his chin, looking from Daphne to me. "A body was brought to the cemetery, dressed in the flight uniform of an RAF pilot—Royal Canadian Air Force insignia, if my memory is serving me. Around his neck were the dog tags of a Lieutenant John Mooney. Your fiancé's identification, no doubt, and yet clearly not your fiancé's body. I happened to be at the cemetery when the German medics arrived with the corpse. They'd come directly from the crash site. Of course, the Germans had searched the body on the journey to Dunkirk—they always do—looking for items of value: a wedding ring, money, or pocket watch. Why, they'll steal the gold out of a filling."

"Ratfinks," I said with my teeth clinched.

"They'd spotted the gunshot wound—they would have, the moment the flight helmet was removed. And yet the helmet was undamaged. Naturally, this raised all sorts of questions. The deceased was brought into the building and the caretaker ordered to strip him. We could all see that his underclothing were German military issue. Then the tattoos became visible." He stabbed the air with his finger. "That's how we knew that the deceased, you see, had a girlfriend named Sabine—a very Germanic name."

"Why would a German be wearing my brother's uniform and dog tags?"

"Precisely what the Germans wanted to know. They swore they'd seen the body removed from the Spitfire with their own eyes. While they argued, I stood at the back of the room in quiet reflection and prayer. Within no time I reached the conclusion that your lieutenant must have escaped wearing the uniform of a German. *Mon Dieu!* A switch! A very ingenious idea."

"Jack is alive!" said Daphne, pinching my arm. "I always said as much."

"Ouch," I cried.

"Calls were made," the Monsignor said, continuing the story. "It seemed a Gestapo agent was missing—the very agent who had gone to investigate the crash site. He must have been careless." The Monsignor shrugged a shoulder, using his cane as a prop. "Sad for poor Sabine," he said.

CHAPTER THIRTY-ONE

I LEFT THE CHURCH AND FOUND Daphne and the Faures waiting for me across the street at a monument. Even Madame Faure was giggling. Daphne and her were already buddies and had their arms wrapped around each other's waists and were kissing each other on the cheeks. Like schoolgirls just named homecoming queen. Feeling pretty good myself, I jumped up onto a water fountain and splashed Monsieur Faure and he splashed back.

On top of everything, I'd been absolved. In a private meeting with the Monsignor, I poured out my confession. When I owned up to taking from the collection plate, he had the idea that I give over the leftover dollars, which he would return to The Holy Mother Church. In exchange he gave me a stack of French francs from his own pocket. "Now consider this a donation to your mission and we're even," he said. For about $30 US, I got 150 francs. Not a bad deal.

Wanting to make what they call a "proper act of contrition," I mentioned the biplane and the Congobar I'd bought using collection money. I went to hand back some of the francs, but the Monsignor waved them off and said for me to consider it a gift from God. Then he offered me a short homily: "But don't take from the plate again. Put something in next time."

"*Oui, oui*," I said, which sounds like wee-wee but means "double yes."

When I confessed to hating Sister Bridget at Saint Brendan's, he gave me his own story: "When I was a boy, I had a nasty nun for a teacher. We boys called her Robespierre. She tormented me every day for an entire school year. I dreaded going to class. I was an exceptional student, but my grades began falling under her tutelage. She preferred the iron rod to a soft encouragement. I lived in fear of her wooden chalkboard pointer. She might have used the guillotine had there been one available."

"So what did you do?" I asked, hoping for advice. Sister Bridget had whacked me more than once with a chalkboard pointer.

"As you see, I became a priest. Upon ordination, I asked to be assigned to the same school I had attended as a boy."

With a sideways, eyes-half-closed look, I asked if he was suggesting I become a priest. A split-second later and I was sorry I'd asked. If he said yes, I wasn't sure I could refuse. Although it sure was a good way to get back at Sister Bridget, and one I'd never considered.

"Only if the Lord calls you," he said.

Well, my options were still wide-open. I wanted to be an Egyptologist and dig up mummies and ancient treasures. Be the Howard Carter of my generation—if not that, than a racecar driver. I asked what he done about Sister Robespierre.

"I put in a request she be relocated."

"Where to?" I asked.

"To Tikai, a small remote island in the French Polynesian archipelago. It wasn't far enough, to my mind. And I made a specific recommendation that she never be allowed near children again."

Now I was worried for the natives of Tikai. They'd have no way of getting away, what with ocean on four sides. Hopefully they were better swimmers than me. My fears were soon put to rest:

"She chose to retire instead," he said. "To a convent, as I had hoped."

I asked for the moral of the story, because there's always one in a homily, guaranteed. The Monsignor laughed though and waved his hand. For once I was spared. "You are absolved," he said, making a sign of the cross above my head. "Go in peace, first saying four Hail Marie's and the Our *Père* for your other sins: stealing the speedboat and lying to your mother, in particular."

With a wad of French francs in my pocket, I wanted to celebrate. I was never one for saving. I'd gotten a piggy bank for my 10th birthday, but that pig was starving. My ma said she was certain I had a hole in my pocket but had trouble locating it when she done the mending. My motto was: *Why spend tomorrow, what you can spend today?*

The Faures walked us over to a café a few streets away. Daphne said, "Champagne for everyone. Even a sip for you, Thomas." The Faures helped decode the menu and I ordered everything strange: frog legs and snails in butter—which they called *escargot*. There was no shortage of them, even in wartime. I ordered something called *Kig ha farz*, just for the sound of it. It ended up being nothing but boiled pork with dumplings, something my ma made all the time. They didn't have champagne, because the Germans were drinking it all, but Daphne ordered an entire bottle of the fizzy water. When I took a sip, the bubbles went up my nose. I was having the time of my life.

Until the bill came.

How could a bunch of snails cost so much? In America we try to get rid of them by leaving bowls of beer, which they jump into, drown and then dissolve. The Faures seen the panic on my face and insisted on throwing in.

Daphne and me were invited to spend the night above the tobacco shop and we headed home. Even though we passed German soldiers, they weren't able to put a damper on our good moods. We stopped at an ice-cream cart, which was attached to a tricycle. The boy served up shaved ice, with more ice than syrup. Daphne passed. Said she had to mind her figure now that she'd be seeing Jack again.

CHAPTER THIRTY-TWO

Somewhere in German-occupied France

THE SUN IS ABOUT TO RISE after a cool night. There's mist in the air but this is clearing. Imagine you're looking at a gatepost and above the post is a sign, hanging crookedly: PARIS ORLY AÉROPORT.

A few years earlier, you might have come to pick up a friend who'd flown in from Algiers. But it's early autumn 1942, and there hasn't been a commercial flight arriving to this airport in quite a while.

A Nazi flag snaps in a gust of wind.

Tilting his cap toward his left eyebrow, an officer of the German Luftwaffe idles his motorcycle at the gatepost. After taking a drag from his cigarette, he lets it dangle from the corner of his mouth. Reaching into his overcoat pocket, he removes his identity papers from a billfold, handing them over to the soldier on guard duty.

The soldier is standing at attention but relaxes as he examines the papers. "*Flieger-Stabsingemieur* Hans Dorfmann?"

The Luftwaffe officer nods and says, "*Ja wohl.*" He returns his papers to the billfold and rides into the air base, in the direction of the aerodrome.

Looking into the window of the operations shack, he sees several pilots lounging in chairs and one curled up on a small sofa. One has his feet propped up on a wooden table that takes up much of the room. He's reading a book that the officer sees is *We* by Charles Lindbergh, who flew from Long Island, New York to Paris in 1927, making the first trans-Atlantic solo flight and becoming a hero to his fellow Americans. Now he's also a hero to the Luftwaffe, having visited Germany at the invitation of Hermann Göring.

The pilots are tired after a long night in their flying machines and are catching a few winks before their replacements arrive and they go to their barracks and rest properly.

A parachute harness hangs from a hook outside the shack and the man puts it on while walking toward the airfield. A Messerschmitt awaits—his very favorite. With his flight boot, he kicks the blocks out from in front of the wheels, jumps up on the left wing and slides the canopy open. Looking at the gauges, he is pleased to see that the tank is nearly full, so is the battery.

He jumps into the cockpit, strapping the harness to a parachute already placed on the seat. The oxygen mask goes on his face—the tank snuggly beside his leg. Flicking a switch, the motor springs to life. He looks through the Plexiglas. The morning sunrise—which is now hovering at the horizon—glares off the windshield and blinds him momentarily. The plane rolls forward and trundles to the airstrip.

The Messerschmitt lifts itself from the ground, flying over a field where black cows graze on gentle undulating hills. When the ignition switch is moved down, the drop in revolutions is barely noticeable. The engine hums monotonously. The oil temperature begins to rise, remaining steady. The needle stops comfortably below the red mark.

The pilot levels at 3000 meters, heading into the sun, which is now throwing orange rays over the French countryside.

He banks his Messerschmitt to the right. And as Luftwaffe pilots do every day, he heads north toward the English Channel. Sometimes he wishes he were a bomber pilot. They do more damage, that's for sure. But after few spins, dives, and a flick roll, he reminds himself that being a fighter pilot is so much more fun.

CHAPTER THIRTY-THREE

FROM THAT MOMENT IN DUNKIRK, when we were certain my brother was alive, Daphne began talking more about her time with Jack before he went missing. She'd been superstitious keeping these stories to herself. Like in the back of her mind she worried they'd be the only things left of Jack and she didn't want to give them away.

"Whenever there's a moment of quiet between sweeps," she said, "the pilots make up crazy games which we girls join in on. One is called Mayday. We play it in a former ballroom, where the boys are barracked. The floor is the English Channel, touch it and you're in trouble. Downed pilots—and that's all of us—escape by jumping to furniture, carpets, tables, and cushions, which we imagine to be life rafts. We swing from curtains and chandeliers, trying to land safely on an island or into a boat. Sometimes, when there's an attractive WAAF—short for Women's Auxiliary Air Force, don't you know—one of the pilots will play the part of a shark. Everyone knows there are sharks in the English Channel."

"Sharks?" I said gulping, thinking how I'd tried to

talk her into swimming over to Belgium.

"And if one need parachute from a Spitfire?" she said, getting my attention. "One must do so by jumping from the fireplace mantel. Ripping fun during the winter when there's a fire roaring below."

"Ripping!" I said. "I wanna play Mayday!"

"Only once did one of us get seriously injured playing the game—knocked unconscious when he fell from a chandelier and hit his head on a metal drinks trolley. His face was cut up by broken glass. When he came to in the medic tent, we were all there to award him with the Distinguished Flying Cross. I played the part of the queen."

No wonder Daphne never told me about the game. As long as there was the ghost of a chance that Jack died in the crash, it wouldn't of been funny.

Daphne kept the stories coming, as we drove the next weekend to Paris. We were driving there in the Faure's car. It was their wedding anniversary and we were getting a lift to what they called, "The City of Love." The description made me squeamish, but I had no choice but to head in that direction myself.

We knew the escape route from Belgium to Spain went through Paris. It made sense because Paris was a big city and a good place for a pilot to hide in. We figured Jack might know about this escape route; he had friends who had evaded capture. Made sense he'd head to Paris and make contact with the French Resistance. Anyway, Paris was as good a guess as any place.

Besides, Daphne insisted we go. She was crazy for Paris and all excited about seeing Great-Aunt Dalia again. We'd have somewheres to stay while we combed the city, that's all I cared about. And we'd eat good, too; because the aunt was buddy-buddy with all the chefs, one of the perks of being a food critic. Daphne said her aunt "favored" cream sauces, ate Hollandaise sauce on her eggs, and knew the best way to roast a quail. She promised we'd be eating truffles before long. Truffles were subterranean fungus, she told me, hunted by pigs. Sounded interesting. My eyes closed and I dreamed about ham sandwiches. With mayo.

"Your aunt must be fat, huh?" I asked, when Daphne woke up from a snooze. Her cheek had an indent from where she'd rested against a strip of seat piping. "And how old is she, anyway?"

"Hmm…good question," she said yawning. "She's my grandmother's elder sister. So she must be 70, at least. Yet she doesn't act it. Such a hoot!" (Daphne hooted.) "And the way she dresses! I'm telling you—straight out of a Pre-Raphaelite painting."

"A pre-what?"

"You know: Dante Gabriel Rossetti, Edward Burne-Jones, John William Waterhouse. Oh, it was all the rage amongst late 19th century English painters. Do you mean to tell me you haven't seen *The Lady of Shallot* at the Tate Gallery?" The blank look on my face made her shove me and say: "Philistine."

Before we left Dunkirk, the Faures managed to get us travel papers, issued by the Germans and required for passage on French roads. Monsieur Faure's sister—using her identity papers—got a pass for Daphne. Madame Faure used Jacques-Yves' birth certificate to get a pass for me.

We should've reached Paris in three hours, but there were roadblocks. A couple times, Germans searched the car, while they made us cool our heels on the side of the road. They were looking for concealed weapons, smuggled Jewish folks, runaway airmen, and contraband food. Not once did they question me about my bow and arrows, pocketknife, or about the slingshot Daphne had in her valise.

I was warned to keep my trap shut if they questioned us. No matter how tempted, I was not to speak German with the soldiers. "And no name calling," said Daphne. "If asked a direct question, bust out crying and cling to Madame Faure. Do. Not. Speak." Humiliating, if you ask me. At every checkpoint, the Germans asked for our papers and fired all their questions to Monsieur Faure. They always ogled Daphne, ignoring me completely.

"Funny," said Daphne as we pulled away from a checkpoint, "but growing up in England, I'd often hide the fact that I was Jewish—you know, from schoolmates and the like. Trying to fit in, I suppose; trying to blend. And yet here in German-occupied France, now when it makes sense to conceal it—life and death, rather—well, I suddenly don't wish to. There's this longing welling up inside me to shout it out for all the world to hear."

Monsieur Faure looked over his shoulder, rolled up

his window, and stepped on the gas pedal.

Daphne said, "Come to think of it, I might raise my children to be Jewish."

"You think Jack will go for that?" I asked.

Daphne fluttered her hand, "Jack doesn't give one fig how I raise my children. So long as they're his too." She sighed and got a dazed look in her eye.

We stopped for lunch in Arras, a pretty town that was rebuilt after the Great War. When the Germans captured the town two years before, 240 suspected French Resistance members were executed in the Arras citadel. Hearing this, I lost my appetite. Then, as we drove out of town, Monsieur Faure pointed to the citadel and I threw up while imagining Paul-Henri x 240. Daphne felt my brow and said, "You must be coming down with something," and I let her think it was true. Madame Faure cleaned up the mess, but the car smelled bad all the way to Paris.

As we neared the city, the stories became sappy and some of them had me wiggling nervously in my seat. "How did you two fall in love?" asked Daphne. The Faures were overjoyed to tell us all the gory details.

"We met in grammar school when we were only twelve," said Madame Faure, batting her eyelashes at her husband.

Twelve! I thought. *Jeez Louise.*

"We sat next to each other at roll call each morning, because my maiden name is Doumer, as you know. No students with a surname beginning with E—thank God. I thought Émile had the most charming smile, the way his teeth were so straight even without the help of orthodontics." I put my hands over my ears, but no one appeared to notice. The Faures continued in full swing:

"And Rochelle had the most beautiful dimples. Still does." Monsieur Faure reached across the front seat and pinched his wife's cheek. This was too much.

"It was love at first sight," said Madame Faure.

At twelve years old, I thought. *Come on!*

"And how about you and Jack?" asked Monsieur Faure, eager as a Cocker Spaniel for a bone.

I skewed my eyes. I'd already heard the saga: Jack approaches Daphne on a crowded London street and offers to take her out for bangers and mash. Two seconds later and they're madly in love. Three long days pass before Jack proposes "whilst" canoeing down the Thames—Daphne shading herself under an umbrella, "whilst" Jack stands paddling. Daphne throws herself at Jack and the canoe tips over, soaking them to the skin on an early spring day. They have to embrace to get warm, harps play in the background. And before you know it they're holed up in some bungalow in Long Island City with six brats and living on franks and beans.

So as Daphne flapped on, I gazed out the window. I seen from a distance a small airplane come from the east and fly over the road we was driving along. The plane was so low I could identify it: a German Messerschmitt AG.

Daphne said, "I could feel his pilot wings pressing against my ches—" then stopped mid-sentence to look at the airplane too, because by now her voice was drowned out by the roar of its V-12 engine.

Monsieur Faure pulled to the side of the road when his wife began weeping. He wanted to wrap his arms around her and needed both of them. We watched as the German fighter plane let loose its guns in a valley below the road, firing on a factory less than a quarter-mile in the distance. There was an explosion, probably when the German pilot fired on a fuel tank.

"Why is a lone Messerschmitt firing at a factory?" asked Monsieur Faure, to no one in particular. "Étrange. Usually it's the British and Americans attacking factories these days, because so many are being used for the German war machine." Shaking his shoulders, like he wanted to forget the scene, he restarted the car.

We continued on our way to Paris, stopping once more as we men relieved ourselves against the car tire. The ladies walked into a stand of trees to do their business. While we waited, Monsieur Faure put his arm around my shoulder and took a big gulp of air. "*Par-ee!* Tommy," he said, wiggling his ears. "Can't you smell love in the air?"

Honest to God, all I could smell was throw-up.

CHAPTER THIRTY-FOUR

IT WAS TIME TO GO OUR SEPARATE WAYS. Daphne and me were headed to her aunt's apartment. The Faures were staying with family. Monsieur didn't seem as gung-ho as his wife. After all, he'd be staying with the in-laws.

"But there's a view of the Eiffel Tower—so romantic," said Madame Faure.

"Out the bathroom window," said Monsieur Faure, lifting an eyebrow.

Madame Faure took a ballpoint pen from her pocketbook but couldn't find any paper. Instead, she wrote her family's address on the back of a used ration book. Daphne tucked it in her pocket where she found a receipt and scribbled the aunt's address on the back. With any luck, we'd be eating Madame Faure's food again. *Cuisine*, they call it.

A whole lot of cheek kissing followed. Then we parted from our friends and searched for the subway. Daphne called it "The Metro" and said it was a short ride to her aunt's neighborhood.

"Couldn't we walk?" I said. "We've been cooped up in the car all day." Daphne agreed and pointed the way.

The buildings were as old as Methuselah and re-sembled the setting of the comic strip, *Prince Valiant in the Days of King Arthur*. Arthur might've been English, but Paris was more Camelot than London. And the city wasn't all knocked to the ground like London. Daphne said that when the Germans rolled in, the French government picked up and blew town for someplace named Vichy, which until then I thought was a potato soup Mrs. Balson had invented for the Sopwiths.

It didn't seem right to me. The only people still fighting were in the Resistance and there didn't seem to be enough of them to do the job. By golly, you wouldn't even know there was a war going on, if it weren't for all the Nazis everywhere: fishing alongside the embankment of the Seine River; fräuleins dressed in uniforms, coming out of chichi shops; a Panzer tank smack in the middle of a park. We saw a brood of Luftwaffe officers go down into the Metro. Nazis were everywhere you looked—like ants swarming all over a birthday cake.

"It's all too sick-making," said Daphne.

We kept passing Nazis who made rude with Daphne by whistling and reaching out to pinch her. She stopped me from hauling off and punching one in the nose.

"They wouldn't do that if I had a yellow star pinned to my jacket," she said.

I knew there were worse things than getting flirted with, so I said: "Better not. It will ruin your *ensemble*."

Daphne laughed. "Your French is really improving, Thomas."

The problem was, her black suit was drawing attention. Even French ladies shot jealous looks her way. I held onto her hand so's she'd feel protected. "I can fend for myself, little brother," she said but didn't let go.

While we walked, Daphne told me about her aunt. She'd traveled a lot, all the way to Tibet and once to Mongolia. Her life's ambition was to write a cookbook featuring dishes from countries not known for their cooking. She'd eaten deep-fried crickets in Thailand, monkey brains in China, and stinging weeds in India. Daphne remembered her aunt saying that Icelandic food was underrated.

"What sort of food do they eat in Iceland? Ice-cream?"

"Fish mostly, I think," said Daphne.

"On Fridays probably," I said.

When Daphne first laid eyes on her aunt, she thought she was a giantess, maybe something out of *Gulliver's Travels*. Daphne was only four, short in other words. The aunt showed up wearing a long flowing robe over wide-legged pants, an outfit she picked up in Shanghai. (First time Daphne'd seen a lady in pants, so that part stood out.) Great-Aunt Dalia had just traveled from Lapland to Russia. She brought Daphne a set of Russian nesting dolls. Come to think of it, I'd seen them in the bedroom back in London. Once little Daphne got over the shock, the giantess became her favorite aunt. But it wasn't until the aunt settled down in France that they really got to know each other.

"Why France?" I asked.

"Aunt Dalia says there isn't a place on earth to compared to France foodwise. And she would know. She loves feeding people—like a Jewish mother. Why, she makes the most amazing schnitzel…and challah bread. Then for Hanukah there's potato latkes, and for Shavuot there's blintzes and cheesecake."

"I love cheesecake. Ever heard of Lindy's? Jack took me once." My stomach growled. I couldn't wait to meet the aunt. "Sounds good to be Jewish. All us Catholics get is a flounder on Fridays, and wafers and wine on Sundays."

"Oh, Thomas, honestly," she sighed.

The walk took longer than I wanted, but we came to the right neighborhood finally. Daphne called it Montparnasse, said it was where all the big-name artists lived. She started rattling off names again, not a single one I ever heard of. I asked if she'd heard of Norman Rockwell, who drew the covers for *The Saturday Evening Post* But Daphne she just rolled her eyes.

We came to a busy road and a building with seven floors if you didn't count the attic. Daphne made a happy exhale. Then she walked on.

"Hey, where are you going?" I said.

Halfway down the block she stopped in front of a monster flowerpot. I tipped it over while she felt around underneath. "Bob's your uncle," she said, and her fingers came out dangling a key. "I hoped it would still be here! My aunt is always misplacing her key fob. Half the time, we have to use this." Daphne opened her palm and said,

"Hello Key, Are you happy to see me?"

The front door was made of black iron, rusted on the edges and left open for robbers. Daphne tore up the staircase, taking two steps at a time and I was right behind her. On the third floor, she inserted the key in a lock. "This *is* going to be a surprise."

And it was.

The door swung open and Daphne stopped short. "Blast," she said. "This isn't the apartment. How very odd." She peeked her head in and glanced left to right before shutting the door. Standing back, she looked at the number painted on a blue tile, while her hand mussed up her hair. I followed her down one flight and she inserted the key in a door at the same spot as the one above. The key wiggled every which way but wouldn't work. She leaned over the bannister and counted, one, two. Looking up she said, "Three."

We climbed the stairs again and she opened the same door as before. "Aunt Dalia?" she shouted, without stepping inside. No one answered. "Odd that. This isn't my aunt's furniture."

"Maybe she redecorated?"

"This isn't at *tall* decorated to my aunt's taste. This is so…Spartan."

"Maybe she moved?"

Daphne walked to the neighbor's apartment and banged her fist on the wooden door. No one was home, not at that door or at any other on the floor. We returned to the lobby, not knowing what else to do, and I took a seat on a bench. It was time to put on our thinking caps, because if Aunt Dalia had moved, we had no place to stay.

"Budge up," said Daphne, making me scoot over. She looked up at the ceiling, her thinking posture. I looked up with her. The ceiling had plasterwork around the edges that reminded me of a wedding cake. We watched a spider string a web between the beams, hanging from a thread when it needed a rest. I daydreamed until the front door creaked open and Daphne shot to her feet. An old lady came in with her back pushing the door, her hands full of parcels wrapped in brown paper.

"Madame Barrault!" said Daphne, all happy.

The lady scowled when a parcel fell to the floor, almost like she was blaming us for making it happen. Daphne rushed over to help. Madame Barrault refused. *Stubborn old bitty*, I thought, and kept sitting. *Let her lug her own parcels if she wants.* The lady bent her knees and reached for the parcel. The other packages tilted and almost tumbled over. Meanwhile, Daphne mimed a catch. Madame Barrault brushed past Daphne, headed for the staircase. Daphne began rapid-fire French, with question marks at the end of every sentence. The lady straightened her crooked back and her nose went in the air like it just caught the whiff of dog poop. Meanwhile she was as silent as the grave, not answering even one of Daphne's questions. *Maybe she's hard of hearing,* I thought.

I looked at my friend. Something was dead wrong, that's all I could tell. The lady took two steps up. Daphne began asking questions again, this time with a pleading voice. *What is wrong with the lady,* I wondered. Daphne shouted, "Madame Barrault! *S'il vous plaît!*" Madame Barrault froze. Then she spun, so that the same parcel slipped from the stack. She finally moved her tongue. Like a snake's it was. Her French was too fast for me to catch much of anything she said, but I got the drift by keeping my eyes glued to Daphne's face. She was hyperventilating. Madame Barrault didn't care. She kept at it: words like daggers.

"What do you mean 'Roundup of Jews?'" said Daphne, slipping into English.

Madame Barrault said, "*Sale Juifs!*"

Daphne blinked. I jumped from the bench with my fist up because I understood what the words meant: *dirty Jews.*

That's when Daphne had what the English call a "wobbler." My eardrums almost burst. A door opened on the floor above and a man came running down the staircase, angry and yelling for us to leave. I pulled Daphne to the entrance. For every insult the Frenchies made, Daphne yelled two back. The man shoved me and I stumbled onto the sidewalk, taking Daphne with me.

The door slammed and metal scraped against metal: barred from the building. Daphne banged her fists against the door so hard her knuckles bled. Her voice was cracking at the higher notes. I begged her to come away. The witch shouted through the thick door. *Police* is one word you don't need translated. Daphne kicked the door over and over but it wasn't budging.

I knew this was the biggest job of my life so far:

getting Daphne away from here so she wouldn't get rounded-up. I jumped up behind her and pressed my hands to her mouth, tight. She was fighting like a boxer. Her diamond engagement ring scraped my cheek and she kicked me in places I won't mention. She slammed an elbow into my rib.

"I'm not the enemy," I said.

She leaned down with her hands on her knees and took deep breaths, starved for oxygen. I thought I'd done the trick, but then she ran at the door, throwing all her weight against it. After rubbing her shoulder, she ran at the door again. Next time she ramrodded the door, her head hit hard against the metal. She looked dizzy but kept throwing insults. They included words like: Hitler, Nazi, pigs, and Bloody Fascists. When I grabbed at her sleeve she bit my hand.

I tried begging and that didn't work. Then I said: "Daphne. Do. Not. Speak."

She weeped, "No! No! No!" and pounded on her chest.

My biggest fear: a group of German soldiers stopped to stare at us, same as if we were a circus sideshow. I made sure not to make eye contact. Daphne made eye contact though, and belted out an ear-piercing shriek; it'd be no surprise to me if window glass shattered up and down the street. The Germans moved off, scared. But here came another group and these ones were SS. Only one thing would save her: The Nutcracker.

My thumb pressed against her Adam's apple, using a Jui Jitsu move Jack taught me to ward off bullies at

Saint Brendan's Catholic School. I guess he never imagined I'd use it to save his fiancée's life. Daphne went limp like a rag doll but was still breathing. I grabbed under her armpits and pulled her to the curb. A bicycle taxi came down the street and I waved like a madman. The boy driving the rig screeched to a halt; his breaks needed oiling. He dismounted and helped me fold Daphne into the caboose.

He said, *"Pas de problème,"* and started pedaling.

Daphne took three gasps, choked for air, and began sobbing into my aching chest. It was the kind of thing might break a heart.

CHAPTER THIRTY-FIVE

WE DROVE AROUND IN CIRCLES until the bicycle driver looked like he'd pass out from exhaustion. I picked Daphne's pocket and found the ration book. A while later we pressed on a bell labeled *DOUMER*. A key landed on my sneaker and we opened the building's big double door. A redhead came leaping down the staircase. I figured this was Sophie, Madame Faure's sister. She went to throw herself into Daphne's arms but stopped short. She was wearing a smock with paint smeared all over the front. Two paintbrushes held up her bun, geisha girl style.

"I couldn't believe my eyes when I looked down from the balcony!" she said. "Émile mentioned you were in Paris. But I didn't expect you so soon."

"We haven't anywhere else to go," said Daphne, pulling on her friend's thumb.

"God, you look a fright," said Sophie.

Her eyes darted around the lobby, worried that somebody seen us come in. Turned out she knew about Daphne being half-Jewish. She threw an arm around Daphne's shoulder, shielding her from harm. It left a

246

good first impression. "*Vite!*" she said, and we bolted up the stairs.

By the time we reached the fifth floor apartment, I was huffing and puffing like an old lady. I'd let my training lapse. Out loud, I promised myself to start up calisthenics again. Sophie heard me. "We'll let you run errands. You'll get in shape in no time, believe me."

When we entered the apartment, another redhead came running to Daphne, squeezing her so she couldn't breathe. I took this to be the mother because of the grey roots. Then a third redhead joined us—*fourth* if you counted Madame Faure, who was nowheres in sight. This one was an inch or two taller than me, but I figured us to be about the same age because she wasn't to the brassiere stage yet. She kissed Daphne on the mouth and turned to kiss my cheeks.

"Wait one cotton-picking minute," I said. "I'll have none of that!"

"I'm Juliette," she said, holding out a hand.

The females started talking French. Feeling outnumbered, I went in search of Monsieur Faure. We'd talk about sports or toss a ball around. I'd teach him a new pitch. Or we'd discuss airplanes, tanks, and battleships. We'd find a map and pins, plot out the whole course of the war like Eisenhower and General Patton. I searched every room, even the bathroom, before circling back to the ladies. The redheads were happy to launch into a blow-by-blow of Monsieur Faure's anniversary plan, which was already in full swing.

The plan included (in alphabetical order):

Breaking the German curfew
Bubbly
Candlelight
Chic dress with plunging neckline
Kissing
More kissing
Oysters (an aphrodisiac)
Romantic chitchat
Stargazing
Stroll along the Seine River
Sunrise watching

Sophie was the first to notice that Daphne was sitting quiet as a figurine. "Look at you, you poor thing. And us rattling on." She rubbed circles into Daphne's back.

Daphne told them everything she'd learned from wicked Madame Barrault. The long and short of it was that the French police arrested Aunt Dalia back in July, along with a whole lot of other Jewish people. The French police were in cahoots with the Gestapo and only doing their bidding. Daphne said it didn't make sense because her aunt wasn't even religious and ate bacon and decorated the apartment with Buddha statues.

The whole time Daphne talked, the three Doumers shot each other nervous looks. I hoped they weren't secret Nazi collaborators. How well did Daphne know these people? The door was only ten feet away. There was probably a fire escape. In the worst case we'd jump five flights. I tried to catch Daphne's eye, but she was crying again.

"*Déplorable*," said Sophie, and I relaxed.

Turned out that everyone in Paris knew about the roundups, when thousands of Jews were arrested and taken to the Vélodrome d'Hiver, a stadium for bicycle racing. It reminded me of stories about the Roman Coliseum and Christians being thrown to the lions. But in this story, the Germans sent the people away on trains.

"To labor camps we've been told," said Madame Doumer. "Same as my husband."

"But Monsieur isn't Jewish," said Daphne with a puzzled look.

"No, but he's a machinist. He didn't want to go, but it was that or prison."

Sophie rose from the couch and found an envelope on a dinette table. It was stamped with a swastika. I tried to read the letter but the handwriting was terrible. Sophie said it was from her papa. The Germans made Frenchmen with mechanical skills work in German factories, so that their own men could fight for Hitler. Forced labor. The papa couldn't say exactly where he was, or what it was he was working on. Probably Panzer tanks or Messerschmitts. And he didn't mention anything about work conditions, which was the same as saying they were bad.

"Maybe you'll get a letter from your aunt," I said, hoping to cheer Daphne up.

"What kind of labor can an elderly woman do?" said Daphne, fitting words in between sobs. "She has arthritis in her fingers and knees. And she's a food critic. What could they possibly want with her?" Madame Doumer handed Daphne a hankie and she blew her nose.

"Whole families were taken, little children too," said Juliette.

The conversation switched to Advanced French and my mind turned to worrying. *Slaves,* I thought, remembering big Jim, Huckleberry Finn's truest friend—abused by wicked Miss Watson the slave master, and forced to escaped on a raft up the Mississippi River with Huck. I pictured Aunt Dalia, with chains on her legs and whip marks on her back, made to pick cotton in the scorching sun. No wonder Daphne was so heartsore. What if Jack ended up a slave too? My palms got sweaty thinking about it. Hitler was worse that a million Miss Watsons. And what about the Jewish children, I wondered: Will the Nazis rip them from their folks, same as the Southerners tore apart slave families? Right then, I missed my ma fiercely. I even missed Da a bit.

"We have to rescue Aunt Dalia," I said.

"Impossible à faire," said Sophie. "No one knows where they've sent people. Most likely to Germany." She pulled a paintbrush from her bun and looked at it troubled-like. Daphne volunteered to help wash the brushes, but Sophie made her stay put.

I wished I hadn't burnt *Mein Kampf.* What if Hitler wrote about his plans, about where he'd be taking people? You couldn't just walk up to a Nazi and ask for directions. We were in a bind, that's for sure. I told Daphne that we needed to find Jack more than ever. He was an expert treasure hunter and would know how to find the aunt.

Daphne squeezed my hand. "You're sweet to call my aunt a treasure."

"Ooooooh," said Juliette, raising her hand. "Didn't you tell us Jacques was an RAF pilot? Surely he'd know the coordinates of labor camps."

Daphne perked up for the first time since we got the news about her aunt. It was probably true that British Intelligence told pilots the location of camps, so's they wouldn't fire at innocent people by mistake. Daphne agreed that Jack was the one to find a solution. "He's so resourceful," she said, breaking into a smile.

"Oui? Comment?" said Juliette, moving to the edge of her seat.

Daphne thought for a second and said, "Hmm... Well, he found my favorite perfume, which was challenging given that French perfume is no longer being imported and there's such high demand for English brands...and he found little pats of butter, too."

Everyone sighed at the same time, all of us thinking the same thing: It was one thing to find butter and another thing to find an aunt. That didn't stop us from agreeing to a plan: we'd find Jack first. After all, he was the only one of us trained for exactly these predicaments.

They started jabbering away in French, so I went to scope out the place again. Teensy-weensy was too big a word for it: packed with bric-a-brac, wardrobes overflowing, crates stuffed under tables, and bookshelves and paintings stacked up the ceilings. Most of them showed naked people. I found Sophie in a closet-sized kitchen, swooshing paintbrushes in a jar of turpentine.

"Life drawing is essential for the artist's training," she said, "the same way medical students must study the human body."

"Uh, huh," I said, but I wasn't buying it.

Sophie had talent. If you stood back far enough and squinted, her paintings almost looked like photographs. I followed her to a bedroom where she showed me what she was working on: a painting of three whitewashed wine bottles. Sophie spread her wet brushes on a towel, just as Daphne stepped into the room.

"Lovely," said Daphne squinting her eyes, something art experts do whenever they look at a painting. "And so like you to be emulating Morandi at a time like this." She threw her arms around Sophie.

"Who's Morandi?" I asked.

"A Jewish-Italian artist," said Sophie. "Banned. Along with Chagall and Modigliani, among others."

"Good God." Daphne rubbed her eyes, red and puffy. She leafed through drawings, impressed with Sophie's progress. They went on and on—about this artist and that artist—about some fella named Picasso, who was living in Paris. The Nazis didn't approve of his work and he wasn't permitted to exhibit. (I wondered if that meant he wasn't allowed to pose naked.) Sophie said the rumor was that Picasso had turned to writing.

"Hitler was a realist painter," said Daphne, as though that explained everything.

I was glad when Juliette invited me to play a game

of cards out on the balcony. It was windy out there and a few cards, from the deck of 52, flew away down the cobblestone street. Even without the Jack of Hearts, a deuce, or the Queen of Spades, I taught Juliette how to play Go Fish. One thing about the game: it depends on each player being honest about the cards they have in their hand. I won the game, proving that Juliette was an honest girl. So I trusted her enough to give me the low down on German occupied Paris.

"They're wicked people, Tommy. They ship our food to Germany along with our fathers. They take the best seats on buses and in the Metro. They sit in the box seats at the cinema and at the ballet. It's because of them the Bolshoi no longer comes to Paris. When *Gone With the Wind* finally plays at Le Grand Rex it will be impossible to get a ticket because the theater will be filled with Germans. And that cinema has 2,800 seats!"

She leaned forward and whispered, "You heard what they did to my cousin, *oui*? Jacques-Yves? We're not to speak of it when my sister is visiting. It upsets her so, to hear him spoken of." (She meant Madame Faure, of course.) We had a moment of silence together where the mood got gloomy. After that I switched subjects.

"*Gone With the Wind*. Bettya the German's hope to learn about American battle maneuvers. Hopefully they'll take their cues from the Confederates."

"Ooooooh! You saw *Gone With the Wind*?"

I told her that everybody seen *Gone With the Wind* in New York, but that we was rooting for the Union. Juliette squinted her eyes, like she was thinking hard.

For a minute I was worried that she'd correct my grammar, which would've been humiliating coming from a Frenchie. Then she asked me if Scarlet O'Hara was as beautiful in life as she was in the book. I wasn't going to lie. I'd only skimmed the last ten pages after cutting them from my sister Mary's copy.

Juliette asked me if I was in school and I explained that I'd taken time off for important war work. I didn't go into the details. Juliette studied at home ever since children began missing from her school. One day she'd go into class and there'd be an empty seat next to her. When her friend Ruth disappeared, Juliette's mother—trained as a teacher—withdrew her from the school and was now teaching her from home.

"My *maman* made inquiries about Ruth's family at the Lycee."

"I take it this Ruth is Jewish?"

"*Exactement.* Her family came from Berlin originally, and fled to Paris when Hitler came to power, thinking it would be safer. Who could have imaged this?" She threw a hand over the balcony, taking in the whole city. "That day, when Maman returned from the Lycee, she was very upset and wouldn't speak to Sophie or I about what she'd discovered. She forbade me from stepping anywhere near that school from then on. All she'd say was that the headmistress was a Fascist."

"Did they torture your ma?"

"I don't think so; I hope not. But I've seen the Germans beat people with club sticks, only for looking at them the wrong way. I've watched as families are dragged from their homes and afterwards all their furniture carted off by the Germans. Get on their wrong side and that's the end of you. Look—I have gooseflesh talking about it!"

She let me rub the bumps on her arm. That had me scared, so I changed the subject again. I asked her what it was like to study at home, if she got to sleep late. Juliette said it got a little lonely, that's all. She thought maybe her ma would let me join in her lessons. "Do you want me to ask? She can teach in English, if you prefer. Maman's English is *très bein*."

"Well, in that case—" I realized that it might not be a bad idea after all. At this rate, I was in danger of being left back a grade, and ending up in Sister Bridget's class all over again. But if I came back fluent in English *and* French, they'd probably skip me to high school.

She asked me what took us to Paris, and I told her the short version of the story, emphasizing the danger to my own life. "I have the Gestapo on my tail right now," I said.

"Then should you be sitting out here on the balcony, in plain sight?"

Juliette had a point, and so we went through the French door and into the living room where the three grown-ups were sitting. The conversation was off Picasso and onto my brother, Jack. Daphne had pulled his photograph from its hiding place in the lining of her valise and was passing it around. Everybody agreed that he looked *très beau,* and *très courageux,* and that he was lucky to have such a devoted fiancée. No mention of the devoted brother.

"Jack," said Daphne, squeezing her knees. "I have a gut feeling he's hiding in Paris."

"Gut feeling? What does this mean?" asked Juliette.

"*Avoir une intuition*," said Daphne.

Sophie suggested we put ourselves in Jack's shoes and think about what kind of places he might gravitate to. We tossed the idea around. I mentioned that my brother was Catholic and asked if they had a church like the one in Dunkirk, one with gargoyles."

Juliette shouted like she was on a radio game show: "*Petit* Sainte Chapelle—it has *très belle* stain glass windows!" Madame Doumer, snapping her fingers: "Saint-Denis Basilica where 32 French queens are buried." Sophie chimed in with: "Sacre Coeur Basilica, don't forget."

"He's not *that* religious," said Daphne.

We went on like this for a few hours, even as we ate our supper and got ready for bed. Daphne was going to bunk with Juliette, Sophie, and the mother. The Faures, if they ever returned, were taking the mother's room. Juliette was worried about the Gestapo coming to take me in the middle of the night and said I'd better sleep in the hall closet or in her toy chest. The sofa looked awfully comfortable.

"Better take the sofa," I said, "so's I can guard you ladies."

CHAPTER THIRTY-SIX

FROM THEN ON WE SEARCHED PARIS for my brother. If Jack was hiding out in the city, he was doing a good job of it. Daphne and me walked for hours everyday, visiting every place we figured Jack might go. Sophie sometimes joined us, when she wasn't painting naked men. Meanwhile the Faures had returned to the tobacco store in Dunkirk, with Monsieur Faure's last words to me being: "Juliette—*très charmant*, no?"

Madame Doumer worked part-time in a shop, gluing feathers onto hats. And all because the Germans hadn't sent a pfennig of Papa's paycheck, even though they'd promised. Off-hours she taught Juliette and me about French history. So while we learned about Louis XVI—his palaces and furniture, his spoiled-brat wife, and their gruesome executions—Daphne searched without me.

When I dropped that Jack liked history, Madame Doumer had the bright idea of combining the search with our lessons. We visited the Bastille, where I got the willies by putting my head under a real guillotine. It was the sort of place Jack liked but he wasn't there. On another field trip we visited the Musée de l'Armée: one of the largest war museums in the world. They had some very impressive swords but no Jack. Maybe he was sick of war.

I had blisters on my heels and toes, and the rubber on my sneakers started loosening from the canvas. If we didn't find Jack soon, I would be walking around Paris barefoot. We spent too much time in art galleries and dress shops: two places Jack wouldn't be seen dead in. Otherwise, we covered the right ground.

Meanwhile, we kept an eye out for people wearing yellow stars. We'd spot an old lady across a wide boulevard and Daphne would perk up, thinking maybe it was her aunt. Then it was: run across the street, with Daphne waving her hands. Until she got close enough for the letdown. She'd drag her feet the rest of the day, with me trying to cheer her up.

Twice we walked by synagogues bombed by the Nazis, so that the Jewish people had nowheres to go to church. Daphne said it made her blood boil and once when no one was looking she bought a flower and laid it at a synagogue door, under a Nazi sign warning people to stay away. I thought she was super brave. That time, I stood around the corner watching.

The next time, I got up my courage and ducked under a fallen beam that once held up the entryway. Using the rubber tip of my sneakers like a bulldozer, I made it to the altar—if that's what you called it—and stood with my mouth gaping. The place was blown to smithereens. A hand trembled on my shoulder: Daphne about to faint.

"Oh, God—how tragic," she said. She spun on her heels, taking in the whole view.

Rain was coming through a hole in the roof and making the marble floor slick. Daphne slipped and fell to her knees. When she stood, I saw she had a little book clutched in her hand. "It's a prayer book," she said, wiping soot from the pages, "a *siddur*." The book was half the size of a paperback and burnt on the edges. Somebody had ripped off the cover.

So, that's what Hebrew looks like, I thought, taking in the strange shaped letters on the title page. Daphne snapped opened her pocketbook, found a white hankie trimmed around the edges with lace, and wrapped the book in a neat little package.

"It shall be very helpful come Shabbat," she said, sighing. "It's got songs and prayers and all sorts of lovely things."

"Should I find more of them?" I said eagerly, struck with the treasure hunter bug.

Daphne's face, I noticed, turned ghost white. She stumbled to a bench, plopped down, and asked me to give her a moment. She covered her eyes and began weeping into her gloves. I figured she needed privacy— the way Ma needed it the day the telegram arrived. So I wandered down an isle, looking under rubble for more of them books.

That's when my trained eye caught something glimmering. It was nailed to a charred doorframe: silver, the size and shape of a thumb. I spit on my finger and wiped soot off. It looked like a ladies brooch, with teeny leaves and branches carved into the .925 silver. A blue sapphire mounted the top. I examined the stone for flaws and noticed a little gold letter—like a W, it was. Using my pocketknife, I pried the nails from the wood, going slow—like archeologists are supposed to do—being careful not to damage the treasure.

By the time I got back to Daphne, she'd pulled herself together.

"Get a load of this," I said, opening my fingers in slow motion.

She let out a gasp, took the treasure in her hand, and tried to hold it up to the light. But the sky had darkened to slate gray since the time we'd been inside the ruined temple, making so that we were sitting in shadow.

Then came a jaw-dropping moment.

Clouds parted above us. A beam of orange light shot through the hole in the roof and flashed off the jewel. I swear to God—it reminded me of Cecil B. DeMille's movie *The Ten Commandments*—the part where Moses holds up the tablets right before the Dead Sea parts in two and Pharaoh and his army are hit with a wave of salt water.

Next thing I knew, we were sitting in pitch darkness.

"It's a mezuzah," said Daphne, fingering the carvings. "Religious Jews attach them to doorframes. I remember now that my grandmother—we called her *Bubbeh*—had them on every doorframe in her London flat."

"Great name, Bubbeh."

"She'd touch her fingers to her lips and then to the mezuzah—each and every time she passed through the door." Daphne shook the thing like a rattle. "Inside is a little scroll, upon which is written the words of Moses."

"His genuine handwriting?"

She laughed. "Goodness, no. The tiny scrolls are written by a *sofer*, a Jewish scribe of sorts. Now…is that a *sofer* or a *shofar*?"

She looked at me like I was the Webster's dictionary. One of the words, she explained, was for a trumpet made from a ram's horn, one for a scribe. Ancient Hebrew was confusing like that. I tried to help her out, mentioning that Lord Sopwith had a *chauffeur* to drive the Rolls. Daphne rolled her eyes, so I tried again and said, "*Am Yisrael Chai.*" It was the best I could do.

Her eyes got wet and glassy. Next thing I knew, she was darting at my mouth with pursed lips. *Smack!* went our lips. You could say it was my first religious experience. There was the faint sound of a choir of angels singing, "Gloria in excelsis Deo." I even had a vision: Jack pummeling me with his boxing gloves. My conscience was having a field day as I watched Daphne put the mezuzah in her coat pocket.

She stood and looked at her wristwatch. "The booksellers will still be out." Without making eye contact she added, "And see here—best not to mention the kiss to Jack. He might misconstrue what was merely a sisterly kiss."

"Oh," I said, trying not to sound disappointed.

We saw the coast was clear and ran from the building, slowing down only when we spotted a row of book-sellers. They lined up along the streets, even on rainy days. That's when they put tarps over the books and waited for the sun to come out. Like me, Jack liked to read. Before the war, he went in for westerns: Zane Grey was his favorite author, and for good reason. Problem was most Paris booksellers didn't sell Zane Grey books. But we were striking out anywhere else.

When we got bushed, we'd rest at a café and people watch. This is what Ma liked to do sitting out on our screened-in porch in East Hempstead. Now the pastime took on new meaning. I kept hoping we'd see Jack walk-ing by, but it wasn't happening like that.

I worried that maybe he was in disguise. "He could be disguised as a street sweeper or a delivery man. Or a gypsy," I said. We'd seen gypsies playing music on the street, and once watched as a gypsy boy pick a French-man's pocket.

"The Nazis are taking gypsies to internment camps, so I doubt that," said Daphne, sipping from a bottle of Fanta we were sharing.

"He might've grown a mustache or a beard…grown his hair long like one of 'em Bohemians we keep run-ning into," I said.

"Jack? A Bohemian? I think not. Even so, I should recognize him."

More than a week passed like this, when during a break back at the Doumer's apartment, I took up my coloring book. It made me sad thinking about Paul-Henri and most of the cars got colored black and grey. I wondered if he had a wife and kids. I hoped for their sakes that he didn't.

I was filling in an Invicta 4½ Litre Sports Model, when I remembered the crossword puzzles Paul-Henri gave me. I brought the crossword book to Daphne, explaining that it might contain a clue leading us to a contact along the Comet Line.

"You waited this long to show me?" she said.

"Paul-Henri getting shot shook me up bad and I plum forgot about the crossword clues. Anyways, I tried guessing the words and gave up. Spelling's not one of my talents."

Daphne clicked her tongue, huffed and puffed, shook her head, and pinched my arm before getting down to solving the puzzle. Her know-how of Paris and French was what was needed to break the code.

"Who is Saint Germain? That's the baffling part," I said, scratching my head. "And what does *Des Pres* mean? Maybe Dédée isn't good at spelling either."

"Wait!" cried Daphne. "Saint-Germain-des-Prés! That's it! It's so obvious. It's a Paris landmark. There's an ancient abbey by that name and also a neighborhood and a street."

"How's about the date? 1927." I pointed to the four horizontal boxes. "That's the year Charles Lindbergh made the flight from New York to Paris. The Spirit of Saint Louis left from an airfield near our house: Roosevelt Field. Did Lindbergh land in Saint-Germain-des-Prés, maybe?"

"No silly, that would have been a mess! He landed at LeBourget Field, I believe. Maybe it's not a date but an address. 1927 Boulevard Saint-Germain-des-Prés. Any Parisian might have sorted out the clues, Thomas."

"You're so smart Daphne. No wonder Jack fell for you!"

"That's definitely the reason, Thomas. You nailed it right on the head." She took a compact from her pocketbook, looked in the mirror and dabbed her nose with powder.

An electric shock went through my body as Paul-Henri's voice spoke from the grave. I grabbed the crossword book and began filling in blank spaces, just as he'd warned me to do. If the book had gotten into the hands of the Nazis, the whole Resistance network might've crumbled. I couldn't let my absent mind ever get the best of me again. Daphne looked on as I scribbled letters into the little boxes.

"The answer to 21 down is VICTORY," she said. "And now, let's not dilly-dally—get your jacket on."

We took the Metro to the Mabillon station, even though there was one called Saint-Germain-des-Prés. Daphne said the connection was better and instead of switching trains twice, we would do it once. She had Paris down like the back of her hand and didn't once look at the Metro map to know where we was going. Saint-Germain-des-Prés was on the left bank of the Siene River, and we traveled under the river to get there, though you wouldn't know it down in the train. When we boarded the first train, it was empty and we got a good seat, but the second train was crowded and we had to stand holding onto an unreachable strap. I held onto Daphne's hand instead. Some people looking our way might've thought I was her boyfriend.

We were lucky to board that exact car, because in walked a poet, who began reciting a poem about a grapefruit named Claudette. I thought it was pretty good myself. A couple people tossed change into his hat when he finished and I went to reach into my pocket, but Daphne stopped me. "Don't encourage him," she said.

At another stop three old men came into our car carrying instruments: one had a cello, one had a violin, and one a guitar. Right there in the train, they played a song, and a few people danced in the crowded space. A French lady started dancing with a Nazi, which ruined the whole thing for us. Still, it was a better experience than taking the subway in New York. On them trains you got stinky hobos wanting your spare nickels and loud-mouth preachers who never get to the good parts about treasures in heaven.

We arrived at the Mabillon station and climbed the stairs to the street level. The place looked like a million other spots I'd already seen in Paris, but Daphne said it was special because it was where the struggling artists holed up—near the university where lots of them studied. There were plenty of bookstores in the neighborhood and we took a look in every one we passed, just in case we might spot Jack hiding behind a paperback.

The building we were looking for was on the corner of Boulevard Saint-Germain-des-Prés and Rue Du

Dragon, which I figured was pretty exciting. No dragons though—driven out by all the artists was my guess. Plenty of those all over the place—standing on the streets with easels in front of them, hoping to get discovered. Daphne said most of them were imitating that Picasso fella, who had turned to writing. Ugly, the paintings were. No small wonder he'd needed to switch jobs.

A young Frenchie, wearing a bowler hat, was painting his girlfriend but it looked like a space ship, not a human being. He was pleased as punch though. He kept standing back from the painting, with the paintbrush in his mouth, smacking his lips and saying, "*Oui. Très magnifique!*"

At number 1927 Boulevard Saint-Germain-des-Prés we found a shop on the ground level. *Les Misérables*, it was called. I figured that they sold corsets.

"There wasn't an apartment number mentioned in a crossword clue, correct?" asked Daphne. "We'll have to ring every bell and also inquire at the shop. The frustrating part is that maybe 1927 is a code for building number 197-apartment 2, or 19-apartment 27—. I wish they'd been more exact. We can't go around telling people we're searching for a RAF pilot. There are Nazi sympathizers all over the city. People are literally in bed with them."

Why can't the Nazis get their own beds? I asked myself.

Les Misérables was a book by Victor Hugo, a French writer. I'd tried to read the tome once but it was over my head and I'd returned to the *Hardy Boys* series. Now I was sorry I hadn't stuck with it.

Daphne gave me the baffled look. "Why is a dress shop named *Les Misérables*? The book hadn't anything to do with fashion." She stepped up to the plate-glass window to check out the merchandise.

I asked her to explain the book's plot, thinking it held a clue. The book was about a man named Jean Valjean, she said, who is running from the police. He spends twenty years in the slammer for pinching bread to feed his family. When he gets out, an evil cop is still pestering him. He's forced to take a new identity: he calls himself Monsieur Madeleine and becomes Mayor of his town. Then, when the evil cop discovers him, poor Jean hightails it to Paris and goes on the lam.

Lowering my voice and pointing to the boutique, I said, "That's what we're looking for Daphne: the skirt shop." She raised her eyebrows like a doubt. "Simple deduction," I said. "Javert stands for the Gestapo. Jean Valjean stands for the British airmen who are hiding in Paris." It was then I pulled the LeReine mint pastille tin from my pocket. I'd eaten all the mints, which didn't matter.

"*Bonjour, mademoiselle,*" said the saleslady to Daphne when we entered the shop. She was ignoring me, same as they always do. I held out my hand to her—palm up with the empty mint pastille tin smack in the center. The lady's penciled eyebrows lifted and she said, "*Un moment*" and grabbed her purse and keys.

We went back out to the street and she closed up the shop—locking three deadbolts and then bringing down an iron gate. She looked around and we followed her to a side entrance. Instead of having to huff it up the stairs, we got into a cage that turned out to be an elevator. It jerked up to the fourth floor. We followed her down a dark hallway with creaky floorboards and the smell of boiling cabbage, and into a one-room apartment with nothing but two upholstered chairs that looked like cats got to them. There were wood crates for tables and added seats. The saleslady rubbed her hands together and then lit a heater that was shoved into a fireplace.

"We were all expecting your arrival much sooner," she said, getting the ball rolling without so much as a how-do-you-do. "Dédée told us to expect your arrival two weeks ago. What delayed you?" She crossed her arms, tapped her toe on the floorboard, and put a sour look on her face. She would've made a great Gestapo agent.

"Didn't nobody tell you about Paul-Henri getting murdered?" I said.

"I know of whom you speak. There was a contingency plan, no?"

We started spilling our beans, leaving nothing out. She didn't say much, didn't even laugh at the funny parts, not that there were many; she just asked a question here or there, always with a poker face.

"You should have come directly here," she said. "It's complicated things. No matter." She waved her hand. "Tonight I'll relay what you've told me to my leader. He'll decide where we go from here. Return to this flat tomorrow at 15:00 hours—that's three in the afternoon.

At that time you can speak directly with him. Understood? Three in the afternoon—don't be late this time."

She walked over to a window, pulled back a curtain, and looked down at the street. "Now go—you two first. And don't stop to speak to anyone on the way."

CHAPTER THIRTY-SEVEN

I HAD TROUBLE SLEEPING THAT NIGHT, what with all the excitement of finding the Resistance and a lead to Jack. While the ladies snoozed, I finished coloring in motorcars of the 1930's and then got bored. Meanwhile, the sky turned from India ink black to cotton candy pink.

We'd be escaping Paris soon as we found my big brother. It was time for me to do a little sightseeing like a real tourist—maybe buy a souvenir or two for Ma. I took the key, locking the door behind me. The Eiffel Tower was my destination: the world's largest Erector Set project. It popped in and out of view all the time—just like when you go to Manhattan and catch glimpses of the Empire State Building from seems like every street.

I zigzagged my way to that tower, trying for the straight-as-a-bird-flies route, which isn't easy in a medieval city. By and by I arrived at a park with a clear view of the tower. There were a few bleary-eyed, chain smoking dog walkers. I passed a German soldier dragging along a toy-poodle and choking the poor mutt. Seeing the Eiffel Tower from a distance, or on a View-Master reel, isn't the same as standing right under the thing. Each leg is bigger than a tower on the Triborough Bridge. They want you to buy a ticket to walk up to the top, but I leaped to the staircase and past the ticket collector. Climbing the five flights to Sophie's flat had brought me back to Olympian fitness—Jesse Owens wouldn't be too far ahead of me in a race. I didn't break a sweat until nearing the top.

On the last flight of stairs, my progress was interrupted when I came to the rescue of a man whose knee was troubling him. On top of bad knees, he was missing an eye and wore a pirate's patch. He leaned on my shoulder and we made the final push together.

"Irish?" he asked after I introduced myself. "I'm going all the way up," he said, "to show Hitler who's on top—even if it means the death of me, a distinct possibility given my scarred lungs."

We made it to the observation deck and the man leaned against the railing, gasping for air. "Maurice Piaf," he said, extending his hand. "Decorated in the last war." I noticed a few tarnished medals and faded ribbons pinned to his tweed coat. "The Germans used chlorine gas on us in the second battle at Ypres." He patted his wheezy chest. "The eye got in the way of one of their bayonets. Still, I was one of the lucky ones. 6000 men lost in the first ten minutes. We called it 'the war to end all wars' and now look." He pointed to a gargantuan Swastika flag hanging from the tower. "The lift was sabotaged by the French Resistance last year. Cut the cables, that's what they did. So that Adolph Hitler would have to walk up if he wanted to gloat over Paris."

I took my hand off the railing—not wanting to touch anything that wicked man might've had his hand on, a surefire way to get the cooties. "Did Hitler do it?" I asked. "Did he get to the top?"

"No, he didn't. That's why I made it my business to succeed where Hitler failed. 1710 steps. At 76 years of age."

"That's the fighting spirit," I said, giving him a slap on the back and then the thumbs up. He appreciated the gold star words I was throwing his way—those stars you get from novice nuns who buy them in bulk at the 5&10 and paste them onto anybody's papers with a B or better. My sister Mary bought the stars on the sly and stuck them to her pop quizzes. I figured Mr. Piaf here deserved a whole pack of stars.

He reached into his pocket and handed me a piece of metal: shrapnel that had been pulled out of his leg. It was his good luck charm, so I handed it back.

When I dropped a hint that I was from New York, by comparing the Eiffel Tower to the Chrysler Building, he slapped my back. "One of the happiest days of my life was when *Radio Londres* announced that the Americans were on their way. My wife and I listen secretly, sitting in the closet with the volume turned down. We celebrated by opening a bottle of 1895 Champagne. It was a wedding gift we'd been saving for our 50th anniversary but we broke it open that very day. It was a cold December evening, with no coal for the fire, but the news warmed our old bones."

"My big brother, Jack, he's fighting Nazis as we

speak. Jack joined up with the British the same day that France fell to Jerry. Only he's missing now—that's why I'm here in Paris. I gotta find him, see? We found his Spitfire." I had to choke out my last words, because I was getting weepy. It happens when I'm around nice grandparent types and telling them a sad story. They never mock you, like kids might do—mock you and maybe even sucker-punch you along with their gang of goons, calling you sissy and words like that. "Jack's Spitfire was broke up bad and we found dried blood splattered all over the instrument panel."

"Well, my wife and I will light a candle every day for Jack's safety. Every day and that's a promise. We do it for all the Allied soldiers, but we'll mention your brother by name."

"That's awfully swell of you. He'll be glad when he hears it."

It was time to be getting back. Daphne would be worried when she found me missing. Maurice said it would be no trouble for him to get down by himself. I said: "I was a Cub Scout, you know," referring to my solemn pledge to help old ladies cross streets. It applied to one-eyed, lame kneed, wheezy old war heroes too.

"Much easier going down," he said. "First I plan to stay up here a while shouting a few insults in the direction of Berlin. That's something this 76-year-old veteran can do for the Resistance." He turned about, getting his bearings, and then shouted, "*Viva Le France!*"

I breathed in as much air as could fill both lungs, so's my chest looked like Mr. Universe. Then I pinched my nose and spun around facing dead east. All the air came out with a shout: "God bless America. Land of the free!" I yelled, so loud my ears were buzzing. Could be that Roosevelt heard me all the way in Washington.

"Be on the look out for Nazis." I warned Mr. Piaf, knowing how much they liked sightseeing. "*Au Revoir*, Maurice." I flew down the stairs, taking three or four steps at a time, sliding on the railing whenever possible and dashing past the ticket collector who shouted for me to stop.

CHAPTER THIRTY-EIGHT

WHEN I GOT BACK TO THE APARTMENT, the ladies had breakfast waiting. It couldn't feed a Chihuahua but I wasn't complaining. I knew the Doumer's were giving us their food. Daphne put her French roll on my plate and began biting her nails. She was worried about our meeting with the leader of the Resistance, I could tell. Then she got out of the borrowed robe and into her black number. She fussed with her hair all morning, first trying braids, then a bun, then a roll. Finally she let it hang loose. The whole time she must've been hoping we'd see Jack later in the afternoon and that he'd sweep her off her feet. Hairdos are important in scenes like that.

We returned to the Resistance flat with half-an-hour to spare. We knocked but no one answered. We heard the elevator working, and then stomping on the plank floors that led to the flat. I guessed right away that the man was Dédée's father—the lady who'd invented the Comet Line. Same Roman nose and cat eyes. He didn't say one word until we were back inside the apartment.

He asked us to call him Paul Moreau, even though his name was really Frédéric De Jongh. I let him know my code name was "The Dauphin" and he liked that. The saleslady came in a few minutes later with a paper bag full of coal. She let me put it in the stove and light the fire. I took a seat on one of the crates and Daphne and Monsieur sat in the two upholstered chairs. The saleslady stood behind a dusty curtain, looking down at the street, on watch for the Gestapo.

"I'm so relieved you've found us," he said. "We assumed that either Paul-Henri hadn't passed on the package, or that a boy couldn't decipher the code. We were very concerned when you hadn't come immediately."

I looked down at my sneakers. "And Paul-Henri?" I asked.

"Paul-Henri was a good man. He'll be missed."

"And what happened to the person we was supposed to meet in Mons—the man carrying bonbons?"

"We don't know. He's missing. We fear the agent was betrayed and taken by the Gestapo. Sad business." He sucked in his lips. "You're here now and we can proceed with plans to get you to Spain."

Daphne shook her head wildly and her hairdo had its most dramatic effect. She wasn't going anywhere without Jack. Dédée's father held his breath. Right before he exhaled, his cheeks looked like they were stuffed with tennis balls. "And tell me again, Mademoiselle Daphne," he said. "Why do you think your fiancé is still alive? Did you actually dig up the grave?"

She said, "I admit the thought had crossed my mind, but…"

"If you didn't dig up your fiancé's grave, how can

you be certain he is not in it?"

I looked at Daphne. She said, "There was no record of Jack being buried in Dunkirk, and then we spoke with Monsignor André—the priest who does the burial ceremonies. The body taken from Jack's plane was a German's—he had a swastika tattoo, for heaven's sake. And a girlfriend name Fräulein Sabine."

Dédée's father lit a cigarette, thinking deeply. His eyes squinted like something was coming to him. He tossed the match into an ashtray before speaking. "A man was in contact with us last week—here in Paris—identifying himself as Lieutenant John Mooney of the RAF 121st Eagle Squadron."

Daphne sat up straight in her chair and clapped her hands. Dédée's father put his hand on hers, stopping her.

"Listen first," he said. "The Lieutenant was to meet with us again to discuss the details for an evacuation. We made him aware there would be a delay. We were stalling for time. You see—we didn't trust this man. We were working under the assumption that Lieutenant Mooney had been killed in action and that his body had been taken to Dunkirk."

"But now you know that it wasn't Jack's body your people saw being removed from the Spitfire. So it had to have been Jack who approached you," said Daphne.

Dédée's father shook his head sadly. "Let me try to explain. We can't evacuate these airmen fast enough. Many must remain in safe houses here in Paris and elsewhere along the line. The Germans know this. They know perfectly well that every airman who gets back to Britain will be returning in a Spitfire—or worse for them—in a bomber. That's why our work is so important. It's why people are willing to risk their lives."

"Go on," said Daphne.

"The man calling himself Lieutenant John Mooney asked to be put in touch with the other Royal Air Force pilots hiding in Paris."

"My brother is probably lonely—on his own for months now—"

He interrupted me. "When things have gone wrong, men we were shielding—men under our protection—have been exposed and taken by the Gestapo. Some have ended up in German internment camps. A few of our agents as well. Have you heard of Ravensbrück?"

Daphne turned white. "Is Jack in Ravensbrück?"

"You misunderstand me," he said.

The saleslady went to a porcelain sink that was fastened to the wall and filled a glass with water. When Daphne recovered, Dédée's father explained everything. Because the Resistance believed Jack was dead, they'd had the Lieutenant followed to a townhouse in the 16th arrondissement—Villa Jocelyn, to be exact. The Lieutenant entered a building that evening, and the agent staked out the place all night. In the morning the same man left the building, but this time dressed in the uniform of a German Luftwaffe major. The agent was a hundred percent certain it was the same man who claimed to be Jack.

I asked if there could be any mistake.

"No. Absolutely not," spit out the saleslady. I wondered if she was the agent who'd stalked the man.

"Our agent followed the Luftwaffe major to Paris Orly Aéroport," said Dédée's father. "The Germans are using it as a military airfield—fighter command, actually. The agent watched as he was admitted into the base. We now know this man to be *Flieger-Stabsingemieur* Hans Dorfmann of the German Luftwaffe. Do you know that Hermann Göring commands the Luftwaffe? Some of these men are evil. And think—who could impersonate an RAF pilot better than a pilot himself? Had they succeeded, there would have been deadly consequences— perhaps for many."

I remembered the pretty town of Arras, where 240 French Resistance members were executed in the citadel. In broad daylight the Nazis lined them up against the church wall and shot them one by one. Their horrified families stood on watching, waiting to collect the bodies.

"Fortunately, Dorfmann failed to get inside of our operation," said Dédée's father.

This had me thinking. So what if a Nazi was impersonating my brother? It changed nothing. Jack was out there somewheres and we needed to find him. Monsieur De Jongh interrupted my thoughts: "This is the troubling part," he said. "We believe the Gestapo knew you were heading to Dunkirk in search of your fiancé's burial place."

"Dédée told the missing agent that I was going to Dunkirk?" asked Daphne.

"I'm afraid so. She told him everything. We believe

also that this is how they knew Paul-Henri would be at the train station in Mons. The other agent was loyal to the bone, but we worry that under pressure—you understand?" He paused for a moment, rose and filled a glass with water, stood by the sink and drank. He was stalling. Setting the glass on the edge of the sink, he returned to his chair. "You say a priest told you there was a German in your fiancé's uniform?

"Monsignor André at Église Saint-Éloi Cathedral," answered Daphne.

"Mademoiselle Daphne. Get used to this simple fact: men can be bought."

I jumped to defend the Monsignor—he had to be legit because he'd taken my confession.

"I'm not surprised," said the saleslady. "And what did you tell him?"

Daphne got hysterical. She jumped up and shouted, "What possible reason could he have had to lie to us?" She blinked back tears. The saleslady walked her back to the chair and put a hand on Daphne's shoulder after she'd sat again.

Dédée's father said, "It seems you were set up to believe that Lieutenant Mooney was alive—so that you would then relay that information to us. This Major Hans Dorfmann—impersonating Lieutenant Mooney—would then approach us and we would have believed him."

I remembered the ledger book at the cemetery. Jack's name must've been written there and then crossed out right before we arrived. The Monsignor—*the dirty rotten*—. He'd probably exchanged my dollars so's he could mail them to the German American Bund. *Double-crosser.*

"But the plot didn't work," I said.

"Because you waited a fortnight to tell us." I knew what a fortnight was.

"All 'cause I forgot about the crossword puzzle?" I sat there frozen. I couldn't even move my pinkie finger. So Jack was buried in that cemetery, after all. I'd stood a few feet from his grave and didn't put flowers on it.

He outlined the plan, but I was having trouble following, feeling like somebody had slipped me a Mickey. I had to ask him to repeat.

"So we proceed with our original mission of getting the two of you back to England. Really, you aren't safe here. The Gestapo will still be looking for you in connection with the events at the munitions factory. They followed you to Dunkirk, they may have followed you to Paris."

"What will be done to stop the Luftwaffe major from impersonating Jack," Daphne asked, anger bubbling up in her. Her nostrils were flaring like a dragon's.

"We have severed communication with him."

"But he'll try to make contact with the Resistance in another way," I said, my head finally clearing and my eyes focusing again after the shock I'd had.

"You may be right, but now that we are aware of his true identity, we'll continue to stall him, making excuses and not letting him know we're onto him. Dorfmann is not only hoping we will introduce him to RAF airmen, but that we'll take him along the line to Spain. They are hoping to expose the entire Comet line. Can you imagine?"

"I want to see this Luftwaffe major," said Daphne.

"Why?" I asked, no fight left in me.

"It's impossible Mademoiselle. And what could be the point?" said the saleslady.

Dédée's father suggested we continue to stay at Sophie's, since we'd already been there for a while without being detected. He warned us to stay inside as much as possible.

We got up to go but Daphne turned and asked if they could help find Aunt Dalia. Both of them shook their heads no. "Out of our scope, I'm afraid," said Dédée's father. "I'm sorry. I know how hard this is for you. We've lost so many good people in this war." He squeezed Daphne's hand. "Return to this flat in three days time. By then my daughter will have arrived in Paris and she'll have made arrangements for your evacuation over the Pyrenees Mountains. She may even want to escort you herself. Come at the same hour. Bring all your belongings. But pack light."

"What a bleeding conundrum," said Daphne, digging her fingernails into her palm.

CHAPTER THIRTY-NINE

I LEFT THE FLAT WITH DAPHNE and followed her down Boulevard Saint-Germain-des-Prés, hoping she'd enter a Metro station and we'd head back to Sophie's. But we passed several by and kept on walking. We crossed over the river and onto an island. My feet were killing me but I didn't say a peep. Soon we stood before a huge church, the largest I'd ever seen in my life—bigger than Saint Pat's in New York City. Daphne went straight inside, even though she was half-Anglican.

"You sure you're allowed in?" I said.

"The synagogues have all been closed. Notre-Dame will have to do."

It was dark inside the church until my eyes adjusted. Even after, the only light came from high-up windows that looked like kaleidoscopes. A million different colors swirled around in the space. Hundreds of chairs were lined in rows and facing the altar, which seemed like a million miles away. I took the seat next to Daphne. She closed her eyes, bent her head, and began to pray. Tears dripped from the tips of her long eyelashes. We stayed like that for ages—Daphne lost to herself, and me looking up at them gorgeous windows trying hard to hold it together and not be a baby.

The windows made me dizzy, especially when they started gyrating. Faster and faster they spun, until I thought they'd fly out of the window frames and kill us. I imagined a hundred shards of multi-colored glass sticking from Jack's body. I closed my eyes tight and ducked, waiting for the end. That didn't help any: colors flashed at the back of my eyelids, pounding on my brain. It only stopped once the sun wasn't shining through the windows anymore. After that, cold came up from the stone floor and into the holes in my sneakers, sending a shiver through my whole body.

Like a ghost's voice, I heard my ma weeping. Then my sister Nancy joined in. Next Da began wailing. Last came Mary screeching like chalk on a blackboard. They were driving me crazy and I ordered the voices to stop.

I wanted to talk, but I kept quiet. Everybody knows it's rude to interupt somebody while they're praying. But at times like that, thinking was a bad idea: the imagination picks all the sad scenes.

My mind was filled with Jack the last time we were together. He'd come home after flight training in Canada, right before shipping out to England. Crossed the border during a leave—illegally, because he'd lost his American citizenship swearing allegiance to the king. Jack was wearing his Royal Air Force uniform with sergeant strips on the sleeves and a duffel bag hung from his shoulder. We went to Jones Beach and all the girls were going mad for Jack, even before he stripped down to his boxers. Two short days and we were seeing him off at the Greyhound station. When the bus pulled in, he grabbed me and whispered in my ear: "Don't forget me, kid."

Why'd he think I would?

A man passed by each aisle and handed me two sheets of paper, one for Daphne, in case she decided to sing along. A girl stepped up on a platform near the altar and a spotlight lit up her white robe. On the paper were the words for psalms and the musical notes to go with them. The words were in Latin, which I happened to know. The girl in the robe began singing. She sang like an angel.

Daphne stayed praying. I focused on the girl on stage, looking at the paper, trying to follow the words—not singing myself. It all had to do with how good God was. About hope and about trusting God. I tried to do that but it was too hard. It came to me then: God had let me down. He'd let down my ma and da, my sister Nancy, and even Mary. Even her. I tossed the papers on the ground and poked Daphne—maybe a little too hard. "Let's blow this joint," I said.

She stood to rise and we left the church. It was getting to be pitch dark. Lights were coming on in cafés and in the windows of apartments. Street lamps were coming on one by one, and the sound was like night.

"What now? I asked Daphne.

"Revenge," was all she said.

"Do we start with the priest?"

"No, with the Luftwaffe major. Then the priest."

"How?"

"An arrow to the heart. I told you, I'm an expert archer."

CHAPTER FORTY

BACK AT SOPHIE'S, Daphne wrapped the bow and arrows in a bedsheet. She looked my way and her eyes gave away what she was about to say. "It's best you stay here, Thomas."

"No, Daphne. No." I stamped my foot hard.

"Bloody hell-O! I'm about to assassinate a Nazi. Thomas, have you any idea what the consequences might be if I'm caught?"

She seen the backbone sticking from my shirt. It told her I was coming with her and there was no way on earth to stop me. "Promise me you'll run if there's trouble," she said. "Promise me you'll run back here."

Behind my back I crossed my fingers, then I promised.

Daphne asked Sophie for a map of Paris, not letting on that our plans were to eliminate *Flieger-Stabsingemieur* Hans Dorfmann. We located the 16th arrondissement, then Villa Jocelyn: a tiny street that ran off of Avenue Victor Hugo, of all places. A street that length couldn't have many houses on it. If the Luftwaffe major returned to his apartment, we was going to know it.

We told the Doumer family we might be spending a night or two away and not to worry. They looked worried anyway, especially Juliette, who hid my socks so's I wouldn't go. That wasn't enough to stop me.

The Metro took us to the Rue de la Pompe station and a few minutes later on we stood in front of a black iron gate. It blocked the entrance to Villa Jocelyn. I rattled the gate, but it was locked.

"It's an *auteuil*, a very exclusive street where fabulously wealthy people dwell," said Daphne.

"Like a country club on the North Shore of Long Island?"

"I suppose so."

The gate wasn't very tall and I climbed over. Daphne tossed her bundle over the fence and then followed it, even though she was wearing a dress. We walked from one end of the street to the other. It took all of two minutes. We picked a position mid-way down the street with a good view of the whole length, just inside a doorway. Daphne unwrapped the bow and arrows.

We waited.

Several times the gate was unlocked and a car came rolling into the *auteuil*, but the passengers were never in German uniforms. The street was quiet and we picked up voices as people walked from their cars to their front doors. Daphne said that all of them, so far, were French.

We started getting drowsy and I came up with the idea to take turns napping. I let Daphne sleep first. She flopped on the ground and rolled up into a tight ball, getting her new outfit dirty. But she didn't seem to care.

"I could die right now," she said before nodding off.

Hours ticked by like this. The French liked to stay out late, and some of the residents arrived home in the wee hours of the morning—drunk as skunks. One lady sang a French song, off key and loud enough to wake the dead. The day began to dawn and still no Luftwaffe officer.

"It's only a matter of waiting and being patient," Daphne said.

We perked up when traffic picked up. Noise came from Rue de Victor Hugo—honking cars and other morning sounds: accordion gates opening, garbage men emptying cans, street sweepers, and boys hawking news-papers. A lady strolled by carrying a bag of French bread, which I was sorely tempted to snatch. Daphne went to fetch herself some black coffee. She brought me back a cup of hot cocoa with marshmallows, only it was imita-tion and tasted like mud.

Then at about ten o'clock, we watched as a Rolls Royce came out of a garage and rolled toward the locked gate. Our eyes fixed on the chauffeur, who got out to open the lock, then drove the car just outside the *autiel* entrance. He parked and got out of the car, so as to lock the gate again.

I heard the roar of a 500cc motorbike, coming out of a side driveway. We watched dumbfounded as a Luftwaffe officer—in full uniform and sunglasses, white silk scarf trailing behind him—came shooting out of a driveway riding a German motorbike. Them things go zero to a hundred in seconds flat. Before we knew what happened, Hans Dorfmann was rocketing down the road, through the open gate and out of sight.

"Well at least we know where he lives," said Daphne. "Now it's simply a matter of waiting for him to return."

We spent the whole day walking back and forth. At all times at least one of our four eyes was on the building where Hans Dorfmann lived. We each took a short break to relieve ourselves in a café bathroom. And once Daphne kept watch while I ran to a market and brought back snacks: *faux* cream puffs to be exact.

Night dropped again and still no Luftwaffe major. My spunk began to weaken—and that's the truth—but Daphne's remained solid as the Hoover Dam.

The gate kept opening and closing for cars, most of them very expensive: Daimlers, Mercedes, and once a Bugatti Coupe. Whenever Daphne spotted a German car she said, "In bed with the Germans." Then she'd spit on the ground. I'd never seen her so sore. Somebody was getting the brunt end of that, and I was glad it would be a Nazi.

At half an hour past midnight Daphne looked at her wristwatch and yawned. The gate opened again, and this time, instead of two headlights pointing in our eyes, there was one. We hid in an entrance across the street from where the Luftwaffe major lived: Hans Dorfmann—the Nazi who was impersonating my brother and threatening to expose the Comet line.

The transmission shifted gears as the motorcycle rolled down the street, its headlight blinding us. Daphne readied her bow and arrow. The motorbike swung into a driveway next to Dorfmann's building. I looked at the Luftwaffe pilot's back, and was close enough—my eyes sharp enough—to see he wore the insignia of a Luftwaffe *Flieger-Stabsingemieur*.

"Are we sure it's him?" I whispered. I'd never killed a man in cold blood and my knees began to shake.

"I'm sure," said Daphne, in a voice so low and yet so fearsome, it made my hair stand up on end. "And besides, what's the worst thing that happens? We kill the wrong Nazi?"

We watched as Hans Dorfmann cut the engine of the motorbike. The headlight went dark. He was hidden in shadow, but there was still enough light for Daphne to sight her target. Dorfmann swung his leg over the motorcycle seat and with both hands on the handlebars he lifted the bike onto its stand. I looked at Daphne, "It's now or never," I said in a shaky voice.

She pulled her right elbow back, right fist and feathers to her armpit, the bow and arrow tip steadied with her left thumb and index finger, the string straining and bending the bow. Her form was perfect, taking the correct body stance: feet spread apart, body perpendicular to her target, left foot pointing toward it. Aiming at the bull's-eye on the side of our barn in East Hempstead, she'd be about to decimate Hitler's nose. She squinted one eye like she was looking in a riflescope. Highlighting every syllable, she shouted his name, "*Flieger—Stab—singe—mieur*—Hans—Dorf—mann!"

She wanted to look the man in the eyes as the arrow flew at his heart. A shot in the back was too good for him. Better that he have a moment to mourn his choices. Her arm pulled the string even more tautly. I was afraid it would break, but Daphne wanted the arrow to make its deadliest impact.

The man turned his face to us and seen exactly what awaited him.

I had my eye on the tip of the arrow and followed its path as it flew from the bow, whooshing across the street and hitting its mark. Even in the dark, I could see the red-feather-tipped arrow sticking out of the Nazi's chest.

He groaned, "Awwwwh," as he began staggering toward Daphne—one hand on the arrow, one unbuttoning his jacket—reaching for his Luger, no doubt.

I yelled, "Run, Daphne!"

Insanely, she took a step out from the entranceway so that she stood illuminated by a street lamp—making the perfect target. I didn't know what got into her. We'd be lucky to make it to Ravensbrück alive.

Then the Luftwaffe major spoke something—one word—almost in a whisper. But the street was deadly quiet and gust of wind was coming from his back, bringing his word to us. Sounded like he'd said "Jeepers."

Daphne dropped her bow, letting it crash to the ground. "Oh no," she said, her voice all choked up.

The man stepped into the light. My eyes were still on the arrow, which I seen had missed its mark and was sticking out of his shoulder blade—not his heart.

"Sweetheart," he said, "I know I haven't written in a

while, but *really* Daphne, this is extreme."

My brother tried to grin but it was hard with the pain he was in.

Daphne started bawling.

CHAPTER FORTY-ONE

WHEN I STEPPED INTO THE LAMPLIGHT, my brother yanked the arrow out of his shoulder, ran across the street, picked me up, hugged me to him, and tossed me into the air. I felt like bursting. My jacket was all bloody but so what?

"I knew there'd be trouble the minute I took my eye off you," said Jack, "but honest to God—I'm flabbergasted." He stood there in the street looking me up and down, his hands on his hips. Scratching his head, the Luftwaffe pilot's cap went lopsided. "I thought the time you ran away to Coney Island took the cake, but this beats all."

This was a real complement. I was beaming. I'd forgotten all about the time I went to beg the rollercoaster operator to take me on as his apprentice. That coaster had an unparalleled 58.6-degree drop and a top speed of 60 miles per hour. A cop ratted on me to my ma. She sent Jack to get me. The two of us took a few spins on the Cyclone. My stomach was so upside down that I threw up on Jack's shoes. On the drive home he said he couldn't blame me for trying. Charles Lindbergh himself said it was the best roller coaster in America.

Jack put one arm around Daphne's waist and one around my shoulder, squeezing it to him. "Awwwwh!" he groaned, clutching the arrow wound. As we walked up the steps, I felt him kiss the top of my head.

"Jack, darling," said Daphne, "You shan't break off the engagement simply because I tried to kill you, will you?"

"Steady on old girl," he said with a British accent. I couldn't believe my ears. I should've paid more attention to Lady Sopwith. He bent down and kissed Daphne on the lips, hard. When they came up for air, he said, "Honey pie, it's only a flesh wound." He said it like a New York cabbie.

My brother was back.

Jack stood straight up, trying to look chipper but staggering a little. "Why, I feel like I got shot by cupid!" He kissed Daphne again.

When we reached the door I was standing so close to him that—by mistake—I stepped on the heel of his flight boot. The townhouse door handle was shaped like a lion's body; into the lion's open jaws you inserted the key. "You do the honors," said Jack, handing the key to me. I opened the door, fingers intact and laughing.

When we entered the townhouse, Daphne let out a hoot. "It looks like Versailles! How ever did you land here, Jacques, darling?"

"I thought you'd like it, honey. I picked it with you in mind."

"Oh get out, Jack," she said. "Really?"

"Actually the place chose me."

"Well, who wouldn't?" She stood up on her toes and they rubbed noses like Eskimos.

Time to do a little exploring, I thought.

It wasn't like any joint I'd been in, unless No-tre-Dame counted. The ceiling was five times taller than me, painted with chubby-cheeked cherubs and clouds, so I felt like I was looking up into heaven. The trim on the walls was, I'm pretty sure, solid gold. A chandelier in the dining room looked like thousands of diamonds. And, if it crashed on you, forget it.

I didn't want to get lost, so I made my way back to the lovebirds. Jack's shirt was open and Daphne was pouring something from a little silver flask onto the arrow wound and swabbing it with a handkerchief. Whatever she was using was strong as moonshine, by the way Jack was moaning.

"Say, this is a mighty swell place," I said. "Who lived here? A gangster?"

"No, a banker—Awwwwh! I take it from the building caretaker, who comes to check up on things—and he's on our side, by the way—Ouch!—that the fella fled to the south of France right before the Germans rolled into town."

"I'm feeling a little light-headed," said Daphne, looking at blood on her hand. "You'll have to take your jacket and shirt off, Jack. Is there an old bedsheet we can use to make bandages?"

Jack looked down at the Luftwaffe uniform and said, "Let me get out of this monkey suit."

"Please do, darling. It's giving me the willies. And why are you wearing it in the first place?"

Obviously he's a spy, I thought, without saying it out loud. I seen the poster in London: *Loose Lips Sink Ships*.

Daphne turned to me, "And while Jack changes, let's you and I see what we can rustle up in the kitchen. That is, if we ever locate the kitchen."

All that we found was a couple tins of ham, a loaf of French bread, a small wedge of cheese with green mold on top, and a half full bottle of cider—the kind that's boozy.

"Jack's living the bachelor life, I'm happy to see," said Daphne.

We took everything with us and made our way back to the living room, where Jack now sat decked out in a tweed suit. His shirt collar was opened at the neck and instead of a tie, a white silk scarf wrapped around his throat. On his feet were brown wing-tipped shoes worn with argyle socks. A felt beret tilted on the side of his head. He looked upper crust—I hardly recognized him. The only thing that spoiled the picture was the sling around his shoulder. When he noticed me admiring his new outfit, he said, "Courtesy of the previous tenant. I hope he doesn't mind me borrowing them."

Daphne sat close to Jack on the sofa, her legs folded behind her, knees resting on Jack's. I sat on the floor near the fireplace. The room was freezing. Next to the fireplace was a nice stack of wood and I couldn't resist. As I made a fire I asked, "Why were you wearing that Nazi suit, anyway?"

"It started when I shot the Gestapo agent who made the mistake of coming to my airplane all on his lonesome."

"Your Enfield service revolver?"

"I was wounded: broken nose, dislocated shoulder and a cannon bullet had come from below and hit my right heel. There was blood all over my face, so it wasn't hard to play dead. The Kraut didn't see it coming."

I said: "You weren't scared, were you, Jack?"

"Call me Jack*rabbit*. Sure I was scared."

"I'd 'a been terrified!" I said in a rush. "I'd pass out with fright! I'd of—I'd have—VOMITED!"

Jack pulled me to him. "I was shaking in my boots, Tommy."

I felt like a paratrooper whose chute opens after the ripcord being stuck. I never had to fake it with Jack. He'd still be my brother no matter what, even if I was a jackrabbit like him, even if being in a war was petrifying and I wasn't brave all the time. So long as I had Jack, my feet were never going to touch ground.

"Well," he said, jumping back into his story, "that's when I had the idea to switch clothes with the Gestapo agent, thinking it might throw the Germans off long enough for me to get out of there. Lucky for me, a couple of farmers came along and helped me get the German into the cockpit. We put his motorcycle in the back of their truck—didn't want to give the whole works away." Jack took a piece of French bread and stuffed it into his mouth.

"Did the Gestapo agent have a swastika tattooed

on his neck?" asked Daphne.

"How did you know?" Jack talked with his mouth full.

"Mother of God!" I said. The priest in Dunkirk—Monsignor André—wasn't lying after all. He told us the truth about the Nazi dressed in Jack's flight uniform—the one with the girlfriend named Sabine and the swastika tattoo. I was terrified by the idea that we'd almost assassinated a priest. There weren't enough Hail Mary's in the history of the world to have gotten me out of that mess.

"Then I had a run in with an SS Waffen *Truppführer*," said Jack. "I was dressed in the Gestapo getup and he struck up a conversation with me. That's when I tried out my German for the first time since high school."

"A nun taught you?" I asked.

"Sweetest nun I ever met," he said. "The SS fella asked where I'd picked up the New York accent. He didn't like the answer."

Jack crossed himself. There was silence in the room—like a church.

Then he said, "The SS uniform came in handy later, when I had to break a buddy of mine out of a German prison. He worked for the Resistance and was my only hope of getting out of here." Jack got a big grin on his face. "You should have seen it—marched right into the prison like I was Adolf Hitler himself. I was in the nick of time too, because my buddy Pierre's face looked like a welterweight who'd stupidly challenged Joe Louis for the heavyweight title. I roughhoused Pierre all the way to the front entrance, acting like a jerk. Pierre was an actor before the war. He started squealing and pleading for his life—me yelling death threats at him the whole time. By then I'd ditched the Long Island accent."

"Did thou do it reading Shakespeare?" I asked.

"You're a funny one!" said Jack. "No, I did it eavesdropping on Luftwaffe pilots."

"Spy work!"

He put his finger to his lips and shifted his eyes around the room. Then he laughed and whispered in my ear: "Wait'll I get together with Churchill. Have I got stories to tell."

He was smiling, but I saw his teeth clench as the light went out of his eyes. Jack was keeping the bad stuff from us, putting the positive spin on his stories. That was Jack: always the upbeat one.

"My God, it sounds terribly dangerous," said Daphne, putting her hands over her ears. "I'm not sure I want to hear this."

Jack looked at me. He knew I was itching for more. I leaned in so's I could catch every word. "It was my friend's idea to find a Luftwaffe pilot and steal his identity. And we picked the right one too, because he had a key for these digs in his pocket." He waved a hand around the room. "The plan was for me to take a Messerschmitt and fly back to England. Risky, I know, but I was getting tired of starvation."

"What went wrong?" I asked. Obviously he was still in Paris.

"Twice I've tried—planes from two different German airfields. Got shot down by the RAF the first time, which I have to say, made my day. I bailed out in the Channel and swam back to France. You know I'm a strong swimmer, Tommy. Remember when I was a lifeguard at Jones Beach?"

He slapped his knee. "Problem was, I had to flip the plane upside down to drop out and I busted up a couple of ribs striking a vertical stabilizer." He opened the buttons on his shirt and showed me the scars. You get the Purple Heart for scars like that. "It was a long and painful swim, that was."

He buttoned his shirt again while still talking: "Second time the Luftwaffe chased me from the base. I managed to get away into the clouds. And the plane didn't have enough fuel. But I shot down a German bomber headed for England before ditching the Messerschmitt in a field. Why, that plane's sitting there right now, waiting for—"

"What happened to your Resistance friend, Pierre?" I asked. "Couldn't he help you get out through Spain?"

"He got caught a second time, and I wasn't able to help him—they sent him east is what I figure." Jack stopped short. His Adam's apple moved up and down and his eyes watered up. "He was as true blue a fella as I've ever known. He was helping Jews to hide, he—"

"Oh, Jack." Daphne started tearing up. "It's all too monstrous."

All the life went out of Jack's face. "Worse than monstrous. Things are rough here for Jewish folks." He took her hands in his. "Babe, we've got to get you the heck out of here. Alaska wouldn't be far enough. No joke, this is no place for the likes of you. I've seen some things with my own two eyes. Got to Paris in time for the last big roundup."

"When they took whole families to the Vélodrome?" I asked.

I knew Daphne was thinking about her aunt Dalia when she said, "Where did they send them? La—lab—our—camps?"

Jack ran his fingers through his hair nervously. "Worse than that," he said. "Pierre had a friend staking out the place where they took people from the Vélodrome, an internment camp outside of Paris—town called Drancy. The Germans were loading people into cattle cars. One of the train engineers was overheard talking about Poland."

I wondered why Jack was delivering such a hard blow, instead of "humoring" Daphne. Then it came to me: he needed her to know what kind of danger she was in. He wasn't pulling any punches. The next punch was a woozy.

"There's talk about death camps." Jack kissed Daphne's forehead, not a sloppy kiss but gentle." Daphne rested her head on Jack's shoulder and was real quiet. She closed her eyes and gulped hard. We both knew Jack was right and we had to get her out of here fast.

"It's a rotten trick telling people they're a superior race," he said. "The world's lousy with it. Now we're getting it from all angles: the "Aryan Race" on one side and the *Yamato-damashii* on the other, everybody in between getting squeezed out."

"What's a *Yamato-damashii?*" I asked.

"Japanese version of the Master Race. Thugs always think they're better than the next guy, that the other fella oughta be his slave: lick his boots and wash his dirty underwear. You know those kids, Tommy, who pick the wings off flies and drown kittens in toilet bowls? Well, if we lose this war they'll grow up to be Stormtroopers."

I shuffled closer to Daphne and put my head on her knee. I felt terrible-bad about her aunt Dalia. Meanwhile Jack was telling us about what was happening to the Jewish Parisians.

"First the Germans took away their radios, then bicycles. Next they disconnected their phones and forbid them from using pay phones. Then came the curfew. They're not allowed in parks or theaters. Not even in cafés."

"No cafés?" said Daphne, sniffling. She started picking a scab off her knuckle. "My aunt Dalia must have been miserable."

"I'll say," said Jack. "Swell lady like that…broke my heart."

We lifted our heads and stared at Jack with puzzled expressions. Daphne was the first to speak:

"It almost sounds as if you actually *met* my aunt."

"Where do you think I headed first thing I got to Paris? I needed a place to hide, didn't I?"

Daphne made a bunch of confuse sounds: "Huh? Uh? Whah?"

Turned out Daphne'd been upset, knowing her aunt wouldn't be able to attend the wedding because of the war. She'd made out an invitation anyway and ordered Jack to carry it to the post office, even though he swore it was a waste of time and a stamp.

"Gold," said Jack. "It's not a name you forget. But the address? I racked my brain to no avail. Soon as I arrived in town, I started asking around. Didn't take long before I was pointed to Montparnasse. Remember? You told me Dalia lived near all the artsy types. From there it was a simple matter of asking at the snazziest restaurants. *Dalia Gold, food critic.* Sure, they knew your aunt. Before long I was knocking on her door, holding out that black & white of you—and introducing myself as the future nephew-in-law."

"She took you in?" asked Daphne.

"Sure she did. And we hit it off like gangbusters."

Half Jack's mouth smiled, the other half drooped. I was waiting for the shoe to drop—boot more like it. You could feel it coming. Daphne's aunt was taken exactly one month after Jack crashed in Belgium. He couldn't of been with her long.

"Soon after that I made contact with Pierre and mentioned where I was staying. He's the one warned me that your aunt's apartment wasn't a safe place, that another round up of Jewish folks was in the works. Then, early morning of the 16th—July this was—Pierre showed up at the door in a panic. Said the French Police were taking Jewish families by the thousands and that we'd better get out fast. And somehow we had to throw the Germans off our tracks."

I clapped my hands, "You used one of the uniforms again!"

"Bingo. While Dalia threw things into a bag, I got into the Gestapo getup. Pierre played the part of an undercover French policeman. We slipped out quiet and then started pounded on your aunt's door—loud enough to wake the whole building. See, we needed an audience so when the real police came calling, the neighbors would say someone'd beat 'em to it. A crowd of well-wishers cheered us on as we escorted your aunt to the waiting car. Would've made your stomach turn, Daphne."

Madame Barrault, I thought.

Daphne rocketed from the couch. "Aunt Dalia! Aunt Dalia!" She ran for the hallway, opening doors and calling out for her aunt—like Jack had been hiding the old lady the whole time, waiting to spring a surprise.

He looked at me and shrugged his shoulders. "It kills me to disappoint her."

By now I'd figured out Aunt Dalia wasn't there. Daphne came back into the room with her hands on her hips. "Where'd you put my aunt?"

Poor Aunt Dalia. Poor, poor, Aunt Dalia. I started to moan when Jack said it:

"A convent."

Nuns!

"Which convent?" Daphne asked.

"I have no idea. A month later and Pierre was arrested. And he's the one who knew the exact location."

Daphne plopped back down on the couch—happy, if you can believe it. I'd go rescue the aunt but there didn't seem to be any way to find her. France had a million convents, Jack said. She might be anywhere.

"We'd better get to Spain then, right?" I said. "We'll get a boat to America!"

"England, please." Daphne looked worried. "My wedding dress is in England."

"Funny you should say that," said Jack. "I've been having the darndest time getting in touch with the Resistance again. I made a new contact after Pierre was taken—this one with a different group—and then the fella vanished. Poof! And since then, I've had a helluva time finding anyone else. If I didn't know any better, I'd think they were trying to avoid me."

"They followed you to this building," said Daphne. "Then watched you leave in the Luftwaffe uniform."

"O—h! Now I get it. So I take it you two have a contact here in Paris?"

"Yes. And if it weren't for Thomas and I being able to vouch for you, you might never have gotten back to England."

"How's Ma?" asked Jack. "Gee, I miss her."

Just then I realized I was headed for the whooping of my life. I'd probably be grounded until I was eighteen and old enough to leave home. But I looked at my brother sitting in front of me—living and breathing and in Technicolor—and right then, it didn't matter.

"It's a good thing we came, huh, Jack?" I said.

He answered by grabbing my hands and swinging

me around in a circle. My feet were flying in the air and they knocked over the bottle of cider.

"Will you be going on any more missions?" I asked.

"Maybe one," said Jack, and Daphne slapped him.

CHAPTER FORTY-TWO

Somewhere above France

IT'S APPROXIMATELY 17:50 HOURS.

Sheldon Edner, who is "Sel" to his friends, and Reade Tilley of the RAF 121st Eagle Squadron, are returning to England and only a few miles from the coastline of France when they spot a German Focke-Wulf 190 on the starboard side, about three miles away. The enemy aircraft immediately sees them and disappears into the clouds.

Edner and Tilley, both flying Spitfires, give chase. They are about 25 miles from the coast when they manage to get within range, and Edner gives the first burst of five seconds and closes in from 300 to 100 yards. He sees the shells ricochet off the enemy aircraft, which goes into a spin and is losing altitude.

But close to the ground, the German comes out of the spin, levels off, and circles back around, taking a position behind Edner's tail.

Tilley gets behind the enemy aircraft and fires a long blast from 100 yards astern. Meanwhile, the FW 190 is firing the whole time at Edner's plane, which takes several hits.

Between the Spitfire and the FW 190, many RAF pilots consider the German plane to be the superior. It sports two 13-millimeter cannons above the engine, two 20-millimeter cannons in the wing roots, and two more cannons in the outboard wing.

Edner is now losing altitude and smoke is coming from his left wing. Tilley attacks the FW 190 once more, using the remainder of his ammunition. The German pilot now drops to 1000 feet to give Edner chase, and Tilley looks on helplessly.

Tilley sees, about a mile from his starboard side, a Messerschmitt at about 9,000 feet. It drops down out of the clouds and comes up along the side his Spitfire. He's so close to the German plane that he's able to make eye contact with the Luftwaffe pilot.

The Luftwaffe pilot gives Tilley the thumbs up.

Tilley looks over dumbfounded and says, "Well, I'll be a son-of-a-gun."

He watches as the Messerschmitt comes within 50 yards of the FW 190 and gives a long blast. Tilley sees dense smoke coming from the FW 190's port engine and slight smoke coming from the craft's starboard engine. The FW 190 immediately loses height and speed, and then goes into another tailspin—this one from which it doesn't recover.

Edner and Tilley watch as the enemy plane crashes in a French field.

Edner assumes that Tilley made the kill.

Tilley knows otherwise.

Sel Edner is on reserve fuel by now, and flying low to the ground, and his Spit is shot up bad. He heads toward the English Channel. He is weaving to the left and right hoping to avoid fire from the Messerschmitt but none comes.

When the two RAF Eagle Squadron pilots cross back over the Channel headed to England, the Messerschmitt tips its wings and heads back toward Paris.

Lieutenant Reade Tilley is going to be making one heck of a report when he gets back to RAF Rochford.

EPILOGUE

I LET JULIETTE KISS ME good-bye. On both cheeks too.

"It will be freezing over the mountain passes," she said handing me back the socks she'd stolen, "you'll be needing these."

Then Dédée escorted us over the Pyrenees Mountains and into free Spain. She guided us to the British Consulate in Bilboa, before making her way back to Belgium. I pray every day that God will keep her safe. I have every reason to hope He will.

From Spain we were taken to Gibraltar—which is really just a big rock that England happens to own. It's stuck out in the Mediterranean Sea, south of Spain.

A fishing boat returned us to England, where Lord and Lady Sopwith were waiting for us with the Rolls. O'Reilly the butler was leering at me as I put my foot back onto English soil. It turns out the Resistance was in touch with British Intelligence and so was Lord Sopwith, because he knew exactly when we'd make landfall. Keep that on the hush-hush, at least until this war is over.

First thing we done was to head straight to a post

office. Lady Sopwith insisted. As Jack handed over our message to the telegraph operator, I could almost hear the telegram boy on the other side of the big ocean yell, "Telegram for Mrs. Mooney."

This one was going to cheer her up.

The Series Continues!

MESSAGE FOR HITLER

By Cate M. Ruane

PROLOGUE

Somewhere in The English Channel

A FISHING BOAT BOBS on choppy waters, as its captain scans the horizon with a spyglass. He tilts his wrist and moonlight illuminates the crystal on his watch.

"They're late," he says.

Inside the cabin, a radio operator taps out a message —the same message he's been sending for more than an hour. He adjusts his headset, as though that will help, then shakes his head, "Negative," he says.

A crewman cranes his neck out the porthole and shouts, "Still no contact, Captain."

Just then, a whitecap rocks the boat, almost capsizing it. The radio operator is thrown against a pile of nets, but manages to hold onto the radio set.

"We have contact!" he yells.

The crewman shouts, "Contact, sir."

"Obviously, you idiots," says the captain as he watches a thousand tons of steel rise from the waters. He waits until the submarine has surfaced, then orders the crew to come up as close as they dare. When the forward hatch swings open, two figures emerge from the belly of the submarine. The crew helps them aboard the fishing boat.

The captain turns toward his new passengers. "Welcome aboard," he says. Noticing their uniforms for the first time, he begins to laugh. He straightens his back and executes a fast and sharp salute, "It is always a pleasure to be of service to the Royal Air Force."

Both passengers turn toward the submarine, bidding its crew farewell. They raise their right arms, palms perfectly flat. "Heil Hitler," they shout in unison. The salute is returned and the hatch shut.

The German U-Boat vanishes below the waters of the English Channel.

The captain says, "Back to England, boys. Nice and slow now."

CHAPTER ONE

London, England

I WAS WARM AND TOASTY in the back seat of the Rolls, on my way to meet my brother Jack in London, when Lord Sopwith—my guardian for the duration—said, "Duncan here will drop me at the Air Ministry, then take you around to the Eagle Club. Will that suit, old boy?"

"Boy oh boy, sir—does it ever!" I said.

My mouth began watering. The American Eagle Club was a joint to boost the morale of Americans serving in the British Armed Forces. They dished up peanut butter and jelly sandwiches on real Wonder bread, and cheeseburgers with fries and a Coke. With any luck, we'd get s'mores for desert—toasted marshmallows and Hershey bars squashed between two crisp graham crackers. Washed down with a Yoo-hoo, it was the perfect meal.

I'd been to the Eagle Club before—a special guest of my brother Jack, who joined up to fly with the Royal Air Force before we Americans had the sense to start fighting off Adolf Hitler. Except for the squadron leader, who was British, all the pilots in my brother's squadron were Yanks. Winston Churchill used the Eagle squadron pilots to get America off the fence. He made sure their photographs appeared in *Life* magazine and *Colliers*, looking dashing in their flight suits, with parachutes strapped on their backs in case they had to jump from a burning airplane. They showed up in Pathé newsreels, dogfighting in their Spitfires against the German Luftwaffe. Getting metals pinned to their chests by the King and Queen of England. A Kansas girl, on a movie date with her Joe Shmoe boyfriend, took one look at those pilots and started swooning. Because of this, every man from sea to shining sea wanted to fight the Nazis. Ma called it propaganda, but it worked.

"I'll be back Sunday night, sir," I told Lord Sopwith. "My brother will take me back to Warfield Hall on a

Triumph motorcycle filled up with high-octane aircraft fuel."

"Then you'll be back in time for dinner, no doubt," said Lord Sopwith, adjusting his 14-karat gold wire frame glasses. "Invite your brother to join Lady Sopwith and me, will you? Just the thing—a good chat with a fly-boy. Puts everything in perspective. Can't have too much theory, what."

Lord Sopwith was an aviation pioneer. His company Hawker Aircraft made the Hurricane—the fighter plane my brother was flying when he shot down his first German plane. My guess was Lord Sopwith was headed to the Air Ministry to discuss his latest invention. He was working on top-secret airplane designs—very hush-hush.

"And you'll be billeted with the squadron?" he asked. "Should be jolly good fun being so close to the action."

We were passing by Downing Street. I rolled down the window, getting ready to wave if I caught sight of the prime minister, Winston Churchill. If you ask me, he got gyped. His house was smaller than the White House pantry.

"Close that window, boy, before we catch our deaths," said Lord Sopwith shivering. He buttoned up his coat and pulled a scarf tight around his neck. Then, to drive home his point, he pulled a handkerchief from his pocket and sneezed into it. I rolled up the window fast. Lord Sopwith is a real gentleman, so he didn't take a look at the booger that came out of his nose. Instead, he folded the handkerchief back into a perfect triangle and tucked it into his pocket.

I said: "I've already sat in a Spitfire, sir. I am learning how to fly one."

Lord Sopwith blew out a puff of air: "It's come to that, has it? God preserve us." He wasn't taking me seriously. It happened all the time, even though I was a hero of the Belgian and French Resistance after rescuing my brother from the Nazis when his plane went down in occupied Europe.

"Really, sir," I said. "I've started my training, just the same way Jack did. He put me in his Spitfire with a blindfold around my head. Had to feel for the instruments and name them one by one. Once I get that right, he'll let me fly the girl. The fellas call it 'feeling the tits and bits.'"

"Rather risqué for a twelve-year-old, what?"

I knew he was dead right, and that my ma wouldn't like Jack using colorful language to refer to the thing that fit into a ladies' brassiere. She wouldn't like him teaching me to fly either. Ma wanted me home to East Hempstead, New York, because she was missing me something awful. Problem was that with the war full on, there was no way for me to cross the Atlantic without getting torpedoed by U-Boats. Last week a German submarine sank the British freighter *Goolistan*. Every living soul on board was now on the bottom of the ocean floor being eaten by catfish.

I was sure grateful to the Sopwiths. While I waited for a safe passage home, they were letting me hole up at Warfield Hall. "It's the thing to do," said Lady Sop.

Everyone lucky enough to own a grand country estate was expected to take in stray children—save them from the German bombs dropping on London. Lady Sop was in cahoots with my ma. Every single day she made me write a letter home, even if all it said was "I'm still alive and kicking." She'd always check the spelling and grammar and make me rewrite the whole letter over if there was one mistake: "Mind your Ps and Qs," she'd say. Which was strange, seeing that I hardly ever used words with the letter Q. I wrote my letters at a special desk made for letter writing. Lady Sop called the desk by its French name, *escritoire*. It had built in letter slots, inkwells, pen stands and matching blotters. There were also secret drawers, designed to confuse thieves. That was where you were supposed to keep the jewels and treasure maps. I checked, but the drawers contained nothing but rubber bands and paperclips. Turned out Lady Sop kept her diamonds in a safe-deposit box at the bank, which was probably a good idea.

If a day came when a letter didn't arrive to East Hempstead, my ma would know I'd been killed in action. Ma knew the Germans were dropping bombs on Southampton, England, near where the Sopwiths lived. There was no hiding the fact—she'd seen it in a newsreel. The Supermarine Aviation Works had factories around Southampton making Spitfires. A Spitfire can go 400 miles an hour and push 600 in a nosedive. That's so fast it will make the pilot black out. When a Luftwaffe pilot sees a Spitfire coming he starts praying. Living at War-field Hall, it being so close to the Supermarine factory, meant my life was in grave peril. Ma was lighting so many candles for me, she said Saint Brendan's Catholic Church looked like the Consolidated Edison power plant.

Duncan, the chauffeur, slid open the glass divider and said, "Whitehall, your lordship." Lord Sopwith pressed a bowler hat to his head, put on a pair of kidskin gloves and waited for Duncan to open the back door.

"Toodle-oo, sir," I said as he exited the Rolls.

The door slammed behind him. He knocked on the glass to get my attention, motioning for me to crank down the window. I figured he'd forgot his attaché case containing top-secrets but then I seen he had it in his hand.

"Promise me you'll stay out of mischief, Tommy," he said. "Remember, you're *my* responsibility. And I must answer the American ambassador for your conduct. So be a good chap and no tomfoolery. Consider this an order from Ambassador Winant himself—on second thought—make that F.D.R."

"Oh, don't you worry, sir. My brother will keep a tight reign on me." I yanked an invisible leash wrapped around my neck, choking with my tongue hanging out.

Lord Sopwith took off his glasses, rubbing at his temples. Him and Lady Sopwith were against me visiting my brother for the weekend. It took all my powers of persuasion to convince them to let me go. Last time I left their house unattended, their Chris-Craft powerboat ended up over in German-occupied Belgium where it was still sitting. Docked next to a German submarine base.

Lord Sopwith hesitated before entering the Air Ministry building. He turned around and looked at the Rolls, troubled like. I knocked on the glass divider.

"Step on it!" I said. As Duncan pulled away from the curb, I added, "Sir." I was the low man on the totem pole at the Sopwith residence, and boy, did I know it.

"Yes, me lord," said Duncan. When I looked into the rear-view mirror he winked.

We were stuck in traffic, which was making me fidgety. I was looking forward to this weekend with my brother. Jack was so busy fight Nazis I hardly got to see him. We had big plans: After lunch at the Eagle Club, he was taking me to see the Crowned Jewels, which they kept in the Tower of London. St. Edward's crown alone contained 444 precious stones and had emeralds the size of Milk Duds. They also had the 105-karat Koh-i-Noor diamond, which had come from India. It was the size of a marshmallow Easter egg, the kind with sugar stuck to it. The Koh-i-Noor diamond came with a curse, which worked only on men—every fella who ever owned it met with disaster. Queen Victoria, on the other hand, was able to wear the rock and go on to become the longest reigning queen since Cleopatra—make that the Queen of Sheba. The curse now applied to King George VI, whose older brother would've been king if he hadn't ditched the throne to marry a twice divorced Yank. The curse: maybe that explained the war. If someone didn't take that diamond off King George's hands, the next monarch would be King Adolf. My fingers started twitching.

Finally, the Rolls pulled up in front of the Eagle Club on Charring Cross Road and I let myself out, tipping my tweed cap to Duncan. I looked around for Jack and didn't see him, so I started toward the front door where a pack of American airmen were smoking cigarettes and bragging to each other. One bragged: "I was flying so close to his tail, could smell the sauerkraut on his breath—"

"Excuse me," I said interrupting them, because I knew this sort of one-upping could go on until Miami froze over. "Have you seen my brother Jack Mooney?"

"Eagle Squadron, right?" said a gunner. "Heard their leaves got cancelled. Heard it from Reade Tilley's girl, who was just here looking for him."

"You mean that woman you just tried to make a date with?" asked an airman, "Ain't right, nosing in on another feller's gal."

"Mind your own business, Bill, if you know what's good for you," said the gunner.

You could tell they were itching for a fistfight. They had that look that tough guys get right before they throw a punch—shifting their weight from one foot to the other, clinching their jaws and widening their eyes so the white showed around the eyeballs. I was scared just being in the vicinity. Innocent bystanders end up with black-eyes exactly this way.

Just then Daphne—Jack's British fiancée, my future sister-in-law—ran up, out of breath. Her cheeks were pink from the exertion, her hair wild and wind-tossed. Like the cover of an *Action Comic*. Gee, was she a knockout. "Thank goodness," she said to me. "I was afraid I'd missed you. Jack's leave has been cancelled, worse luck."

I looked down at my sneakers and kicked the ground, "We were going to see the Crowned Jewels in the Tower of London."

"Well, you would have been disappointed in any event, because the jewels were moved to a hidden location in '39. Can't let Hitler's girlfriend, Eva Braun, get her hands on them."

"But—we could've at least seen where Henry VIII's wife, Anne Boleyn, had her head chopped off. They've got the actual block with her dried blood on it. And I know you won't take me, because you faint at the sight of blood."

"Hey doll," said the gunner, interrupting and making googly eyes at Daphne. "How's about you and me go for a hot-toddy?"

Daphne sneered like a Doberman. Bill grabbed the gunner by the shoulder, spun him around and socked him in the nose. "That's Jack Mooney's fiancée," he said. The gunner was flat out on the pavement, blood gushing from his left nostril.

"Thanks William, but you needn't have," said Daphne, pulling me back. "I'm capable of defending myself."

When, really—she was about to faint.

"My pleasure, miss," said Bill, clutching his aching knuckles.

Daphne wrapped her arm around mine, so's she

wouldn't fall down. "See here," she said, "let's go back to my place. I've already rung Lady Sopwith and you have her permission to stay the week's end with me. And you don't have to look like such a sourpuss. If the Luftwaffe takes a break, Jack might be able squeeze in lunch tomorrow—a sandwich on the airfield with one eye on his Spitfire. We'll take the train and cross our fingers the whole way. Mum's got a nice wicker picnic basket and then there's the tartan blanket we can sit on." She stopped short, took a little notebook from her coat pocket and added to a list she'd already started. "Do you like vegetable pasties? Mine you, they'll have to be eaten cold," she said. "But we shouldn't get our hopes up, because he might be flying." Her face fell, like she'd just said the saddest thing imaginable.

The airmen were now on top of each other, landing fists left and right and yelling out nasty names. Daphne put her hands over my ears. Even so, I was pretty sure I'd heard a jaw crack.

"My goodness," she said, "why do we need the Germans, anyway?"

I heard a whistle blow and saw a cop—the kind wearing one of those foot-tall hats—rush up swinging a night-stick. I wanted to stick around, but Daphne grabbed my hand and pulled me in the direction of a subway station.

"Boys will be boys," she said, shaking her head.

Message For Hitler
By Cate M. Ruane

When visiting RAF Rochford, Tommy begins to suspect that a Nazi spy is working mischief at the base: airmen are mysteriously wounded; Spitfires are sabotaged; someone has been poisoning the food. No one escapes Tommy's radar, especially after Daphne falls ill and is hospitalized. That night the base is attacked, setting off a chain of events that will either prove Tommy to be a fool or a hero. *Release date: July 2018.*

Letter Via Paris
By Cate M. Ruane

Back at Warfield Hall, Tommy gets a call from Daphne, his brother's fiancée. They've received a letter from Paris, written in invisible ink. The letter is from Juliette, begging Tommy and Daphne to return to Paris and help find her sister, Sophie, who has gone missing. There is no way that Daphne is returning to German-occupied Europe—unless, that is, Tommy can find a way to drag her there. A mystery involving a stolen masterpiece, communist Resistance members, and a foolhardy attempt on the life of Hermann Göring, leader of the Luftwaffe. *Release date: August 2018.*

GOOD REVIEWS ARE BETTER THAN MARASCHINO CHERRIES!

If you enjoyed *Telegram For Mrs. Mooney*, kindly write a review. It will make the author do an Irish jig. Just go to www.amazon.com and type in the title of the book. And, while you're at it, write one at: www.goodreads.com.

BONUS CHAPTER: DAPHNE GETS A LETTER

By joining our mailing list, you'll receive bonus chapters, rare photographs of the true-life characters, historical backstories, advance notice of new books in the series, and more. We'll begin with a peek into Daphne's mind, as she dreams about her fiancé, Jack, and reads a letter she's just opened from his little brother, Tommy Mooney. We hope you enjoy!

Sign up at: www.catemruane.com

Telegram For Mrs. Mooney is a work of fiction, but some of the characters are loosely based on real people who lived and died during World War II.

Tommy is based on my own da, Thomas Robert Mooney, who was a child when his oldest brother, Flight Lieutenant John "Jack" Mooney, flew with the RAF Eagle Squadron.

Jack was a 20-year-old Spitfire pilot, engaged to marry a 17-year-old London girl named Daphne. About all I know of the real woman comes from a newspaper article quoting a letter that she'd written to my grandmother when Jack was missing: "I've put away the trousseau for a while but I'll be taking everything out again soon as I know he'll be back." The character of Daphne is built entirely from that one line.

Much of Jack's story, up until June 16, 1942, is either true or as near to it as I could get. Some of his flight maneuvers come from his actual flight reports; it's true that in a dogfight a few days before his fateful crash, he had shot down two German fighter planes within minutes of each other. At the Imperial War Museum in London, you can ask to see a two second film shot from his Spitfire as he fires upon a German mine-sweeper.

After finishing the book, I learned that he'd actually gone down just over the Belgian border into France—somewhere along the train track near Bray-Dunes—on his way back to England from a rhubarb to Oostende.

He's buried at the Dunkirk Town Cemetery.

On 29 September 1942, the three Eagle squadrons were officially turned over by the RAF and RCAF to the U.S. Army Air Force. Eagle Squadron pilots are mentioned in the book: Hugh Kennard, Sel Edner, etc. All are listed on a monument in Grosvenor Square in London, near the American Embassy. Seventy-seven American and five British members were killed during their time in the RAF. Several spent time in German prison camps. Sel Edner, Jack's best friend, was caught in Paris in 1943 and not freed until the Americans liberated the Stalag Luft III camp—made famous by the film *The Great Escape*.

Andrée Eugénie Adrienne De Jongh, nicknamed Dédée, was the young Belgian woman who founded the Comet Line. She was betrayed and captured in January 1943, at the last stop on the escape line before the flight over the Pyrenees. She was interrogated by the Gestapo and tortured. She was sent to the notorious Fresnes prison in Paris and then to Ravensbrück and Mauthausen concentration camps. Released by the advancing Allied troops in April 1945, she was later awarded the United States Medal of Freedom. As far as I know, she wasn't a Communist. (I say that just in case her association with my fictional Paul-Henri might cast her in that light.)

Her father Frédéric De Jongh was also betrayed to the Gestapo and was executed in 1943.

The Vel'd'Hiv Roundup was a raid and mass arrest of Jewish families in Paris by the French police directed by German Nazi authorities on 16 and 17 July 1942. The roundup was one of several aimed at reducing the

Jewish population in occupied France. According to records of the Préfecture de Police, 13,152 victims were arrested, including more than 4,000 children. Most of those arrested ended up at Auschwitz. Yet, it's true that the French Resistance was able to rescue several people, arriving just ahead of the French police. It was about this time that a man named Jan Karski, a Pole, was making his way from Poland to the French Resistance in Paris and onward to England with evidence showing that the Germans were conducting mass exterminations of Jewish families. So our fictional characters are placed in Paris at the right time to have heard rumors of death camps.

Sir Thomas Octave Murdoch Sopwith (who wasn't actually knighted until 1953) was an English aviation pioneer and yachtsman. His *Endeavour* challenged the America's Cup in 1934 and 1937. Warfield Hall is in Berkshire; I have taken the liberty of relocating it to Hampshire.

My grandmother, Tommy's ma, did get back to Ireland once before she died. She brought me back a four-leaf clover glued to a card.

To take a train from Mons to Dunkirk, via Lille, you would have had to return to Brussels and switch trains. For the purposes of the story, the train goes direct Mons-Lille-Dunkirk.

In September 1942, the Eagle Squadrons were transferred from the RAF to the Eighth Air Force of the U.S. Army Air Forces. In *Telegram For Mrs. Mooney* I've delayed the transfer by a weeks...at least.

And lastly: Crayola didn't come out with Canary Yellow until 1998.

ACKNOWLEDGEMENTS

To THE MANY PEOPLE who have helped shape this novel, thank you.

To Caradoc King, Mildred Yuan, and Millie Hoskins at A. P. Watt, United Agents, London, for the many hours and heart you put into reading multiple drafts, making astute suggestions, and for talking the book up all over the place.

To my early readers: Victoria Fisch, Renee Rushing, Rachel Devenish Ford, Josiah Goodman, Sarah Clatterbuck, and the late Ian Brown. Especially to Chrys Goodman for excellent copy-editing. And to an expert on all things World War Two: my brother, Kevin Mooney.

My next-door neighbor, Frances "Frank" Simmons, of Asheville, NC, was a navy fighter pilot in the war. Frank answered nit-picking questions about every aspect of flying a fighter plane. He passed at age 92, one of the last of a brave generation.

And finally, to Kevin and Glenda Mooney—for your faith in me, which seems to know no bounds.

ABOUT THE AUTHOR

CATE M. RUANE spent years working as a copywriter and art director at advertising agencies in New York City and San Francisco. Born and raised on Long Island, she now lives in Asheville, N.C. This is her first novel.

www.catemruane.com

Fonts used in this book

The headline and subtitle font is LD Telegram,
by Inspire Graphics, licensed from LetteringDelights.com.

The text font is Adobe Caslon Pro.
Englishman William Caslon (1672-1766) first cut his
typeface Caslon in 1725.
His major influences were the Dutch designers
Christoffel van Dijcks and Dirck Voskens.

Printed in Great Britain
by Amazon